EXTINCTION

A Selection of Recent Titles by Carol Anne Davis

SHROUDED
SAFE AS HOUSES
NOISE ABATEMENT
KISS IT AWAY
ELECTRIC AVENUE
SOB STORY

EXTINCTION

Carol Anne Davis

CRÈME de la CRIME

This first world edition published 2011
in Great Britain and in the USA by
Cremè de la Crime, an imprint of
SEVERN HOUSE PUBLISHERS LTD of
9–15 High Street, Sutton, Surrey, England, SM1 1DF.
Trade paperback edition first published
in Great Britain and the USA 2012 by
SEVERN HOUSE PUBLISHERS LTD

British Library Cataloguing in Publication Data

Davis, Carol Anne.
  Extinction.
  1. Psychotherapists–Fiction. 2. Widows–Fiction.
  3. Suspense fiction.
  I. Title
  823.9'2-dc22

ISBN-13: 978-1-78029-013-3 (cased)
ISBN-13: 978-1-78029-511-4 (trade paper)

All Severn House titles are printed on acid-free paper.

Severn House Publishers support The Forest Stewardship Council [FSC],
the leading international forest certification organisation. All our titles that
are printed on Greenpeace-approved FSC-certified paper carry the FSC logo.

MIX
Paper from
responsible sources
FSC FSC® C018575
www.fsc.org

Typeset by Palimpsest Book Production Ltd.,
Falkirk, Stirlingshire, Scotland.
Printed and bound in Great Britain by
MPG Books Ltd., Bodmin, Cornwall.

For Ian
1957 – 2009

ONE

He'd kill her today, before she had time to mention him to anyone else. That way they'd never be linked together. She'd be his second victim and no one had ever proved that he'd murdered the first.

He smiled at her encouragingly. 'This drop-in centre closes at midday, but I feel that you need more time. My office is only a ten-minute walk away so we could continue the session there.' *Come into my parlour said the spider to the fly.*

'Is there a charge?'

Only when I plunge in hard. 'No charge for the client – the charity pays my fees.'

'That would be brilliant.'

It certainly would. She was thirtyish, with long blonde hair and equally long legs, a living Barbie doll. He liked the pretty ones as they were used to men doing them favours and paying them compliments. The look on their faces when he forced himself on them was priceless as they went, in seconds, from ice queen to distressed maiden, as Red Riding Hood met the Big Bad Wolf.

'I wouldn't bother going to the police,' he always said afterwards as they lay there sobbing or shaking silently. 'I mean, it's your word against mine that it wasn't consensual. And you were showing everything in that tight top and short skirt, and just how much did you have to drink?'

He enjoyed watching the dawning realization in their eyes as they admitted to themselves that he looked good, a well-spoken and immaculately dressed man, and that they looked cheap and available. That was why he'd chosen them in the nightclub, of course, because they were the type of girls who wouldn't impress the constabulary, would look like whores if it ever went to court.

Not that he merely planned to rape this one – no, he wanted to rape and kill. It had been a year since his last murder and the urge had built and built. He'd killed, that first time, in a cold-blooded rage, wanting to punish his wife as she had plans to leave him.

He'd seen it as a way of starting over cleanly, without the need to go through a career-damaging and potentially expensive divorce. But the rush that he'd felt as he watched her fall to her death was better than cocaine or Ecstasy or even doing-it-with-a-virgin sex. He wanted to kill again, only much more slowly, more up close and personal. He wanted to feel them struggle, hear them plead, eventually watch the light go out of their eyes.

It was imperative that he didn't leave a trail now, nothing to link him with – what was her name? – Hannah. She'd called in here on impulse, having seen the Bereavement Drop-In Centre sign, so hadn't had a chance to mention the place to anyone else.

'Here's my card,' he said. 'If you come to the side door, it leads straight to my study. I'll see you there in fifteen minutes or so.'

'Shall I just walk with you?'

Hell, no. He could just imagine a lookalike playing him on the *Crimewatch* reconstruction. Ironically, he looked a bit like a forty-year-old Ted Bundy, albeit slightly less smug.

'No, I have to lock up here and, to be honest' – he rarely was – 'I'm supposed to put new clients on a waiting list.'

'That's what happened when I phoned my doctor – he said that it would be five months until I could see a counsellor one-to-one.'

'We're very overstretched,' he said, sounding apologetic. 'But sometimes I bend the rules when someone is clearly distressed.'

The blonde nodded. 'It's just that she was more like my best friend than a sister and with us having lost our mum last year . . .'

'A double bereavement. I understand.' He'd done his best by reading all of the counselling books but it was like looking through a glass darkly: he never could understand other's emotions. But he knew that bereavement counsellors attracted vulnerable people, which is why he'd taken the training course and started reeling new victims in.

'Plus it's only been ten days,' she said.

'It's all so very raw. Well, I promise that I can give you lots of time.' He wasn't kidding. She had three orifices that he wanted to explore.

'No one expected her to die so soon.'

'It's a challenge when you have no time to prepare. Well, I'll see you in fifteen minutes,' he said again, trying to keep the edge out of his voice. He wanted her to fuck off before the other counsellor that he was working with today at the drop-in centre entered this particular room and realized that he was no longer alone.

'Adam – I'm locking up in five.'

Talk of the devil. He tensed as his colleague, Beth, popped her head round the door. She grimaced apologetically. 'Sorry, I didn't realize that you were with someone.'

Getting up quickly, he strode to the door, murmured, 'She was upset, wanted to see someone on a one-to-one basis so I brought her in here for additional privacy.'

'No problem,' Beth said in a stage whisper. 'My regulars have left so I was about to shut up shop.'

'She's just going.'

He shut the door on Beth, turned back to Hannah.

'Honestly, these clock watchers!'

She nodded sadly. 'I thought that there would be better services for the bereaved.'

'It's patchy, depends on where you live.' He opened the door again, looked tellingly at her.

'See you in a few minutes,' she said, smiling tiredly and walked out into the spring showers. He was pleased to see that there were no observers in the vicinity. He exhaled hard then went in search of Beth.

'She's young to be widowed,' Beth said.

'She's not widowed – she lost her mother.' He wouldn't mention the sister, didn't want her to remain in the counsellor's memory.

'Do you think she'll come back?'

'Mmm? Doubt it. She said something about being here on holiday. To be honest, she might just have wanted to shelter from the rain.'

'Oh, is it on again? It never stops these days.'

That suited him fine. People kept their heads down in the rain or hid under oversized umbrellas. Hannah hadn't been carrying a brolly, unless she had a telescopic version in her shoulder bag, but she was wearing a mac and had raised the hood as she left the hall.

He spent the next few minutes turning on the charm, wanting

to get Beth in his corner. If she liked him, she'd be less suspicious of his behaviour and would praise his conduct if the police ever came sniffing round. Life was a gamble at the best of times and he'd always been a heavy-betting man.

'So, how are you spending your afternoon?' she asked.

With a helpless victim, he thought and felt his penis twitch. 'Oh, you know, working.'

'Your private counselling work – is that also bereavement based?'

'No, it's everything – hyperactive children, adults who are clinically depressed or bipolar.' The latter was on the increase as more and more people self-diagnosed.

'And you?' He pretended that he cared.

'Oh, I'm going back to the hospital, running the canteen.'

She seemed too bright and alternative for a management position but he'd find out about her later – for now, the beautiful Hannah was waiting for him, waiting for death.

She was there when he arrived home. Good. He felt almost surprised that it was this easy. Some killers spent weeks following their prey, learning their daily and nightly routines, but she had delivered herself straight to his door.

'Nice place,' she said, appraising the whitewashed side wall and adjacent garden.

'My wife chose it.' If she thought that the little woman was at home, she'd be off her guard.

'Mum had a bungalow just like this.'

'You'll find that everything brings back memories at first,' he murmured, inserting his key in the lock.

'I'm home,' he shouted, hoping that they had the house to themselves. His lodger, John, was normally at work in the gym in the early afternoons – but, even if he was home, he knew better than to disturb a therapy session. 'My study is through here,' he added, leading her to the back of the house, furthest away from listening ears.

'Is your wife a counsellor too?'

'She is.' She genuinely had been. It was surprising how screwed up most psychologists and counsellors were, often going into the therapeutic field with some vague hope of curing themselves.

'Doesn't sound like she's in.' Hannah followed him to his office, took off her mac and hung it on the clothes peg behind the door.

'She sometimes does outreach work.' She was definitely out of reach all right, though he doubted that people did anything from beyond the grave.

His newest client sat down on the chair opposite his desk but he indicated the long armless settee which was parallel to the wall.

'You'll be more comfortable there.'

'The psychiatrist's couch!' she laughed.

It was more like the rapist's bed – though the two words, put together, made therapist – but he was indifferent to semantics. He exhaled as she got up and crossed to the settee, lay down.

Gotcha. He covertly took the handcuffs from between the encyclopaedias on the bookcase, walked over and swiftly straddled her, pushing her wrists together in front of her and cuffing them.

'What the . . .?'

He was pleased that she was able to talk. Some of his rape victims went mute with fear at this stage which took a lot of the fun out of it. He wanted them to shout or plead for clemency as it made him feel more alive, more powerful. A couple – true optimists – had even prayed.

'We're just going to have a little fun,' he said as he locked his study door and pocketed the key. He wouldn't tell her yet that she was going to die – he'd save that for later. For the moment, he'd let her assume that he only wanted sex.

'I won't tell,' she said, and he saw her start to shake.

'I'm glad to hear it. Of course, even if you did, the police would believe that it was consensual, given that you came to my house despite the fact that we'd only just met.'

'You're right.' She was reasonably smart, this one. In other circumstances, he might have enjoyed a longer conversation with her. There would still have had to be a pay-off, however – a hot date, a job opportunity or money for him somewhere down the line.

'I'm going to cut your blouse off now.' He watched her trembling increase then hurried to his desk drawer, returning with the scissors. He was pleased that she hadn't made a run for the window and made some futile attempt to break the glass. She was a realist, then, would be easier to manage. She hadn't watched any of these unlikely Hollywood movies where the good girl always got away.

He straddled her, slashed the military-style khaki T-shirt down the front and cut the sleeves off. It was easier than trying to get it over her head when she was cuffed. She was wearing a body-tone coloured bra and he cut the straps and the material between the cups, peeled it from her. The cups were padded so her breasts were smaller than he'd envisaged, a minor disappointment. Still, she'd do.

He realized that she was staring at the scissors with trepidation, probably assuming that he was going to cut her. But he wasn't a sadist – or, at least, not so sadistic that he wanted to mutilate anyone. He just liked to do exactly as he pleased and totally take charge. No chocolates, no flowers, no coy kisses, no will-she-won't-she? No compromise.

He put the scissors carefully out of her reach, unbuttoned her jeans and pulled them off. She helped a little by lifting her hips, obviously wanted to placate him. He watched her run her tongue across her bottom lip and hardened at the thought of her licking and sucking his cock.

'Now for your panties,' he said. They, too, were what his mother would have called beige, but which he knew was now called body-tone. Women often wore separates when they were single and kept their matching sets for when they were seeing a lover, which made him wonder if she was in a relationship. Or was she one of those you-never-know women who were always up for casual, spur-of-the-moment sex?

'Nice underwear,' he murmured as he slid it down her hips, thighs, knees and ankles. He contemplated leaving on her shoes but changed his mind when he noticed her utilitarian cotton ankle socks. No, on second thoughts he'd strip her totally naked. After all, he'd want to bury her whilst she was nude. The longer that it took the police to find and identify her body, the less likely that the trail would lead back to him.

A noise at the window made him pause, then he realized that it was just next door's Maine Coon cat, Tilly, thudding onto his outer ledge. He always made a fuss of it as its owners – a middle-aged couple – kept an eye on the house for him whenever he went on holiday, something that he liked to do each time that he had a sizeable gambling win. The back of his property wasn't directly overlooked but he decided to belatedly shut the Venetian blind for additional safety: it would be just his luck if some child climbed the fence in search of his frisbee or ball.

'There – now we have some privacy!' he said when he returned to her.

'What shall I call you?' she asked.

Ah, that old trick, trying to get to know your rapist in the hope that he would see you as an individual rather than as a victim.

'Just think of me as your nemesis.'

She looked blank, obviously wasn't making use of her thesaurus. Call me what you like, he thought, and bent his head to her nearest nipple, teeth grazing slightly as his fingers held the breast's full weight. He transferred his attention to the other breast, knowing that he could squeeze as hard as he liked or ignore them completely. This wasn't foreplay. Instead, she belonged to him utterly.

He felt almost drunk on his new-found authority as he tugged at her pubic hair and she obligingly parted her legs.

'I'm Hannah,' she said tremulously.

'I know.' He'd brought the file that he'd written up about her this morning, would destroy it after her death.

'I never meant to lead you on . . .'

'You didn't. You were just in the wrong place at the wrong time.'

'Have you done this before?'

'Of course.'

'And do you really have a wife?'

'I did.' Like this girl, his wife had done too much talking. He wanted action now, wanted it fast and hard. 'I'll just fetch the oil,' he added and felt her quivering increase.

He was aware of her watching him intently as he crossed back to his desk drawer, took out the bottle of lubricant and box of condoms. Rape victims rarely got wet so it was just as easy to take them up the ass. She put up a token resistance when he tried to flip her over but soon succumbed to his determination and superior strength.

Afterwards, he felt a momentary rage when he saw her blood on the couch. Damn, why did she have to be a bleeder? Fortunately it was just a light spray, doubtless caused when he withdrew from her backside.

'Don't move,' he said, and she remained obediently on her stomach, weeping quietly. He unzipped one of the cushion covers and put it under her belly then told her to get onto her back. Now she'd bleed into the cover and he could dispose of it somewhere at the other side of town: he'd read lots of forensic books, knew just how to protect himself.

He squeezed and caressed her until he grew hard again then told her to lick him, but her heart clearly wasn't in it. He managed a second, faltering orgasm under her tongue then knew that it was time for her to die. She obviously wasn't telepathic as she lay back on the couch and wiped her mouth with her handcuffed hands before exhaustedly closing her eyes.

Bye bye Hannah. He flexed his hands, grabbed for her throat and tightened his grip. Her eyes opened wide and she began to make loud retching sounds and kick wildly. He kept going, tighter and tighter, amazed that such a slender girl had so much fight. She bucked up, twisted from side to side, drummed her feet on the couch and tried to pull her knees up. He kept straddling her and increasing the pressure, every memory of feeling different and unattached and unworthy in his grip.

Eventually – how long had it been? – she went slack but he continued to force his bruised fingers to make the connection as he didn't want her to open her eyes and look at him, perhaps create a momentary guilt. Only when the stench of ammonia permeated the room, indicating that she'd lost control of her bladder in death, did he release her and sit back on his haunches to relax.

By the time that he'd showered and washed and tumble dried the washable cover from the settee and the cushion cover, it was almost time for his lodger, John, to return. After replacing the fabric coverings, he left his study and locked it from the outside, putting the key carefully in his back pocket. He'd wait until dark before disposing of the body in the great outdoors.

As usual, John managed to look apologetic for no particular reason.

'Good day?' Adam asked as the younger man walked into the lounge.

'Quiet. You?'

'I was counselling at the bereavement drop-in centre.'

'Would you like to split a pizza or . . .?'

His lodger, one of the most socially inept youths that he'd ever met, was the master of the non sequitur.

Suddenly he realized that he was starving: rape and murder obviously used up vast amounts of energy.

'I'll get us one each. My treat.'

He tipped the delivery guy well when he turned up on his motorcycle with two stuffed-cheese-crust meat specials. Apart from the throbbing in his hands, he felt great.

'I appreciate this, mate,' John said as they munched, drank ale and watched reruns of *Top Gear* on the Dave channel.

'No problem.' One day, in the future, John might have to be his alibi: indeed, he'd chosen the twenty-four-year-old because he was affable but awkward, clearly in awe of him. If questioned by police, John would tell them that he, Adam, was a great guy who loved to help his clients and who made instant friends with everyone else that he met.

They made casual conversation about the TV as the night progressed but he was pleased when, at just after ten thirty, John stretched and said that he was off to bed.

'I'll hit the sack soon myself – got an early client tomorrow. He's claustrophobic, can't travel at busy times as he hyperventilates.'

'Want me to air the rooms or . . .?' The smell of stale cheese and pepperoni hung heavily in the lounge.

'No need – I'm seeing him at the Counselling Centre as he'd feel trapped in my office.'

He liked to work for several different organizations: it stopped him from getting bored so quickly and it was easier to keep prying colleagues at bay.

He waited for twenty minutes after John's bedroom door closed, then went to his study, unlocked it, entered and quickly relocked the door. The room smelt of blood, now, and something else that was less familiar. He looked at the body and it had gone a strange, almost luminous beige. Her eyes must have opened of their own accord, seemed to stare at him accusingly and he felt momentarily edgy, wanted her out of the way.

Fortuitously, he'd bought a cheap sheet, with cash, for this very purpose, purchasing it from the supermarket a few weeks ago when the urge to kill had become almost overwhelming.

Going into his cupboard, he brought out the king size piece of bedding and rolled her awkwardly into it, surprised that such a slender body was so difficult to manipulate. She'd stiffened so he had to half carry and half drag her through the darkened bungalow and out to his car.

She was too rigid to bend into the boot so he put her on the back seat, still mummified in the sheet, and forced himself to drive slowly to the vast sprawl that was Weston Woods. Fortunately, at this time of night, only the most determined dog walkers were still active. He waited until the coast was clear before dragging her as far as possible from the path, removing the sheet and rolling her under a big clump of bushes. She was still visible so he fetched his secateurs from the boot and cut several branches from nearby shrubs and saplings then piled them loosely at each side. He threw several others around so that his disguise didn't look too obvious: the foliage would soon start to wither and would blend in more.

When she was out of sight – if not yet out of mind – he returned to his Fiesta and drove around until he saw an area littered with bin bags rather than the more commonplace wheelie bins. Putting the sheet in a bin liner which he'd brought with him, he dumped it with the rest of the refuse before driving home. If his luck held out, she wouldn't be found for weeks, allowing decomposition to obscure the timeline and making it harder for the police to ascertain her final movements. He was probably home and dry.

TWO

That murder victim looked vaguely familiar, Beth thought, as she studied the photograph on the front page of the local paper, the *Weston Mercury*. There again, she saw so many people through her work at the hospital – staff, patients and visitors all made use of the restaurant.

There were relatively few murders here in Weston-super-Mare, but more in the neighbouring city of Bristol. Many of them were domestic or were drunken fights between young men whereas the motive in this case appeared to be sexual. The body had apparently been hidden under some bushes but dragged out by foxes or badgers and briefly feasted upon.

The young woman, Hannah Reid, had gone missing last Monday but her body had only been found on Sunday by the inevitable man walking his dog. It had doubtless featured on the local news but she, Beth, had been too busy to tune in, thanks to her busy working and social life. It was only now, on Thursday, when the new edition of the weekly paper came out, that she realized they had a killer in their midst.

'Hannah was a sensible woman who wouldn't have gone off with a stranger so we think that she knew her killer,' the detective leading the case was quoted as saying. Good, Beth thought – she herself lived alone and hated the prospect of a man preying on random females. Not that Hannah had deserved to die for attracting Mr Wrong.

'Beth – the rep hasn't turned up to restock the snacks machine.'

Everything was put out to tender nowadays at the hospital which was a problem if a company or individual became unreliable.

She smiled at her assistant. 'No problem. I'll phone them and sort it out.'

She went into her office and made the call. She also increased their order for fruit and salads. The warmer weather would be here any day now and the spring sunshine briefly encouraged people to get fit. The canteen would have a week or two of requests for healthier choices then the patients' relatives would revert to their usual depressed state and go back to choosing sausage rolls and pies. She suspected that many of them only managed a portion of baked beans by way of vegetables, fell far short of their five-a-day.

When she returned to the serving area, her newspaper had gone. That was typical of some members of the general public. If you didn't nail it down, it walked. Still, she couldn't complain: she'd met lots of caring people since becoming a young widow, and she usually enjoyed her job.

At 3 p.m., she finished for the day and strode through the corridors, looking forward to walking home and having a long bubble bath. She'd have a lazy afternoon and a late evening meal as she wasn't meeting her boyfriend at the pub until nine.

As she reached the front doors, she saw a petite brunette, dressed casually in jeans and a denim top, sitting in the otherwise empty waiting area. Her head was buried in her hands and she was weeping silently. The receptionists behind the desk were both gazing awkwardly at their computer screens; it wasn't the British way to get involved.

Beth hesitated. The girl might be clinically depressed, in which case she had to be referred to the mental health ward, or she might merely be distressed, but, on balance, she couldn't just leave her. She'd never forget her own first year of widowhood, how wretched she felt. Ever since, she'd felt compelled to reach out to people in a crisis, to get them through their most difficult times.

'Can I help you? I work here at the hospital but I'm also a counsellor.'

The girl looked up. 'My husband was killed in an accident.'

'Recently?'

'This afternoon. He was walking to the supermarket when a car . . .' Her voice cracked.

'Is there anyone that I can phone?'

The girl – who could only be in her mid to late twenties – shook her head and her crying resumed. When she at last calmed down she said, 'My parents are dead and Zak grew up in children's homes.'

'Do you have work colleagues, then?' She'd surely be reassured by familiar faces.

'We work from home – he does accountancy, I make curtains and do dress alterations.'

Beth realized that the truth of her husband's death hadn't quite sunk in, that she was still speaking about him in the present tense.

'How are you getting home?'

The girl shrugged. 'I suppose I'll walk.'

'I could give you a lift.'

It amazed her how little the hospital or social services did for a new widow. They invariably let her see the body for a few minutes, gave her a booklet on bereavement services and sent her on her way.

'Thank you. I feel so shaky that I was scared I would collapse.'

'That's shock,' Beth said gently. 'I know. I was widowed three years ago when my husband died of leukaemia.'

'I'm also being sick a lot. I'm four months pregnant,' the girl said.

It never rains but it pours.

'I'm Beth,' Beth said gently.

'Olivia.'

'My car's in the car park.' She helped the young woman to her feet. 'Where do you live?' she asked as they left the building and walked into the afternoon sunshine.

Olivia named a fairly central location.

'Oh, that's handy for the supermarket,' Beth said.

She glanced at the younger girl's pale face and realized that she was probably thinking that she'd never want to shop for groceries, far less eat anything, again. She'd doubtlessly enjoyed today's lunch with her young husband with neither having the slightest notion that they'd never share another meal.

She told Olivia about the bereavement drop-in centre as she drove, reassuring her that she could just turn up on the first Monday morning of the month, that she didn't need to make an appointment.

'It's not formal counselling, unfortunately. There's a waiting list for that. This is just a chat with someone who understands.'

'Just me and you?'

'And anyone else who turns up,' Beth admitted. 'It's for all kinds of bereavement so we get people who have lost their parents, children, siblings or a spouse.'

'But I'll get to see you?'

'Or my colleague, Adam, if I'm already talking to several people. We had a third volunteer for a while but unfortunately she moved away.'

'And I can come in any time?'

She'd already given out this information, but the younger woman's concentration had understandably gone. 'Unfortunately no – they are only held on the first Monday of the month.' She parked outside Olivia's house, went into her bag for a card with the drop-in centre address, and wrote the date of the next session on it. 'In the meantime, I suggest that you put your name down on the waiting list to see a counsellor on a one-to-one basis – the details will be in that booklet you got from the hospital.'

Olivia looked blank for a moment then belatedly stared down at the little white pamphlet that she was clutching. Beth knew, from bitter experience, that she would find it disappointing, that most of the organizations were aimed at older widows and widowers. Even for this age group, help was mainly only available in the bigger cities, a postcode lottery.

'Can I come in and make you some toast and tea?'

Sometimes, if you gave food to the newly-bereaved, they would eat it on automatic pilot. Olivia had to keep her strength up as she was with child.

'Zak hadn't reached the shops when . . . We're out of bread.'

'I'm sure that we can find something,' Beth said gently. She followed Olivia into a clean and reasonably neat flat.

For the next two hours she stayed and talked, even persuaded the widow to nibble at a little dry cereal. Should she cancel her date with Matthew and spend the rest of the evening here? He would survive without her. She was still debating what to do when Olivia's lids began to flutter and she lolled back against the cushions then immediately opened her eyes.

'Sorry, I'm exhausted.'

'You get some sleep. I'll let myself out and I'll see you soon,' Beth murmured and headed for the door.

By the time that Matthew collected her from her home, she had showered and changed and was feeling slightly more lively. Still, she was glad that they were going out to eat as the food would distract from the fact that Matthew could be very quiet. Going out for a drink with him could be a challenge unless she carried the conversation, something which was tiring if she'd spent all day talking to the bereaved or managing the hospital restaurant. He loved his job as a locksmith but talked little about his work, though she tried hard to draw him out.

'I missed you,' he said as soon as he entered the hall.

Beth hugged him tightly. She'd only seen him two days ago so hadn't had time to miss him in return but it was lovely being paid so many compliments.

'You're so cute,' she said, keen to sound as warm as he. It

was more difficult for her to show emotion, she acknowledged
to herself, as this was her first serious relationship since her
husband's death. In contrast, Matthew had been divorced for
almost a decade and had dated several divorcees since.

'And you're so lovable.' They'd only been dating for six weeks
but he was already hinting that he was in love.

At the restaurant, she told him about Olivia and her unborn
child.

'She's lucky that she can see you at the centre,' Matthew said,
touching her knee under the table.

'Well, me or Adam,' Beth said. 'I'll give him all of the details
so that he can meet her needs.'

She was glad that Adam was fitting in so well at the bereavement drop-in sessions, was pleased that the unfortunate young
widow would be in such capable hands.

THREE

R
ise and shine – well, rise anyway. He'd never managed
to be a little ray of sunshine. In fact, even when he was
feeling happy, people in the street often told him to cheer
up. John shuffled towards the kitchen, intent on making himself
some coffee, but stopped in the hall and sniffed the air. The house
smelt different, sickly sweet, as if something had gone off: it
was similar to the smell that remained when a mouse ate poisoned
bait and began to decompose behind the fridge or in a cupboard
and it made him feel strangely ill at ease. Walking into the lounge,
he scooped up the leftover pizza crusts and cartons from last
night and put them in the kitchen bin but the stench remained.
He'd better keep tidying, put the rubbish outside.

As he exited via the side door, he was surprised to see that
Adam's car was still in the driveway. Hadn't his landlord said
something about an early appointment? He, John, must have
gotten the details wrong – there was no way that someone as
together and organized as Adam would ever sleep in. There again,
it looked as if he was behind with washing his admittedly modest

car: there was a reddish brown smear on the boot, presumably mud.

After being out in the fresh air, the bungalow smelt worse so he opened several windows before making himself a much-needed cup of instant and two slices of wholemeal toast, lavishly spread with butter. As a personal trainer, he was supposed to eat a more balanced breakfast, something which included a reasonable portion of protein, but, at this time in the morning, toast was all that he could face.

Why couldn't he be more like Adam? The older man could eat a full English breakfast (grilled of course, rather than fried), find a parking space and get offered every job that he applied for. He also did very well with women – he, John, often stumbled into some giggling blonde or brunette in the hall, invariably wearing nothing more than Adam's shirt and a smile. Admittedly they didn't hang around for long, but Adam had explained that he was playing the field as he recovered from the shock of his wife's suicide.

It was hard to imagine any woman wanting to kill herself when she shared her life with a bright, funny man like his landlord but apparently she had suffered from clinical levels of depression. She'd also self-medicated with alcohol which had only made the problem worse.

He, John, could identify with that: he'd been deeply depressed himself as a teenager, what with being the thinnest and weediest boy in the class. He'd also struggled to find conversational gambits. Even his folks had said that he was so quiet that they had to take his pulse to ascertain that he was still alive. That was why he'd been so pleased when he and Adam had clicked, when the older man had hired him as his personal trainer. They'd only had a few sessions together before the psychologist's workload became too onerous but by then the room that he rented out had become vacant and he'd happily moved in.

Talk of the devil. He smiled as Adam walked into the lounge.

'Bit cold in here,' the older man said.

'The place smelt odd so I've opened the windows.'

Adam sniffed the air. 'Probably the wind blowing our way from the dump.'

'No, I've been outside with the pizza boxes and the air's

fine. The odour is in here. Maybe something spilled inside the bin?'

'I'll clean up later.'

'I thought you were working first thing?'

'He cancelled, seems to have totally gone off the idea of psychotherapy. I'm beginning to think that he's schizophrenic as well as claustrophobic.'

'Double trouble!' John said and laughed at his own joke. 'Talking of mood changes, I'm doing this motivational weekend in London in a couple of months.'

'Sounds like a plan.'

'It had better work, considering how much it costs.'

'A girlfriend or your money back,' Adam laughed.

Damn, was he really that obvious? There again, his landlord was a shrink.

'I'd also like some more work.'

'Wouldn't we all!'

'At least you're paid well per hour,' John said wearily. Personal trainers were ten-a-penny so he had to keep his charges low.

'You could branch out a bit, maybe teach a course on healthy eating? Or the glycaemic index or whatever is the latest trend.'

It was a good idea, John thought, as he walked, mini-gym strapped to his back, to meet his first client of the day. Hopefully, by the time that he'd been on that motivational weekend, he'd have come up with other plans of his own and found the confidence to follow them through, start to find his true potential. Maybe, in time, he'd become more like Adam and lead the perfect life.

FOUR

They'd had to draft in officers from neighbouring forces to investigate Hannah Reid's murder, but everyone was working well and they already had several significant leads. Entering the Major Incident Room – or Murder Room as it was more colloquially known – Detective Superintendent

Bill Winston spoke, in turn, to several of his inquiry team officers.

Every relevant piece of information was being logged into their computerized investigation system. He watched with quiet satisfaction as his indexers typed industriously away, inputting the data, whilst a team of readers studied the incoming information and statements and identified which actions needed to be taken next. A dedicated exhibits officer was dealing with the cigarette ends, drinks bottles and other detritus taken from the woods, which might have been discarded by Hannah's killer, could have traces of his DNA. They knew that the killer was a man as she'd had abrasions indicative of rape and sodomy, but unfortunately he'd worn a condom, was forensically aware. On the upside, even the most careful of murderers sometimes left a handkerchief behind after it fell out of their pocket, particularly if they were trying to roll a body down an uneven slope, wrestling with the undergrowth in a darkened wood.

Bill Winston knew that having the right personnel was vital to this murder enquiry. And he had something that he'd had to work hard to convince the authorities that he needed – an under-cover cop.

Most of the violence that he'd investigated here in Weston had been relatively straightforward, usually involving one drunken or drugged male friend beating another. The police were called to certain streets, where drug addicts and alcoholics lived, again and again. Only the skill of the local surgeons prevented many of these stabbings from resulting in a murder charge: instead the culprit was charged with GBH. The few murders were equally straightforward, caused when one substance-abusing man fell out with his equally mad mate and kicked him to death.

But everything pointed to the fact that Hannah hadn't been killed by a friend or relative. She'd led a peaceful life, enjoyed good relationships with family members and hadn't indulged in any risky behaviour. She was single, and her last three boyfriends had cast iron alibis. Her next-door neighbour had been able to give them masses of information about her social activities, as had the other women with whom she'd worked alongside. No, it was showing all of the hallmarks of a stranger murder, Category A.

But the killer wasn't a stranger now, at least not to the force. No, they thought they knew who he was, just had to prove it. One day, hopefully in the near future, he would arrest Hannah's killer and see him brought to trial.

FIVE

I t had been a trying eight weeks, what with the police constantly making new pleas to the public to help them catch Hannah Reid's killer, but, at last, things were getting back to normal. He'd scrubbed the soft furnishings and carpet in his study, polished the furniture and successfully rid the room of that slightly sweet, decomposing scent. Two of his female clients had even commented on how spic and span the place was looking so he'd been careful not to do further housework – if the police came round, he wanted the place to look normal rather than deep-cleansed. Last night he'd deliberately left a couple of opened beer cans – his and John's – on the coffee table, so that the place seemed more like a typical bachelor pad.

That said, he had a hell of a lot less money than most bachelors in professional jobs. He'd lost heavily again at the casino last night and had done badly last month with spread betting. His late wife had often begged him to stop gambling, but where was the fun in that? He needed the excitement of the big win, the possibility that tonight could be the night when everyone else at the blackjack table was in awe of him. And what were the social options? He didn't want to pick up a new girl every single night, not now that he'd turned forty, and propping up the bar with a male mate had never appealed to him. He also found spectator sport moronic and he was bored senseless by most modern theatre and films.

He ideally needed a few more clients but it was hard persuading people to take the first step into psychotherapy. They saw asking for help as a weakness when it was really a strength. He'd tried to counter this with an advert in the local version of the Yellow Pages, emphasizing that everyone had the right to enjoy life despite having a difficult start.

His own start had been beyond bad, with a heavy-drinking mother and a recently-imprisoned father; it was a textbook example of parental neglect. But he'd been fostered at six months by the Neaves, the couple who eventually adopted him before going on to have Nicholas, their biological son.

Nicholas had quickly proven himself to be the good brother, the one who brought home stray animals and fed them, the child who was always given the class guinea pig to take home for the school holidays. Despite being two years younger, Nicholas had always completed his homework on time whereas he, Adam, copied from the brightest or most bribe-inducible kid in class. Fortunately he was more ideas-orientated than his more plodding contemporaries, had been able to play catch up before the exams.

Nicholas – probably on account of being such a home-based bookworm – hadn't started dating until he was seventeen, and had gone on to marry his first girlfriend, Jill. In contrast, he, Adam, had lost his virginity at twelve and had fucked hundreds of girls since then.

There had been Mummy Neave, Daddy Neave and little Nicky Neave, the three musketeers, carved from the same altruistic stone, in thrall to the god of good causes. He'd been the outsider, hewn from a different flint, always on the periphery, looking in.

What the hell – he liked who he was, wouldn't change it. Having principles just held you back. He simply pretended that he had some, had been delighted to accept voluntary work at the bereavement centre because of the obvious perks. First, it made him look generous with his time and that would impress both his fellow colleagues in the psychology field and the general public. Second, it gave him a doorway to the world of the newly widowed, one of society's most vulnerable groups. How many men had access to tranquillized, partnerless women? How many men would love to be in his handmade leather shoes?

Adam flicked through his half-empty appointments book. His next client was Brandon Petrie, a sixteen-year-old schoolboy with ADHD, attention deficit hyperactivity disorder. He was one of the easiest of his young patients to deal with now that he was on sustained medication which made him less jumpy and allowed him to concentrate on one task, or one concept, at a time. Brandon was highly intelligent and precocious so Adam quite enjoyed their sessions. The boy was like the son that he'd never had – and would never want to have. What was it about most people that made them think their DNA was so special? Why did they insist on further cluttering up an already over-populated world? Ironically, Brandon, too, was adopted, though he'd been taken on at birth by his adoptive family. Many of his, Adam's, clients, hadn't been rescued from their biological parents until they were toddlers or even older, had endured years of abuse or neglect.

He answered the door to the boy and waved to his mother who was parked at the end of the drive. She sped off and he said, 'Come in, Brandon. Can I get you a soda?' It was soda water which he served as the youth had to avoid soft drinks which were full of additives. Research, admittedly controversial, had linked cola with obesity, mood swings and energy slumps so he was keen to keep Brandon on a purer diet, especially when his parents were paying him fifty pounds an hour.

'No,' Brandon said.

'Remember what we talked about last time?'

'No, thanks,' Brandon corrected with the world-weary air of an old man.

'Tea, then?'

'No . . . no thanks.'

'It's like fake it until you make it, pal. Being polite keeps the oldsters happy. Save your battles for the big issues – don't sweat the small stuff, as they say.'

'Sometimes I just forget,' Brandon said, throwing himself on the couch.

'I used to forget too – but it gets easier with practice.'

The kid looked really small on the settee, more like twelve rather than his actual sixteen. He'd been brought here straight from school so was still wearing his uniform, a dark-coloured outfit which made him look sallow and thin.

'They're all so small-minded,' he muttered, picking up one of the new cushions and turning it over and over in his hands.

'They are, but it's easier to play the system than try to beat it. Just act nice and everyone around you will back off, leaving you alone with your thoughts.'

'I wish I had a lock on my bedroom door.'

'Hey, two years from now you could have your own place in a student pad at university.'

'But my folks keep interrupting me!'

'They've been scared because of the times that you've threatened to hurt yourself.'

'It was only threats. I haven't done it.' He held out his thin arms, presumably to show that they were unscarred.

'I know – but when you talk about throwing yourself out of the window if you don't get your own way, your parents understandably fear the worst.'

Brandon, he thought, was easy to counsel because he was a kindred spirit, a freedom-lover. The kid probably wished that he, Adam, was his father or at least his older brother. They were both much brighter than most of their contemporaries, a state of being that could lead to you being ostracized. They'd probably both been spawned by wild, hedonistic free spirits, only to be raised in safe but dull family groups.

By the time that the teenager was collected by his over-anxious mother, he was comparatively mellow.

'I don't know what we'd do without you, Mr Neave,' the woman said.

'Call me Adam,' he murmured pleasantly as he did every week. It didn't hurt to be mildly flirtatious towards females who were paying his fees. Not that he'd ever want to take it further with her type: she looked frigid and as if she'd been born old.

'Same time, same place?' she asked, checking her woefully-empty diary.

No, I thought we'd schedule the next session in Nairobi.

'It's a date,' he said and gave both mother and son his best smile.

Good, they'd gone and now he had this place to himself as John was on that motivational weekend. He'd been talking about it for ages, was convinced that it would change his life. He, Adam, wasn't so sure – after all, some people bought self-help book after self-help book. The people who were screwed up to begin with tended to remain that way. It would take more than a few seminars to cure most neurotics of their character flaws, fears and obsessions. He'd had some clients who had stayed with him for years. His wife had gone into therapy after she married him, though he'd only found out about her deception later. Fortunately her time with the psychiatrist – time in which to criticize her husband – had been limited as it was on the NHS.

But now it was time to eat, drink and be merry. At 9 p.m., he got himself a chicken madras and a pineapple rice from the take-away and ate half of it. He wanted to be fuelled up as he was going to Bristol to get himself a girl.

Excited for the first time since Hannah's murder, Adam began to put his rape kit together. He always kept everything separate, between date rapes, in case the police searched his house. Now, he gathered together duct tape, handcuffs (a new pair – he'd thrown away the ones that he'd used on Hannah), a gag, a knife and his pièce de résistance, the date rape drug Rohypnol. He was a psychologist rather than a psychiatrist so wasn't medically qualified or allowed to prescribe such medication, but was able to buy the pills on the black market in various pubs. He could have bought them more cheaply online, of course, but that would have meant leaving a paper trail . . .

A couple of hours from now, some pretty vacant girlie was going to regret acting so cheap. He'd have a lot of fun with her then leave her house before she regained consciousness. He always gave them a false name and lied about every aspect of his life, plus he used a condom, so was really hard to trace.

He was so looking forward to penetrating new flesh that he made the fifty-minute journey to Bristol in thirty-five minutes. That was foolish, he reminded himself as he entered the over-priced car park of a central nightclub: if he'd earned a speeding ticket it would be proof that he'd been here in the city rather than at home in Weston-super-Mare.

It was late when he arrived at the club – intentionally so. Some girls thought they'd failed if they didn't find a guy to walk them home and, as the night progressed, they became more and more desperate. They were also more drunk, less able to make careful choices or to resist. His ideal date was a twenty-five-year-old who had recently been chucked by her boyfriend; she was temporarily vulnerable and keen to hook up with someone, was young enough to still have a fit body but old enough to know that a jury wouldn't necessarily regard her with sympathy.

Opening the door, he was hit by a wall of sound and winced visibly. Why did you face deafness nowadays when you wanted to get laid? On the upside, it made conversation difficult so he wouldn't have to come up with too many evasions and outright lies. Lying could be tiring, especially at night when the mind wanted to let go of the stresses of the day.

He paid his entrance fee (a street walker would have charged less for a hand job; he used them occasionally for variety) and walked into the disco, casually scanning the legs, butts, breasts and, lastly, faces. He wanted someone who was showing off a lot of skin. Unfortunately the fashion was for longer tops and leggings – or jeggings if they were made of denim – but he persevered until he saw an inexpensively dressed but respectable thirty-something sitting on her own.

'Lost your friends?' he asked – well, shouted – and was rewarded by her look of gratitude.

'We've fallen out,' she yelled back.

'Their loss.'

'Thanks.' She sounded working class and not particularly well-educated, the type that needed a man to complete her. In other words, she was perfect for his plans.

'Care to dance?'

She staggered slightly as she rose to her feet. Better and better. She was wearing high heels which would make it harder for her to run away. Why did young women essentially cripple themselves with stilettos and cheap cocktails? Had they no sense of pride?

As they reached the dance floor, the music changed to a slower beat and the singer wailed about lost love. He held out his arms and she went eagerly into them.

'Been here before?' he asked.

'No. You?'

'My first time,' he said honestly. 'Do you live around here?'

'Uh huh – St Pauls.' She named an area of Bristol which was often in the news for drugs and crime.

'I'm from Fishponds,' he lied, naming another region of the city. 'Do you work locally too?'

He had to sound like a potential new boyfriend, someone in her league.

She named a tacky fashion store and he pretended to be impressed.

'Can you get me staff discount?'

She giggled. 'I can get you anything.' They danced for another moment, his hands firmly on her waist, before she added, 'What do you do?'

'Personal trainer.' He always stole John's identity at times like this. People thought that they knew what a fitness instructor did so they didn't ask too many questions. It also saved him from inventing an office or regular workplace – he just said that he went to the client's house or to the nearest gym.

'You're fit then,' she slurred.

Fit enough to fuck you into the middle of next week. She was so easy that it wasn't really a challenge. Still, he loved the next bit, when the girl slid into unconsciousness and he could do exactly as he wished.

The slow dance ended and he steered her to the bar.

'What can I get you?'

'A gin and tonic.'

'Two gin and tonics, bartender,' he said.

'You mean you drink that too?' She obviously thought that it was karma.

'That or lager,' he said, not wanting to appear too obvious.

He carried the drinks towards the table nearest the door, managed to slip the little white pill into one of them.

'Left hand,' he repeated to himself again and again, determined not to serve himself the spiked drink.

'Makes you thirsty, all that dancing,' she murmured and downed a third of the doctored gin. He sipped his and watched her covertly. In ten minutes she'd start to feel confused and dizzy, so he wanted her out of here in five. When she started to shiver – going hot and cold was another potential side-effect – he put his arm around her and helped her to her feet.

'Time that I walked you home. Where do you live?'

She told him the name of her street. 'Oh, I have a client there. Which number are you in?'

'237,' she said woozily.

'Alright, sweetheart, let's get you safely back.'

He steered her out into the car park, manoeuvred her carefully into the front seat of his intentionally-nondescript vehicle. By now, he could see that her motor skills were impaired and he had to put on her seat belt for her. She started a sentence but gave up after attempting a few barely-coherent phrases, slumped back in her chair and stared glassily through the windscreen. He programmed his satnav but remained alert as he drove, determined not to get waylaid in some muddy lane or cul de sac. So far he'd managed not to draw attention to himself or to her and he was hell-bent on keeping it that way.

'Flatmates in?' he asked casually as he drew up outside her far-from-desirable residence.

She shook her head, looked as if she was verging on the comatose.

'OK, I'll just get the door open then come back and get you, see you safely inside.'

Taking her clutch bag from her nerveless right hand, he opened it and fished out a key which was attached to a key ring with *Kylie* etched on the fake gold fob. He left her sitting – well, lolling – in the front seat and hurried to the mid terrace dwelling. He entered the house and listened intently for signs of life.

'That you, love?' a woman called.

Shit, did she actually live with her parents? After closing the door quietly, he raced back to the car, started the ignition and drove off. Should he just assault her in the vehicle before dumping her somewhere? There again, she could die of exposure and the last thing he wanted was the police sniffing around.

He glanced at her, noted that she'd fallen forward and that her top had slackened, showing her impressive breasts and part of her nipples. His pulse quickened; he could squeeze and nibble on these for hours. What the hell – he'd take her back to his place and she'd be left with the impression that they'd had a consensual one-night stand. The roofies would wear off in, at most, eight hours, so he'd have to give her Valium as soon as she perked up. That way, she'd be too dozy to figure out his real name, address or any other identifying details, would remain in a loved-up haze until he returned her to Bristol tomorrow night.

Satisfied that he had it all figured out, Adam drove back to Weston-super-Mare at a leisurely pace, parked in his drive and carried Kylie in the side door. She felt heavier than she looked and he almost stumbled as he lurched towards his bedroom with his unconscious prize. After dropping her none-too-lightly on the bed, he returned to the still-open outer door, shut it and locked it from the inside, pocketing the key.

'Good night?'

He jumped at hearing a man's voice, turned to see John in the hallway.

'Thought you were in London,' he stammered.

'I was, but the speaker's gone down with that throat bug so they rescheduled for a fortnight ahead.'

'You mean you went all the way to London and came back the same day?'

He'd have hit the strip clubs and Soho bars, partied like a maniac. He especially loved these peep show places where you could tell the girl what to do, make her take down her panties and dance a jig.

'Well, I was there before midday so had time to cancel my room in the travel lodge without charge.'

Fair enough – he knew that his lodger earned peanuts, couldn't afford a hectic social life.

'So, John, what are you going to do for the rest of the weekend?'

Go to Timbuktu, hopefully. Leave me to fuck my bimbo.

'Nothing much. Probably do a bit of sunbathing in the garden tomorrow if the weather stays hot.'

Bugger, he'd have to keep his conquest away from the windows at the back of the house. It was lucky that he always had a plentiful supply of tranquillizers on the premises, ideal for keeping a girl subdued.

'Right. Well, see you in the morning,' he said, faking a yawn.

John looked sad. 'They're showing back-to-back episodes of *24* if you want to stay up and have a pint or two.'

'Can't.' He indicated his bedroom. 'I've got a hot date waiting for me in there.'

'Alright for some. Does she have a friend?'

He hoped not.

'Sorry, kid, it's just her and me.'

'Story of my life,' John said and offered a lopsided grin.

The youth's life, Adam thought, feeling mildly irritated, was not so much a book as a pamphlet. He had no past successes to talk about and his future wasn't looking too bright.

'Well, I'd better not keep the lady waiting,' he murmured, beginning to back away.

She was lying on her stomach on his bed when he entered the room. He locked it carefully behind him and put the key under his pillow. Reaching under her unconscious body, he unbuttoned her pencil skirt and pulled it down and off. She was wearing a white thong, a garment which he'd always hated, and now removed with equal haste. Her clingy top was harder to take off but he persisted with patience, determined not to tear anything. Her clothes had to be undamaged in case this ever went to court.

'That's it, sweetheart. You want me to feel your pretty breasts.' He murmured encouragement as he unclipped her bra, knowing that people sometimes remembered things which had been said to them when they were borderline conscious. He kept up the chatter, giving the impression that this was consensual sex – the words might permeate her psyche, make it impossible for her to eventually cry rape. His job was to cause confusion, to make her doubt herself. Fortunately, most women were awash with uncertainty.

When she was naked, he sat back and enjoyed the view. Her smooth back curved into a small waist then swelled out at the hips. Her thighs were larger than he liked but without a trace of cellulite. The wisps of pubic hair that he could see indicated that she wasn't a natural blonde. Kneading her buttocks, he felt and saw himself grow hard, realized that it was time to fetch the lubricant.

Either she'd done it up the chocolate freeway before or the drug had loosened her muscles: sometimes it did that. He certainly wasn't complaining as he slid all the way in. She moaned and he murmured, 'You like it that way, don't you sweetheart? Oh yes you do. I can tell.' Leaning forward, he reached under her and palmed her breasts, thrust harder. He was going to come quickly but that was fine; after all, they had the rest of the night and tomorrow, locked together in his room. Fortunately the drug caused urinary retention so she wouldn't need to use the loo.

He'd have to let her phone her mum in the morning, of course, to reassure the older woman that she was alright. He'd give her his new pay-as-you-go mobile – to be disposed of later – which had no connection with his name and address. After she'd told mummy dearest that she was staying with a friend, he'd bring her a cup of tea, doctored with a heavy dose of tranquillizers. Valium was only a tenth of the strength of Rohypnol, but it would do. She'd return to the twilight zone whilst he fucked her again; sometimes, he got so excited with his virtual sex slaves, that he climaxed a third time. And, much later, he came again and again at the memory.

He'd arrange things so that he was back in Bristol by the time that the sedatives were wearing off, would take her to her door and promise to call her on Monday. Sometimes he did call, just to keep the pretence going, but always found a reason not to see the girl again. There were lots of girls like her, with only their looks to offer. They lacked ambition and humour and intellect.

He orgasmed with his usual loud shout, crying out into her hair. She moaned again but remained immobile. After a few moments, his penis shrivelled and slipped out of her, so he moved back to what he always thought of as his side of the bed. He also rolled her onto her side: he didn't want her sinking deeper into the pillow during the night and perhaps suffocating herself.

'Let's get some sleep, Kylie,' he said gently. 'We can have a lot more fun tomorrow morning.'

Well, he would at any rate.

SIX

Did women orgasm more quietly than men? John lay on his bed and listened as Adam let out his trademark shout but it wasn't followed – or preceded – by his partner's climax. Yet, in the porn he'd watched and in the self-help books on love that he'd read, he'd been given the impression that women came hard and long. Was that Adam's one failing, that he was poor in bed or a selfish lover? Sometimes his landlord seemed too good to be true.

Never mind – it wouldn't be long until he took that much-lauded motivational course and would be primed as to how to start a relationship and maybe one day Adam would bump into him and his lover in the hall and would ask longingly if she had a friend. Not that he wanted a series of one-night stands – no, he longed for a caring steady girlfriend, one who might, in time, become an equally devoted wife. Had Adam gone to sleep, leaving his hot date unsatisfied? John fancied that he could hear his landlord's legendary loud snores.

He woke up in the morning to find that the lovers were still in bed; leastways there was no sign of either of them and Adam's car was still in the driveway. Making the most of the midday sun, John took his book – a second-hand copy of the old classic *I'm Okay, You're Okay* – out into the back garden and fetched a deckchair from the garage.

He'd just started chapter three when he heard a noise, glanced up and saw next door's Maine Coon cat on Adam's bedroom window. A few slivers of stone cascaded to the ground and he tensed, afraid that the large animal was going to pull the sill away from the stone wall and hurt itself. The bungalow was an old one which hadn't been particularly well maintained by the previous owner, a senior citizen, and Adam simply didn't have time for DIY.

'Shoo,' he said, running towards the affable creature.

Purring, she jumped down and rubbed herself against his legs.

Belatedly, John realized that Adam hadn't pulled down the blind, that he was staring into the man's expensively-carpeted and beautifully decorated bedroom. A naked blonde girl lay on her side, facing away from her new lover, her features obscured by her long hair. He, Adam, was partially covered with a duvet and similarly fast asleep. Feeling unaccountably saddened, John returned to his deckchair. He'd hold his own girl all night, he thought, and would bring her breakfast in bed every morning. He'd remember every birthday and anniversary and would also buy her other presents just because.

Not that he'd had any luck so far. In fact, he'd even been turned down when attempting to join a paid-for dating site. The message that the firm had sent him had explained that they turned down twenty percent of applicants because they were too unusual, would be unlikely to find mates.

He had to find a mate soon or he'd die from lack of love, a

sort of emotional malnutrition. He had to become more like Adam if he was ever to succeed.

'What can I get you, angel? Tea and toast?'

Adam put his arms around Kylie's waist then pulled away; she felt oddly cool despite the sunshine blasting through the window.

'Warm enough?' With difficulty, he rolled her onto her back and realized the awful truth: she would never be warm again. Fuck, she'd only gone and died on him in the middle of the night, probably reacted badly to the Rohypnol. What the hell was he supposed to do now?

Leaving her in bed – and trying not to think about the hours he'd spent sleeping beside a corpse – he left his study, locking the door behind him. He showered, dressed and made himself eat the remains of yesterday's curry; he had to keep his blood sugar levels high if he wanted to think.

He'd taken Hannah's body to Weston Woods but he couldn't do that with Kylie as that would signify that a serial killer was operating in his home town. As it was, the police had stated that they were looking at Hannah's past boyfriends and acquaintances: they were assuming that she'd been killed, as most victims were, by someone she knew.

And he daren't take her corpse back to her native Bristol, especially when he'd briefly parked outside her house last night. What if someone had seen him and remembered some of his registration number? The police might be looking out for a vehicle just like this now that Kylie had disappeared. No, he'd have to keep her here for a while until the heat died down and he could devise a plan.

'Alright, boss?'

He jumped and dropped his fork as John joined him at the kitchen table.

'Just finishing last night's curry.'

'Worked up an appetite, have you?' The younger man grinned.

What? It took him a moment to remember that he and his lodger had spoken last night, that he'd mentioned bringing a girl back. He certainly hadn't burned off any calories this morning, not being a necrophiliac.

'Just a few,' he said with an understated smile. 'I think I've worn her out. She's gone back to sleep again.'

'She was out for the count when I saw her,' John murmured then went very red.

'You saw . . .?'

'Tilly was damaging your window sill so I shooed her away and couldn't help but see in. Sorry about that.'

'This morning? We were probably both unconscious.' He gulped as a little curry-flavoured acid rose in his throat.

'Good night, was it? Where did you go?'

To his chagrin, he almost said Bristol. 'Bath.'

'I went there once with the school.'

I should care? He forced himself to sound friendly, normal. 'So, John, what are you up to today?'

'Oh, just hanging about. I didn't make any plans cause I should have been on that course.'

'There's an indie cinema day on in town.'

'I'm waiting for my new distance glasses, couldn't see the screen.'

'A dog show on the Beach Lawns.'

'I'm allergic.'

'An all day breakfast for three quid at that place on the Boulevard.'

'I'm saving my money for the London trip.'

'Have it on me,' Adam said, going into his wallet and handing the youth a fiver.

'You wanting rid of me?'

'It's not personal. It's just that Kyl . . . Miranda is too shy to meet my flatmate, won't come out until we have the place to ourselves.'

'I could take my book,' John said.

No wonder he never got dates, Adam thought, when he read self-help books in public places. He might as well have had 'geek' tattooed on his forehead and 'virgin' on his chest.

'Excellent idea. Well, see you anon.'

'I should give you change . . .' The youth started to search through his jeans pockets.

'No – keep it.'

Stay in the cafe drinking tea for as long as possible. Go, go, go, go, go.

'You're a good mate, Adam.'

'And you're a very good lodger.'

He was, too – always paid his rent on time and normally didn't pry.

He waited for ten long minutes after John left before starting Operation Recovery, hurrying to the garage and emptying most of the bulk-bought frozen foods out of the chest-style freezer. When he'd finished, he went with equal haste to his bedroom, wrapped Kylie in a sheet and carried her quickly to the cobweb-strewn outbuilding, hoping that none of the neighbours were at their windows or peering through the hedge.

Fortunately her body had remained pliant, perhaps due to the heat, so she was comparatively easy to lower into the cold depths, unlike Hannah who had been a challenge to fold into his car boot.

When she was lying as flat as possible, he piled all of the food back on top, shut the freezer and locked the garage. Taking his key and the spare, he hid them both under a plant pot in his study, a room which his lodger rarely entered. Now no one could unlock the garage to rummage through the freezer and find a lot more than lamb chops and family-sized bags of green beans.

He was sitting in the deckchair reading the Sunday papers (delivered at a ridiculously early time, as per usual) when John returned.

'I'll join you,' said John, heading for the garage. He returned a moment later. 'It was open earlier when I got the chair out but now it's locked.'

'Oh, I did that – the cat was trying to get in.'

'Have you got the key? I want to get another chair.'

You don't really.

'Have mine. I've got tons of work to do.'

'On a Sunday?'

''Fraid so. It's one of the worst days for mental health. The vulnerable go to pieces when they've got time to themselves.'

He went into his study for a while, keeping one eye on John as he sat, reading, in the garden. When he dozed off, Adam went into his bedroom and pulled the blind. The room smelt of sex and perspiration and, perhaps, of death so he put the duvet and its cover plus both pillowcases in the washing machine then returned to scrub the furniture. He put his remaining fitted sheet on the bed and made a mental note to buy another to replace the one which the increasingly-frozen Kylie was currently wrapped in. It was proving to be a lucrative month for the local bed linen stores.

Sorted. He was relaxing in front of the television with a beer, when John appeared.

'Can I have the garage key so that I can put my deckchair back?'

Damn him.

Adam made a show of going through his pockets. 'I appear to have lost it.'

'Do you have a spare?'

'No, it went AWOL months ago.'

'I could break in,' John offered.

'Nah, I've been running down the freezer for a while anyway so that I can give it a good clean. There's next to nothing in there.'

'What about the deckchair?'

'Just put it down the side of the boiler in the utility room.'

'If the weather stays like this, we'll need to get hold of the other chair,' the youth said anxiously.

'I've got a spare one in the loft,' Adam lied.

He must, he thought, buy another one soon in order to keep John from trying to enter the garage. Kylie's corpse might be there for some considerable time.

SEVEN

Could his brother have had anything to do with Hannah's murder? He'd wondered about that as soon as a news report had said that she'd been mourning the loss of her mother and sister, as he knew that Adam offered bereavement counselling. Apparently they were still hunting her killer and had drafted in further officers from Bristol to join the Major Incident Team.

Nicholas Neave sighed and switched off his TV. He'd suspected for years that Adam was capable of almost anything. He'd seen the casual cruelty that the older boy had meted out to the family pets when they were growing up. Later, when his brother was a precocious twelve, he'd started to seduce the local girls and he'd seen their tears and disbelief as he bedded and then ignored them. His parents eventually had to fork out the cash to end three teenage pregnancies.

But the worst thing about Adam was the way that he targeted anyone pure. He'd singled out a shy girl who was saving it for Jesus and had wooed her for weeks with honeyed words and little – doubtless stolen – gifts. He, Nicholas, had warned her that Adam had had a string of girls, that he only wanted them for sex, but she'd chosen not to believe him, had fallen helplessly in love.

He'd had sex with her for a week or two before moving on to his next victim: he loved a challenge. Nicholas would never forget her tears, the way that she'd begged him to intervene. He'd even tried to talk to his brother but the youth had just said, 'You fuck her if you like.'

'But she loves you.'

'That's her problem.'

'She says that you told her that you loved her.'

'Has she got it on tape?'

Once again his parents had become involved and had gone to see the girl's mother and stepfather. Once again, they'd attempted to talk to Adam, to make him feel another person's pain.

And, years later, they'd all talked to Helen, begged her not to remain involved with the man, explained that his relationships were invariably destructive. But, rather than listen to them, she'd married him, and it had probably cost her her life. The police had been convinced that he'd pushed her to her death rather than let her leave him; they merely lacked proof.

Could he have killed again since then, safe in the knowledge that he had already gotten away with murder? And, given his ongoing need for excitement, what would he do next?

Why hadn't Adam Neave responded to any of his phone messages? Dr Edward Frazer returned home from the latest conference on ADHD and checked his answering machine.

Usually, fellow professionals got back to him within days but he'd been waiting to hear from this particular psychologist about Brandon Petrie for over a month.

The conference had been fascinating, if controversial, with its suggestion that children inherited the brain disorder from their parents, inheriting duplicated or missing DNA from the same sections of the brain which were implicated in schizophrenia. Had Brandon's biological parents passed on the chromosomal abnormality? His notes said that he had been adopted at birth.

He'd only seen Brandon twice, but was convinced that the teen had a serious conduct disorder rather than simply an attention deficit. In short, the youth might well grow up to become antisocial, setting fires and torturing animals or hitting his girlfriends. He could become a burglar or a professional shoplifter, would use every opportunity to defy authority. Denied suitable medication, the boy would give in to serious impulses without caring about – or even fully understanding – the implications. If he was angry, he could lash out repeatedly. If he felt lust, he might rape. As an expert in the field, he wanted to talk to the psychologist about his patient's propensity for violence but Neave was clearly ignoring him.

He'd planned to screen the youth more thoroughly but had been thwarted by Brandon's mother, who'd explained that they'd found him a new psychologist – Adam Neave – who thought that the teenager's problems were easily solved, that he'd grow out of them. This was the case with many straightforward cases of ADHD, with up to a fifth of cases resolving themselves by the time that the child reached his or her late teens. It seemed miraculous to some of the parents but simply meant that their offspring's brain had matured and the defects in the neurotransmitter metabolism had lessened or disappeared.

Conduct disorder, however, was different, much more alarming and had long-term implications. He couldn't diagnose it after just one session but wanted to see the boy again or at least talk candidly to his new therapist. He didn't want to put his concerns down in writing as it was far too early to label the youth. And yet . . .

Was Adam Neave so busy that he couldn't make a five-minute phone call about a potentially dangerous patient? How could he justify this level of professional indifference?

EIGHT

'So, how have you been?' Beth asked, trying to keep her voice matter-of-fact. Widows always cried more if you showed too much sympathy and she felt that it was more important that Olivia talk than sob. Doubtless she'd been weeping at home on a daily – possibly hourly – basis for the past few weeks, now she needed to shed words rather than tears.

The girl swallowed visibly. 'There are just so many memories . . .'

'I know.' It was only when her own husband died that she'd realized just how many associations they'd made together. Suddenly everything from a song played on a passing car radio to seeing his favourite foods in the supermarket became a source of pain. Seeing other couples together – especially those who were happily moving through old age together – had also underlined her sense of loss.

'I've cleared away all his things.'

'A lot of people find that helps.'

'Well, it made it bearable,' Olivia said and her lip trembled again.

'Have you managed to join anything?'

It worried her that Olivia was so isolated.

'A book group on Tuesday mornings. Everyone else there is at least twice my age but I don't care.'

'Anything else?'

The twenty-five-year-old shook her head. 'I haven't really had time. I had to go back to the hospital to get Zak's things and go to the registrar's office to register the death. A few days later I went back for copies of the death certificate and I've been mailing them to the bank, building society, DVLA . . .'

Beth nodded, remembering. The paperwork could take months, especially when the deceased was self-employed so you had to take over or close down their business, with all the additional form-filling this involved.

'And have you been eating properly?'

She could tell that the girl had lost weight, which was an especially bad sign when she was in her fifth month of pregnancy.

'I've had some milkshakes for the baby and I'm OK with trifle or fruit mousses but almost everything else comes back up.'

'You should see your GP.'

'I have and he's given me these huge vitamin boosters,' Olivia said. 'He says that the baby gets the nutrients first, that it will be fine.'

'But we want *you* to be healthy too!'

'I know. It's just so hard.'

'I remember,' Beth said softly. 'I can only promise you that it does get easier.'

She broke off as the door opened and Adam walked in. 'Sorry I'm late – problems with the car.'

'That's fine. It's just Olivia and I so far this morning.'

She introduced the young widow to the counsellor.

'I'll leave you to it,' Adam murmured, taking a seat at a table at the other end of the hall. Ten minutes later, an elderly man walked – well, hobbled – in and Adam beckoned him over and began to chat.

'Is he your boyfriend?' Olivia asked sadly.

'Adam? No! In fact, he only recently joined us.' She wondered if she should mention Matthew, decided that it wasn't particularly appropriate.

'And you're all volunteers?'

'We are. And unfortunately most of us have personal experience of widowhood.'

'You seem so sorted,' the younger woman said.

'Well, I am now, as the pain has become manageable. But I was shaken to the core when my husband died three years ago. It just takes time.'

Both clients stayed for the full two hours and were visibly reluctant to leave.

'He's just lost his wife,' Adam said to Beth after the session ended and they prepared to lock up.

'And Olivia just lost her husband.'

'How old is she?'

'Twenty-five, with no living relatives. She's completely on her own.'

'If she wants more extensive counselling . . .'

Beth frowned. She knew that Adam had come to them with first-class references but wasn't sure that it was ethical for him to suggest that clients to a free monthly drop-in centre should becoming paying patients at his home.

'She'll probably get help from the NHS in time, especially as she's pregnant.'

'She doesn't look it.'

'I know. She's actually been losing weight.'

'Are you going on to the hospital now? I'm going in that direction, so could give you a lift.'

'No, I've got the rest of the day off.'

'All right for some! I've got an obsessive-compulsive coming round later, though, on the upside, I won't have to clean the door handles for a week.'

'She cleans them for you?'

'Wraps a tissue around each one before opening it and puts a paper towel on the couch before sitting down.'

Beth laughed. 'Maybe she's normal and you just have a particularly dusty house!'

'Used to, but nowadays I have a lodger with time on his hands so he keeps the place looking reasonable.'

'Send him to me,' Beth said with feeling. 'Brian used to do all the cleaning, so now . . .'

She tailed off, and they looked at each other sadly for a moment, widow to widower. If only the cancer had been caught before it reached grade four, Beth thought for the billionth time.

'So, are you doing anything special this evening?' Adam asked.

Was he about to ask her out? Beth hesitated; she had to admit that he was a very attractive man and that she and Matthew hadn't agreed to become exclusive. But the latter seemed so involved that it would be cruel to date someone else.

'Going out with Matthew again. Just to the cinema.'

'I've heard good things about that new thriller.'

'Unfortunately it's a romcom – his choice!'

'A romantic man? You should hold on to him,' Adam said as they walked into the May heat.

'I intend to,' Beth said, then felt the inevitable flicker of doubt. She feared that he was too quiet for her, and was sometimes left with the impression that he was a shallow thinker. But he tried very hard to please her and was always kind.

That night, as they drove to the Odeon, he switched on the CD player and the car filled with a song about overwhelming love. Beth felt suddenly sad – the only person that she was in love with was her late husband. Despite her attempts to move on, he was always in her heart.

'Who's that?' she asked, forcing her voice to remain neutral.

'Eva Cassidy.'

He sang along, casting sideways glances at her. It was nice to feel cherished, Beth acknowledged to herself, even if she couldn't yet reciprocate.

Matthew held her hand throughout the film and, when they got back to her house, they curled up on the settee and watched a half hour comedy on DVD.

'I'm happiest when I'm in your arms,' he murmured afterwards as they walked upstairs together, en route for bed.

He seemed extra keen to please her tonight, Beth thought, as he kissed his way down her body then began to lick her labial lips – but would he really be able to stay down there long enough to make her orgasm? Her husband had always – as he jokingly put it – hand-started her, sometimes switching to oral when she was halfway there.

As the minutes passed, the sensation built and built, but Beth couldn't quite relax, aware that Matthew's tongue must be increasingly exhausted. She was vaguely aware of a slight change of pace and realized that he was now using his lips to stimulate her instead. He always seemed like a man on a mission, that mission being to make her climax. Ironically, it put her under pressure and had the opposite effect.

Still, she thought that she could get there in the next few minutes if he kept up the same gentle pace, so she was shocked when he suddenly put one finger inside her and another on the outside and started to jiggle them really quickly. Almost immediately, she felt all of the sensation fade. He'd done the same thing the last few times when she was moments away from coming, reverting, she presumed, to the harder touch which must have taken his wife over the edge.

Feeling suddenly low, she sat up and put her hands on his hair. 'Come and have a hug,' she murmured gently.

'You can't quite get there?'

'I need such a soft touch . . .' Translation: *don't rub*.

She held and stroked him for a few minutes until she felt his hardness against her thigh, then guided him inside her. He knew that she couldn't come from intercourse so wouldn't hold back.

Afterwards, as usual, he felt asleep within seconds. She'd have to teach him to be gentler with her clitoris, Beth admitted to herself. She wondered, briefly, if she should bring herself off, but the moment had passed. Though she was still too wired to sleep, she reminded herself that she was fortunate compared to all of the newly widowed who were, at this very moment, lying alone, shell-shocked and rootless, in empty beds.

NINE

Excellent – she'd been introduced to Adam as a weeping widow whom Beth had befriended by chance at the hospital. It was perfect. There was no reason for him to suspect that she was an undercover cop.

Olivia let herself into the house that she shared with her husband, Marc – still very much alive – and removed the thin layer of padding from around her stomach. How on earth did women cope with a genuine pregnancy? She felt ungainly and overheated and kept bumping into things; it was like having premenstrual water retention, only worse.

She'd wanted to have a baby for years, but had daydreamed more about the end product than about the actual gestation period. Now, for the first time, she realized that she'd find the last few months very difficult. She'd always been petite and enjoyed feeling light and lithe when she was walking, loved the admiring looks that she got from men.

That said, she had to admit that the police psychologist who had briefed her had been absolutely right. He'd thought that Beth would stop to comfort a stranger and knew that, upon finding that she was widowed, the older woman would invite her along to the bereavement drop-in centre. It meant that Adam viewed her as one of Beth's patients whom she'd met at a remote location, that he'd have no reason to suspect that anyone was checking up on him. Beth could also unwittingly bolster her story by mentioning that she'd been to Olivia's house.

It wasn't, of course, her real house but one which had been taken over for the duration of the enquiry by the police department. She, Olivia, had to go there from the bereavement centre any time that she might be accompanied by Beth or followed by Adam Neave. Fortunately he'd still been at his workplace when she left today so she'd been able to take the train home to Dorchester. Because she didn't live locally, he wouldn't spot her by chance with her real husband – and *sans* bump – whilst they were doing the weekly shop.

The bump had been the psychologist's idea, of course.

'This man will strike fast if he feels lust, and, in these circumstances, we can't guarantee a surveillance cop's safety, so we need a way to slow him down, to find out exactly how he operates. He'll be attracted by your youth and vulnerability but we believe that he won't want to rape a pregnant woman, so we'll have several months to learn his strategies.'

They'd made clear from the start that they believed he was an unpredictable man.

'He married this really shy woman, a new-age therapist, who was fourteen years older than him – they wed within weeks of meeting. We know from his family that he quickly became cold and controlling and they got the impression that she was afraid of upsetting him, that she'd initially do anything to keep the peace.'

'And his parents told you this openly?' In Olivia's experience, families closed ranks against the police and other outsiders. It was unusual for them to volunteer anything.

'His brother came to us after Helen Neave's death, said that he didn't believe that it was a suicide. Apparently her religion forbade this and she took it seriously.'

'Didn't you say that she was into some kind of New Age . . .'

'Yes, for her work. Off the record, we think that she was a bit of a basket case. She offered this odd mix of past life examination and crystal healing. A very pretty woman, but damaged and susceptible.'

Aren't we all, Olivia had thought, but she hadn't said so. You simply didn't rise through the ranks if your superiors believed that you had mental health problems, yet everyone she knew within the force had baggage and issues and a level of neuroticism, plus lots of officers used alcohol to take their minds off the horrors that they had seen.

'If she was so damaged, isn't it possible that she killed herself?'

'We doubt it as she became perimenopausal and it made her stronger. It happens with some women – they produce less oestrogen than before and become more male, more aggressive. She saw her GP and got herself a referral to an NHS psychiatrist, though she apparently didn't tell Adam. But she confided in her brother-in-law Nicholas and his wife Jill.'

'So she was moving away from Adam emotionally?'

'Big time. Nicholas had the feeling that she was getting close to leaving the marriage as she'd started applying for full-time jobs.'

'And if he was one of those men who need total control over a woman . . .' Olivia had murmured, knowing that women were often murdered by their violent partners when they tried to leave.

'Exactly. He might have decided that, if he could no longer have her, no one would.'

'So how do you anticipate that he'll act with me?'

'We think that he'll be chivalrous for the first few sessions until he believes that he's gained your trust, then he'll become more flirtatious and increasingly unprofessional. We don't think that he'll actually try to seduce you until after he believes that you've given birth.'

'I know that you can't guarantee that,' Olivia said, determined to sound – and be – strong. This could be the operation which would make her career and, having attended self-defence classes for years, she believed that she could take care of herself. It was too risky to wire her, but there were going to be detectives watching from the house across the road. She only needed to appear in the window momentarily and they would storm the therapist's place and, if necessary, taser him.

'Should I try to get him to talk about Hannah?' she'd asked, aware that they were attempting to link him to the recent Weston murder.

'No, just talk about your own bereavement and encourage him to talk about his late wife. Don't steer the conversation in any particular direction, but take careful note of anything that he says about her death.'

'And if he clams up?'

'Don't push it. He's a bright man, so it won't take much for him to suspect that you're part of a surveillance team.'

'I'll be subtle,' Olivia said. She was aware that her heart was beating faster than usual. This was going to be the most exciting thing that had happened to her in years. Adam Neave was possibly a double killer and she was going to use all of her charm and intellect to reel him in.

TEN

He'd rape Olivia a few weeks after she'd had the baby – screwing someone who was pregnant didn't appeal to him and, in the days after she'd given birth, she'd be all torn up and horribly slack. He'd counselled husbands whose wives were suffering from post-natal depression and some of them had joked that it would have been nice if the surgeon had put in a couple of extra stitches when he was sewing up the vaginal tears.

He'd use Rohypnol again. Oh, it had led to Kylie's death but he'd just been unlucky. He'd used it several times before without incident. He'd rape Olivia in her own home so that she woke up in her own bed and would feel comparatively secure, albeit achy. Women often convinced themselves that they had the combination of a hangover and twenty-four-hour flu. Even if they had flashbacks, they rarely went to the police, especially if they'd met the man whilst they were out drinking and invited him back to their place. The drug caused memory problems so how could they prove that it wasn't consensual sex?

Olivia would be especially confused, unable to reconcile any vague sexual flashbacks with the kindly counsellor who had helped her throughout her pregnancy. He'd only met up with her for two therapy sessions at the centre so far but she already seemed to have a crush on him, had spent much of the time widening her eyes and slightly parting her legs and laughing too loudly and too long at his jokes. After the drugged rape, she'd think that she was experiencing some illness-induced hallucination or letting out some previously-suppressed fantasy. Freud had believed that most female patients fell in love with their therapists and some therapists even encouraged this, regarding it as an inevitable part of the therapy.

He was seeing Brandon Petrie at 4.30 p.m. Ten minutes before the teenager was due, Adam opened his study, bedroom and lounge windows. It might just be his imagination but he felt that the house still smelt strange, as if Kylie had left her mark on it. Thank goodness he'd stashed her away in the freezer within an hour of discovering the body; if he'd left her in this overheated house, she'd have rapidly decomposed.

'Brandon – nice to see you again.'

'Yeah?' the teenager muttered then apparently did a double take and muttered, 'Nice to see you too, Mr Neave.'

'Adam.'

'Whatever.'

'Fake it until you . . .' he prompted

'Nice to see you, Adam,' the youth said with a mirthless smile.

'Isn't it amazing weather, Mrs Petrie?'

The not so yummy mummies always liked to discuss the weather. It was a safe topic, non-politicised. They couldn't bear too much reality.

'It is. You know, it's so long since it rained that we've started leaving the sun loungers out overnight.'

'Same here.'

It suddenly occurred to him that he could take the other deck-chair from the garage as long as he didn't unlock the door when John was around. Why on earth had he considered buying a new one? He couldn't have been thinking straight.

He saw that Brandon's mother was staring at him expectantly, realized that he'd forgotten to politely dismiss her.

'If you could return for him in two hours?'

'That long?'

Yes – I need the extra money now that I'm constantly replacing my bedding and soft furnishings.

'It's best. We're making such good progress that I'd like to increase the momentum. Especially when he has his exams next week.'

'I suppose that I could go to that new cafe in town,' the woman said doubtfully.

That was half of the problem, Adam thought – Brandon was an exceptionally bright boy but was stuck with parents who were measuring out their lives in coffee spoons.

'I've heard that it's good,' he lied. It was best that she stayed exactly as she was – after all, if her outlook on life improved so might Brandon's and he couldn't afford to lose the weekly fee. At the moment, she fussed around the boy and added to the stress that his ADHD already put him under, so, as a result, he acted out and required further therapy. It was Adam's task to get him to act superficially better, whilst still being odd enough to require ongoing counselling.

'So, what have you done to earn brownie points this week?' he asked after Mummy Dearest had gone off to buy a cream tea.

'Tidied my room, said please and thank you to everyone, babysat for my cousin Ethan.'

'Yeah? How old is he?'

Brandon shrugged, seemed to belatedly notice Adam's frown and said, 'Four.'

'And your mum leaves you in sole charge?'

He could imagine Mrs Petrie still chaperoning Brandon when he was twenty.

The boy shrugged. 'Not exactly. I have to take him to the woman next door if he becomes unduly distraught.'

'So, why have they asked you to babysit now?'

'Well, my grandmother used to do it but she died recently.'

'Oh, I'm sorry.'

'I'm not. I mean, thank you. His mum goes out a lot and my parents have to shop.'

'So, do you mind looking after him?'

Another shrug. 'He doesn't have a father so I'm in loco parentis.'

The teen's vocabulary was excellent for his age – for any age.

'That's great, Brandon. It really is.' He decided to level with the kid. 'Sometimes you have to do really dull stuff at home or school to get kudos but it pays off in the long term. You look after this cousin now and your mum and dad will see you as a balanced person, are much more likely to fund your years at university.'

'A room of my own which I can lock – that's all I want,' the youth said, as he said during every session.

'Trust me, you're getting closer to it all the time.' He grinned. 'Listen, I'll outline scenarios and you tell me what you usually do and what you think that the new you should do.'

'Conceptually? Be polite, listen actively, make good eye contact.'

'Hell, we haven't even started and you're sorted!' Adam said.

Almost two hours later, he waved the boy and his mother goodbye, sat back and sipped a glass of white wine. This was like taking milk from a baby. With his almost constant movement and bursts of defiance, Brandon had been the hyperactive-impulsive type. He'd also shown an inability to delay gratification, limited social skills and difficulty in sustaining interest in a project, all of which had made him a challenge both at school and at home.

He, Adam, had recognized that the boy's medication was actually keeping him awake and agitated throughout the early hours, had suggested to his doctor that they cut his late-afternoon dose to half a tablet. As a result, he now slept through the night. He'd also talked to his mother privately on the phone and suggested that she use a strategy called 'extinction' when her son behaved badly, in essence the withdrawal of a reward. Brandon was motivated to retain access to his computer and his PlayStation, pure escapism, so his behaviour had improved.

Adam smiled to himself as he poured a second glass of Riesling. The boy was going to be one of his biggest success stories and his mother would recommend him to everyone she met.

Christ, that shrink was easy to deceive – he thought that he was cool and clever but he just came over as arrogant and smarmy. His idiotic parents were paying over the odds to someone who didn't have a clue. But that suited him, Brandon, just fine: the last thing he wanted was a psychologist who understood him. He wanted to do his own thing and to hell with society's rules. Oh, he took the shrink's point that he should pretend to respect his desperately conventional elders and his play-by-the-rules teachers, but he had no intention of living like them.

'Ethan – fucking stop it,' he said as the four-year-old began to wail.

Ethan stopped, doubtless remembering the slaps that he'd given him last week for being too noisy. Slaps were a good bet as they faded long before his parents got back from the weekly shopping trip or Ethan's downbeat mother returned from the pub. She was his aunt, his father's sister, the black sheep of the dull but respectable family: the others had become accountants and bank tellers but she'd settled for being a single parent and a drunk.

'Hungry,' Ethan said, threatening to cry again.

'Here, have some crisps.' There were fish fingers in the freezer but he couldn't be bothered putting on the grill, was immersed in his guitar playing. Anyway, his folks would be back with laden carrier bags within the hour and the little brat could choose something from one of them. 'Fake it until you make it, kid – it'll stand you in good stead in the long term,' he said to the little boy, echoing Adam's words.

Did the man really think that his pathetic homilies were going to infiltrate his, Brandon's, sophisticated psyche? There was one born every minute as his recently-deceased grandmother used to say.

ELEVEN

'Are you sure, Mum?'

As soon as he said the words out loud, Nicholas Neave realized how ridiculous they sounded. Of course she was sure – she'd just returned from an hour-long conversation with the consultant. It was ovarian cancer and it had spread so widely that it was inoperable.

'I'm sure, son. You know how I've been below par?'

Nicholas nodded and took Jill's hand. How often had they sat here on his parents' couch, enjoying hot drinks and snacks and exchanging anecdotes? It must have been so hard for her to summon them here today to break the news.

He heard his wife clear her throat. 'I thought that the doctor said it was just IBS?'

'They thought that for a few months when my stomach puffed up but the new diet didn't help and I was taking so many pain-killers that I passed out in the supermarket and further tests showed that I was anaemic. Then I blacked out again and they did a scan . . .'

'Isn't there anything they can do?'

Nicholas looked helplessly at his dad, only to see that the older man was crying silently. He'd only once seen him weep like that, after his daughter-in-law Helen's unexpected death.

'Just give me painkillers to keep me comfortable,' his mother said. 'Hey, I've had a good life and made it to seventy. Nobody lives forever, son.'

Seventy's not old nowadays, Nicholas thought dazedly. He looked at his three-year-old son, Tim, playing with a big plastic truck on the floor. How many more times would he see his grandmother before she became too ill for juvenile visitors? Would he even remember her when he grew up?

'Mum, Dad, I'm so sorry,' he said, hating the inadequacy of the word. He'd thought that his parents would have at least another fifteen years together as they'd always been so energetic and healthy. They'd only retired last year from running a florist's, with all of the early-morning trips to market and hectic Saturdays which that entailed.

'We haven't been able to get hold of your brother yet,' his mother said sadly.

Good. He bit back the word. Mum loved Adam, her chosen son, whatever his faults and was always reaching out to him, but the sonofabitch only got in touch when he wanted favours or cash. They'd recommended him to a few of their less-balanced customers when they owned the florists so he'd been angry when they sold up.

'Maybe you could speak to him for me? Explain that I don't have long left.'

Nicholas fought back tears. He'd march his adopted brother round here in person if necessary. He'd even pay him if that was what it took.

'I'll talk to him, Mum. Promise. You know how busy he gets.'

Busy screwing hookers, probably. He'd seen him hanging around the rougher parts of the town where it was easiest to score sex or drugs. Much as he despised the man, he'd phone him as soon as he got home and would underline the fact that this was an emergency.

He forced himself to dial as soon as he got back. The phone rang and rang and he was expecting it to go to answerphone when his brother eventually said a breathless, 'Hello?'

'Adam? It's Nicholas. You know how Mum's had all these symptoms? Well, she saw the specialist today and it's not good news.'

'Spit it out.'

'It's ovarian cancer and it's terminal.'

The other man's voice didn't miss a beat. 'How long has she got?'

'They haven't told her yet. She goes back next week to find out about timescales and palliative care.'

'So what do you want me to do?'

'Visit her. Pretend that you care. Make her last weeks as happy as possible.'

A slight pause. 'You know that I've never gone the happy families route.'

'Oh, I'm well aware of that, but she's asking for you and—'

There was a click and he realized that the phone call had come to an abrupt and unsatisfactory end.

TWELVE

'**A** woman has gone missing in nearby Bristol and the police there are convinced that she's met with foul play.' Detective Superintendent Winston studied the missing persons report and had to admit that there were similarities with Hannah's death. Both women had led blameless lives – Kylie worked in a clothing store during the day and spent most evenings with her disabled parents. She'd disappeared during a rare night out with friends. Her mother thought that she'd come home and then had a change of heart: they'd heard the outer door open and close, then a car start up. Neither parent had heard from the young woman since.

But the man that they suspected of Hannah's murder was a controlled and intelligent individual, so it was unlikely that he'd have killed again so quickly, assuming that Kylie was actually dead rather than merely being held someplace against her will, like an outhouse or basement. All that they could be sure of was that she hadn't left voluntarily; she'd been happy with her life and was really looking forward to her sister's impending wedding. Moreover, her modest bank account hadn't been touched.

Could their suspect – if only they had the funds to mount twenty-four-hour surveillance – be keeping her as a sex slave? The police psychologist had said that this was highly unlikely, that he'd tire quickly of one body, would prefer new flesh. So it might well be that one man had murdered Hannah and that a different man was keeping Kylie in his basement or some outbuilding which was off the beaten track. In other words, they couldn't afford to zero in exclusively on one individual, the Detective Superintendent told himself as he reviewed the latest intelligence. They had to keep an open mind.

THIRTEEN

His lips were on her clitoris and he was licking her so sweetly that she couldn't keep still, was inwardly begging him to continue. She had her hands entwined in his lovely, thick dark hair, wordlessly encouraging him as she pushed her pubis against his tongue, as the ripples built and spread . . .

Olivia came long and hard and woke up to find her sex was pulsating. She slid down an exploratory finger, found that she was hot and wet. She'd orgasmed in her sleep, a first for her. It wouldn't have been a problem if she hadn't been dreaming that she was in bed with Adam Neave.

A part snore, part whistle brought her more fully back to the present and she turned on her side to look at Marc, her husband. She'd been fourteen when he first asked her out, and he'd been a whole year older. He'd seemed mature and exotic in those days, particularly given his Anglo-French heritage.

They'd married three years after they first met, in defiance of both sets of parents. Then, life had been full of possibilities – foreign holidays and new hobbies and, they'd hoped, eventually a child. But Marc had tired of travelling, lost interest in his squash club and seemed to blame her for their failure to conceive, though tests had shown that both of them were fertile and no one could explain exactly why their frequent sex sessions had never resulted in a pregnancy. Gradually, they'd made love less and less and Marc had also lost interest in socializing. Nowadays, he was content to stay at home and watch Sky Sports in the evenings whilst she still wanted to have fun.

'Marc, can you lie on your side?' She poked and shoved at him with increasing irritation until he moved, but the nocturnal noises continued. Had he been playing with his cousin's dog? She was sure that he was allergic to the beast and ended up with nasal congestion as a result.

'You in a bad mood again?' he muttered, his shoulders hunched.

'No, just a bit tired with all this extra travelling.' Until recently she'd both lived and worked in Dorchester but now she was commuting to Weston-super-Mare, Adam's locale.

Hug me, she thought, but Marc remained turned away from her. Make love to me – I'm already open and wet. She turned and slid her hands around his waist and was about to move them down towards his groin, but her efforts were met by yet another snore.

How had he become so old, so tired all the time? In the early years of their marriage, they had gone out frequently, even if it was just to friends' houses. Then these same friends had started to have babies and the shared pizza nights had come to an end. They'd still socialized as a couple, though, getting joint gym membership and also attending karate classes. But Marc had become increasingly involved in an engineering project at work so she'd started exercising alone.

Now she was doing more and more things alone, including having sex with herself, often when she came home from a shift at the police station and needed to relax.

They'd been married for thirteen years, so was this their second dose of the seven-year-itch, arrived early? Olivia turned on her side and tried to get back to sleep again but she was all too aware of the wetness streaking her thighs, of the fact that Adam Neave was inadvertently responsible. It was understandable, really, as she was being encouraged to make a connection, to flirt with him. She was also playing the part of a woman five years younger than her real self, as the police psychologist was sure that Neave would be drawn to younger women, seeing them as easier to manipulate. Fortunately they'd allowed her to use her own first name as she'd struggled to answer to the other names which they'd tried out.

Had he similarly dreamed about her? The police psychologist had warned her that he would want to act out his fantasies, that he might pounce at any moment. They'd said that he was a predatory individual, but, in the wet dream that she'd just had, he'd merely been masterful. She had to remind herself that he was at the charismatic stage and trying to get her into his corner, that he would become increasingly inappropriate as time went on.

Marc muttered something in his sleep and Olivia stiffened, wondering if it was another woman's name. They'd been through so much in the past thirteen years that she couldn't wholly blame him. Life hadn't worked out the way that they'd planned.

Suddenly feeling closer to him, she turned on her side and slid her arms around his waist for a second time, wincing momentarily as her hands traced a roll of fat. He'd had such a lovely body when they married, had kept so fit.

'Want to make out?' she murmured, using the words that she'd used when they were in their teens.

She had a momentary suspicion that Marc was awake as his breathing stilled, then he let out another snore. Could he fake such a noise? It was an ugly sound and she felt her desire subside. No one could blame her for being attracted to Adam, she thought;

after all, he was sexual, handsome and intelligent. But she had
no intention of ever acting on her stupid lust. She was a professional, paid to lure him out of his complacency and she would
never lose sight of her original goal.

FOURTEEN

'Tilly's gone AWOL so I wondered if you could check
your garage and shed. She loves dark hiding places.'
John blinked at Mrs McLellan, his neighbour, for a
moment then realized that she was talking about her cat.

'Oh, she can't be in either – we haven't been able to get into
the garage for weeks as Adam's lost the key. And we only ever
go into the shed to get the lawnmower and, as you can see, we
haven't found time to cut the grass!'

'Well, if you hear anything . . . She normally only goes into
your garden and the one on the other side. She's such a home-
body. My husband was so upset when she didn't come home last
night that he couldn't sleep.'

'She's a lovely animal,' John said. She was too, very affectionate. If he ever had a home of his own he'd want a similar
cat.

The woman left and John fetched his deckchair from the utility
room and settled down in the back garden. He was doing so most
Sundays now that summer was here. He felt more relaxed after
a sunbathing session and knew that he looked better with a tan.
Maybe he'd even gain a little much-needed weight with all of
this lying around; considering the amount of exercise that he did,
his muscles had failed to bulk up and he could fit into the smallest
size of men's jeans.

Was that a feline cry? He looked in the direction of the sound
but saw nothing. It came again and he realized that it was coming
from the garage. Looking closer, he could see Tilly pawing at
the dusty glass from the inside and looking increasingly panicky.

How on earth . . .? John walked all around the building until
he saw the hole in the back of the roof. She must have squeezed

through, jumped or fallen down and now couldn't find her way back again. He went and alerted the McLellans and they all rushed back to the securely locked garage.

'It must be stifling in there. Can you get in?' Mr McLellan asked.

'I can, but I'll have to break down the door. The key's missing.'

'I'll happily pay for any damage,' the older man said. 'She's the best cat we've ever had.'

'I'll take a run at it and hit it with my shoulder,' John muttered doubtfully, remembering the cop programmes that he'd seen where detectives easily effected an entry. He walked backwards for a few seconds before racing towards the heavy-looking door. Seconds before he connected with it, he heard a shout.

'What the fuck?'

All three of them jumped and swirled around. It took John a few seconds to recognize his landlord. He'd never seen the man look so wild-eyed before.

'Adam! Tilly's trapped in the garage so I'm breaking in.'

'No need. I found the spare key the other day,' Adam gasped. 'Forgot to tell you.'

He appeared to be breathing heavily, as if he'd speed-walked there.

'You've got perfect timing,' John said admiringly as Adam fished out his key ring. He noticed that the McLellans looked discomfited, presumably because Adam had sworn.

'How did she get in?' the therapist asked.

'Through a hole in the roof.'

He opened up, the cat shot out and Adam made to relock the garage.

'Hang on. I'll get the other deckchair out.'

'No need – I already did,' Adam replied.

'Do you want to get some more of that rice out of the freezer? I thought that I'd make chilli con carne tonight.'

'We're out of rice, I'm afraid, but we can have pizzas on me.'

'Thanks, Adam,' Mr McLellan said. 'I'm glad that we didn't have to force an entry.'

Mrs McLellan, who was holding a purring Tilly, waved the cat's paw at them as she walked down the path.

John felt a momentary sadness that he hadn't been the hero

of the day, a genuine action figure. Adam, he concluded, was one of life's more valiant characters, whereas he was just an average guy.

'Beth's busy with someone but I'd be delighted to talk to you,' Adam said, ushering Olivia into the other room at the drop-in centre. He'd suggested to two of his more depressed patients that they call in here and talk about their long-dead fathers, then he'd made sure that he turned up late so that Beth had to deal with them – that way he'd been able to get the pretty and hugely vulnerable Olivia all to himself. He'd enjoy running his hands all over her petite body and penetrating every orifice on multiple occasions, just as soon as she was free of that horrible bump. Why did women make themselves undesirable for several months in pregnancy, and – for those who didn't lose their baby fat – for years afterwards? At least this one wasn't eating, would soon look svelte again.

'So, how have you been?'

'Lonely.'

Good.

'Have you managed to make any new friends?'

'Well, I joined a national group for widows of my age but there's no one in my area and as I can't drive . . .'

As usual, she made her eyes so wide when she looked at him that he was surprised that she didn't get dizzy. She was seriously cute.

He kept his voice low, knowing that women found this more attractive. As a boy, he'd had a slight lisp but had worked hard to overcome it, to sound more masculine.

'Do you take the bus to your antenatal classes?'

Their conversation was desultory but he could sense the sexual tension between them.

'I used to but, since Zak died, I keep sleeping in and turning up halfway through.'

'Sleeping too much or too little is very common.'

'Is it?' Olivia looked relieved. 'I thought that it was just me.'

'Do you also find that your concentration's gone?'

'Totally! I can read but I can't watch TV for more than fifteen minutes as my mind keeps wandering. And it's so hard to sit still . . .'

'And you're also more accident prone?'

'Tell me about it.' Olivia rubbed the bare knees peeking out from her denim dress and he belatedly noticed that they were marked with both newly red and older yellow bruises. Widows lived in a daze, bumped into things all the time.

'Are you managing to eat now?'

Beth had told him that the girl was still vomiting, a sign that her upset system was producing too much stomach acid.

'I am, but I don't enjoy food anymore.'

'That's also common.' He gave her one of his most sympathetic and understanding looks.

So far, the petite brunette was a textbook widow. She'd also have no libido for months and would find it difficult to fall in love if she did start a new relationship. Not that he cared . . .

'I keep having these dreams in which I pull him away before he can cross the road.'

'They'll fade in time. Trust me, it does get easier.'

'You're widowed?' She looked at him curiously.

'Sadly, yes. My wife became depressed and committed suicide.'

'Oh, I'm so sorry,' Olivia said. 'That must have been shocking.'

She looked as if she meant it, was a typical bleeding heart. Why did some people care so much about others? He'd seen the same traits in his parents and brother but had never felt it himself. He had no desire to see his adoptive parents, except when he needed money, yet they called repeatedly. This week, Nicholas had left three messages on his answerphone, all saying that their mother was pining for him, that this was his last chance to please her before she died. He'd ignored the calls, would get in touch in his own good time – in other words, on a day when there was no prime pussy around.

What was it that this piece of ass had just said? Something about his wife's death being shocking. She was looking at him expectantly so he gave her his best manly look, the one that he practised in front of the mirror. 'It was over a year ago, and, as they say, the first year is the worst. I've learned to cope.'

'Was that what made you become a counsellor?'

'Well, I was already a therapist, specializing in child psychology, but after Helen's death I took a bereavement training course.'

'I might like to do that one day,' Olivia said tremulously.

'Leave it for a while so that you have some perspective.'

They hadn't let him train immediately, had told him that he had to go through his own grieving process, but had accepted him after six months. He'd waited another few weeks before starting to date as he might be under surveillance and had to convince the police that he was desolate. Widowers statistically started dating sooner than widows, and those who were bereaved under the age of fifty, or who were childfree, often started after six to eight months.

'Oh, I won't rush into anything, Adam. I'll wait and get more of an idea of the work when I reach the top of the NHS waiting list.'

Damn, he didn't want her to see another therapist. She might attach herself to them, could stop coming to the monthly drop-in sessions. He wanted her to bond solely with him.

'Off the record,' he said casually, 'If the NHS has too big a backlog of widows, it sometimes sends some of them to private therapists like me. Problem is, it pays at a lower rate so we can't spend the same amount of time as we do with our private clients. You'd be better off seeing me privately.'

'How much would that cost?' Olivia asked then winced visibly at his reply.

'It seems a lot, I know, but it gets you back to work more quickly, gets you earning. Plus, you're probably entitled to a one-off bereavement payment from the government and could pay for it with that.'

Olivia nodded. 'The registrar at the Deaths Office gave me a form, something to do with Zak's national insurance payments, but I've never got round to filling it in.'

'Then do it tonight. In the meantime, why don't we schedule a few sessions at my office and you can pay me when you have the money?' He felt almost guilty at the look of gratitude which swept across her face. Within seconds she'd whipped out her journal and he'd accessed the diary that he kept within his mobile phone.

'See you next week,' he murmured as she left the centre clutching his business card, having arranged to visit his home office. A few months from now, he'd be seeing a lot more of her as he stripped off her bra and pants.

FIFTEEN

'**a**nd the company is refusing to pay out,' the woman concluded tearfully.

. . . It was, Beth thought sadly, a familiar story. Life insurance companies declined one percent of claims each year, leaving a thousand people without collateral at the time when they were least able to fight back.

'What reason did they give you?' Beth asked.

'That he'd ticked the non-smoking box when he filled in the form but had later started again. But it's madness because he was a passenger in a car which was involved in a pile-up on the motorway. What does his smoking have to do with it?'

'I worked for a life insurance company when I was younger but gave it up because I found their practices unethical,' Beth admitted. 'I remember one woman died of pneumonia and the company refused to pay her husband because her medical records showed that she hadn't told them that she'd had surgery on her ankle thirty years before. All the company has to say to refute the claim is that medical information wasn't disclosed – they don't have to prove that it's linked to the death.'

'It's criminal,' the widow said.

'It may well be. Some people claim that they're rushed through the completion of the forms by the insurance companies, that it's a deliberate ploy to catch them out.' She studied the woman for a moment, wondering if she was strong enough to fight her case. 'You can contest their decision, take it to the Financial Ombudsman. It can take two or three years to get the money but he finds in the customer's favour in over two thirds of cases so your chances are good.'

The widow hesitated. 'Yes, I will fight. Jack paid into that policy for years so that, if the worst came to the worst, I'd get the mortgage paid off.' She looked squarely at Beth. 'So, what happens now?'

I cancel my coffee with Matthew, Beth thought. She put her

hand on the woman's arm. 'I'll talk you through the process. If you'll excuse me for a moment, I just have to make a quick call.'

Hurrying to her office, she phoned Matthew's mobile to cancel their meeting here, in the cafe, at 3 p.m. He was on a call-out to Weston this afternoon and had suggested, at short notice, that they meet up. They'd managed to do so twice before when he had local customers and he'd called in at her house.

Matthew lived in Clevedon, a half-hour drive away, but she much preferred it when they stayed at her place as she was happiest when surrounded by her own belongings. He didn't have a hairdryer and there wasn't a plug for the bath so she had to settle for a shower. He didn't even have a lock on the bathroom door, ironic given his job . . .

'It's me,' she said when he answered. 'Sorry, I can't make this afternoon after all. I'm with a widow who needs further information.'

'Drat. I'll miss you.'

Try as she might, Beth couldn't say that she would miss him too. Was that the price of bereavement, that you remained in love with a dead man so weren't capable of loving anyone else?

'I'm still on for tomorrow night, though.' She didn't want him to think that she was losing interest.

'Good. Apparently they're a great group.'

She knew that he'd bought two tickets for the concert weeks before, not long after they'd started dating. He'd been keen from the very start.

'I'm looking forward to it.'

She was, too. It was nice going on dates again at night, almost like returning to her years as a student. Admittedly, at thirty-five, she needed more sleep than she had at eighteen, but the fun of getting dressed up and drinking a little too much vodka were the same.

'Sorry about that,' she said as she returned to the table.

'It's me that should be sorry, making you change your arrangements.'

'Not at all. It was just a vague offer of coffee –' she gestured around the cafeteria – 'and there's no shortage of that here!'

'Still, I should probably have come to your home office or

proper place of work to talk about Jack's death. Maggie said that you do formal counselling?'

'At the bereavement drop-in centre, but you've just missed our last monthly session. It's the first Monday of every month at 10 a.m.'

She gave the woman the address.

'Would I be able to bring my son along? He's been playing up since his dad died.'

Beth nodded enthusiastically, realizing that Adam would be the ideal person to help.

'One of my colleagues specializes in child psychology as well as all kinds of bereavement, so I'll make sure that you get to spend the session with him.'

'Bye, darling,' Matthew murmured into his mobile before reluctantly returning his attention to his work. He quite understood that Beth couldn't see him this afternoon, not when she had another widow to counsel. She was the sweetest, most philanthropic woman that he'd ever known. She did lots of informal counselling for patients' relatives who came into the hospital cafe after losing their loved ones as well as working in the bereavement drop-in centre for free as a volunteer. It was good to know that not everyone put profit before people; he himself was always doing favours for his friends.

Beth had a cute face and a perfect body and she didn't seem to care that he was ten years her senior. She was perfect. If only his wife had been as caring, he'd never have had to get divorced. She'd demanded a separation, claiming that he criticised her endlessly, that she could no longer do anything right in his eyes, that he was distant. But what did she expect when she'd gained weight and lost interest in socializing and in their sex life? In contrast, he'd eaten healthily and always kept himself in first-class shape.

He looked good for his age, thanks to doing lots of walking, often whilst carrying a heavy toolbox. If a call-out wasn't an emergency, he thought nothing of parking in a free zone and strolling the half-hour journey to his client's office or house and back.

Several of his previous girlfriends had commented that he had the muscle tone of a much younger man – and the staying power.

He could easily hold back until his lover was satisfied. Beth hadn't come from intercourse yet but he was sure that it would just take time. She simply had to relax more to fully appreciate the pleasure available from thrusting, had to put aside her previous misconceptions and let go.

He'd been unlucky in the past with his choice of women but was sure that she was a keeper, was The One.

SIXTEEN

She'd been seeing Adam for weeks now and they'd become superficially close but he still hadn't given up any information about Helen, despite her own increasing hints that she'd been failed by Zak, that the marriage had had its difficulties. Belatedly, the police psychologist had decided that her supposed pregnancy was getting in the way, so they'd decided to tell Neave that she'd unexpectedly given birth. They'd brought the date forward by six weeks, and now she had to phone and tell him, using the dedicated police line. A machine was recording their every word.

'Adam? It's Olivia. I've become a mum!'

'Well done you! How do you feel?'

'Quite good, actually. She's tiny, having arrived so early, so it was a comparatively easy birth.'

She giggled in what she hoped was a provocative way, wanting him to think of her as tight and ready.

'Have you got a name yet?'

'Mia.'

'Mia Marsden. Sounds just right. So, are you still in hospital or . . .?'

'No, it was a home birth.'

'That's unusual for a first child.' She could hear the surprise in his voice.

'I know. I was booked in, but she arrived so suddenly that I didn't have time to call an ambulance. My neighbour took me there after Mia arrived but I discharged myself the next day. I can't stand being around strangers. You know how much better I am at one to one.'

'You are indeed.'

She could hear the warmth in his voice. Was it really faked? She reminded herself that her colleagues would hear this call, to keep it measured.

'Well, I won't keep you, just wanted to let you know. See you at the same time later this week.'

'You've got a babysitter already?'

'No, she's still in the hospital, but the nurses have said that I mustn't stay there round the clock, that I need a break.'

The police psychologist had thought that this might make her sound selfish, more like her target. They were desperate for her to reel him in.

'See you on Friday, then.'

'I'll look forward to it,' Olivia said lightly. She put down the phone and realized that it was true.

Her brief now was to get Adam to ask her out, or at least spend more time with her. The police thought that he might let his guard down if he thought that he'd found his soul mate, would tell her a few home truths about his marriage, about being failed by his late wife. At the same time, she mustn't flaunt herself as that would be setting up a honeytrap and would be unethical. Cases had been thrown out of court for less.

After making the call, she went round to her sister's house, keen to discuss Adam with someone. She wasn't supposed to talk about her undercover work but had sworn Cathy to secrecy.

'He thinks I've had the baby,' she said, settling down in her usual chair and accepting a glass of white wine.

'So, is he more likely to pounce?'

'According to the police psychologist he is. There again, he also thought that the guy would have become suggestive by now and he hasn't. In fact, he's been really supportive and nice.'

'It's his job, Olivia.'

'I know that.' She felt a moment of irritation; Adam had been exceptionally solicitous and helpful and seemed to share her sorrow at prematurely losing a spouse.

'So, when do you see him again?'

'Next week.'

'And you've got back-up if he tries anything?'

'I've got half the police force watching from across the road. Plus my body, as you know, is a lethal weapon.'

'Just don't take any chances,' Cathy murmured, setting down her glass.

She'd always been the staid sister, Olivia thought, the one who waited until she was a mature woman before she married, the one who settled for a safe job in an office. She'd never have coped with the excitement and uncertainty of undercover work.

The days passed slowly until her appointment, days of paperwork and nights of TV dinners. Olivia pasted on her widest smile as she rang Adam's bell, heard the psychologist approach the door. She hadn't brought her supposed baby with her today and wouldn't on subsequent visits. The police psychologist, the same one who had recommended a fake pregnancy, was now worried that the child was getting in the way. That said, they'd arranged for her to have access to another policewoman's child if Adam asked to see Mia. She also planned to take the baby along to the drop-in centre to show Beth.

'Hi there,' she said, looking up into the therapist's eyes. With his dark T-shirt and tight black cords he looked more like a rock star than a psychologist.

'Good morning, Olivia. And how's the little one?'

'Out of hospital, but making a hell of a noise about it so I left her with a neighbour.'

'And here I was, about to set up a free crèche.'

'I could use one for myself,' she joked as she followed him into his office. 'I quite fancy a couple of hours in the Wendy House. I never have any time nowadays just for me.'

It was sort of true, she reflected; what with commuting, work and tidying up after Marc, she was always on the go.

'Consider this your "me" time,' Adam said as she sat down on the couch. 'But I know what you mean. Widows tell me that they miss that one-to-one relationship, the feeling of being nurtured.'

'Too right. It's hard doing everything alone.'

'What do you find most difficult?' He was, she had to admit, kindness personified and seemed to view her as a person rather than merely a client.

'Being both Mum and Dad and sole breadwinner. Oh, and I struggle with DIY.'

'You've gone back to work?'

'I've had to, for financial reasons. I'm so lucky that I work from home.'

'I was thinking about your situation the other day, checked out a few subsidized childcare groups,' Adam said, riffling through a sheaf of papers. Olivia accepted a typed list from him. 'I also have a list of local plumbers, electricians and so on who have been vetted by one of the charities for senior citizens.'

'That would be brilliant. I'm terrified of letting one of those cowboy builders through the door.'

The psychologist rummaged through one of his filing cabinets and brought out a booklet, handed it to her.

'If you have similar practical problems, let me know. I'm in touch with various charities who supply volunteers for gardening work and so on.'

'My main problems are social,' Olivia murmured. 'Now that Zak's dead, I have no one to go out dining or dancing with.'

For the best part of an hour, they spoke about her sense of sadness that her husband would never see his child, her feelings about being different from older widows. She also told him about her insomnia and he recommended exercise earlier in the day and meditation at night. She felt a slight pull of disappointment as the session ended, had begun to feel very relaxed as she stretched out on his couch.

'Is there anything else that I can help you with?' he asked as he walked her to the door.

Olivia took a deep breath, grinned and said, 'A boyfriend would be nice!'

He smiled back. 'Unfortunately I'm not running a dating agency.'

'Don't you know of anyone?' Her heart beating faster, she touched his hand.

'If any of my more eligible friends become single, you'll be the first to know.'

Fortune favours the brave, she thought and took a deep breath. 'Do you have a twin?'

'If I do, we were separated at birth, but I'll keep my eyes

peeled for you,' Adam said, then winced. 'I wonder who coined such a horrible expression?'

'A masochist,' Olivia replied and they both laughed.

'Same time next week?' he asked.

'Maybe sooner? As I said, I haven't been sleeping.'

'Try that aerobics class I mentioned plus the mindfulness of breathing programme and I'm sure that you'll see a difference.'

'I'll give it my best shot, then,' Olivia said.

She walked down the path feeling thwarted that he hadn't returned the pressure when she touched his hand, that he was in no particular rush to see her again. She'd pretended that she'd like to go out on a date with him but he hadn't risen to the bait. She was beginning to think that they were targeting the wrong man, that Adam Neave genuinely had lost his wife to suicide. She also doubted that he'd strangled that local woman, Hannah, far less gone to Bristol and murdered a second girl. If her own experience – and that of Beth, his colleague – was typical, he was a caring and dedicated professional who was helping his patients to get the most out of their lives.

SEVENTEEN

'If you don't visit soon, she'll cut you out of her will.'

Adam felt the rage surge through him as he listened to Nicholas's latest message. He hit the delete button and felt a momentary pleasure when the automatic voice said, 'All messages erased.' He'd like to erase the goody-two-shoes in person so that he, Adam, was the preferred brother instead of the prodigal son.

He honestly didn't believe that he was doing anything wrong. Why should he visit these boring geriatrics just because they'd chosen to adopt him? After all, they must have been bored or unfulfilled to start with, had a baby-sized hole in their lives. They'd chosen to create a family because it hadn't occurred to them not to. They were dull traditionalists who had tried to fit him into their limiting mould. He'd done his bit, giving his mother an excuse to avoid work throughout his early years. He wasn't sure exactly what his father had got out of it, but then he'd never understood the older man.

But he'd put up with them until he left home, so he surely deserved to benefit financially when his mother snuffed it. It would be a financial reward for never telling them exactly what he thought of them. He'd always been careful not to overstep the mark, aware that they were a source of emergency accommodation, home-cooked meals and ready cash, though he'd sometimes had to help himself to the latter from his father's money box or mother's purse. His financial precariousness and his determination to sow his oats as a young man had earned their disapproval, but he'd subsequently given the impression that he'd shaped up, and they'd been delighted when he went to university as a mature student, graduated and prospered in his chosen career. But Nicholas had written him off by then, had made it clear that he despised him, that he was no good.

Now, he dialled his parents' number and his father answered.

'Dad? It's Adam. I've been away on a course, just heard about Mum.'

He listened to the man's ramblings, was surprised to hear that his mother had been hospitalized already. Hadn't she only been diagnosed recently? He'd assumed that she had a few months left.

'She's sleeping most of the time but when she wakes up she's very confused,' his father continued, his voice trembling. 'We stayed all night but Nicholas insisted that I come home for a rest and a change of clothes.'

'I'll go now, Dad.' He got the details, took the car to the hospital. He might see Beth there if he was lucky, could chat her up a bit more.

A middle-aged nurse took him aside as soon as he arrived. 'She's been asking for you.' She looked at him sourly.

'I've been away, just got back at lunchtime.'

'She already has two visitors.'

That would be Nicholas and Jill, given that his father was at home having a shave or eating a microwaved spaghetti bolognese whilst watching *Deal Or No Deal* or yet another repeat of *Cash In The Attic*. He'd always had such proletariat taste.

'I'll take over then, give them a break.'

He smiled at her and she smiled back. Gotcha.

'I'm so glad that I got back when I did,' he added, donning his most sincere expression.

'It's just as well.'

'You mean . . .?' He deliberately tailed off, made his eyes wider.

'We thought that she had three weeks but she's deteriorating rapidly.'

He took a deep breath. 'How long has she got, Sister?'

'It could be as little as three days.'

Would he get any money then or would he have to wait until his father snuffed it? And then share everything with their biological offspring, the favoured son? Nicholas always remembered the Mother's Day cards, the birthdays and anniversaries, whereas he, Adam, was too busy living his life.

She was in a side room, the type that they put you in when you were close to death. He knew the drill thanks to his bereavement counselling. Nicholas and Jill were sitting holding hands with each other, though Nicholas also had his left hand on top of his mother's. Adam felt both estranged and claustrophobic just observing the scene.

'Dad asked me to give you both a break,' he said.

'We're OK,' Nicholas said stiffly.

Jill smiled at him wearily, or was it warily? 'No, we need to get a coffee, stretch our legs.'

'OK, but we'll be back in fifteen.'

They left and he sat on the seat that his sister-in-law had vacated. It was still warm from her body and he briefly thought about fucking her. He'd love to make her break her wedding vows, if only for a day. The ideal, of course, would be to impregnate her and make sure that Nicholas knew that the child was born of adultery.

He stared at the morphine drip but turned his attention to his mother when he heard her voice. She sounded like she was dreaming, but she was staring straight at him, though her eyes were filmy.

'Nicholas, I want you to make up with your brother.'

He opened his mouth to explain that he wasn't Nicholas then

promptly closed it again, curious as to what she was going to say.

'All right, Mum.'

'I'll never believe that he killed Helen.'

Aha, so his brother had actually accused him of being a murderer.

'But the police suspected him,' he murmured. 'You know they did.'

'Only because you went to them.' With what seemed to be a Herculean effort, she turned her head to face him more fully. 'Nicholas, promise me that you'll tell them that you were wrong. I don't want to die knowing that you two are still fighting.'

Jesus, so Nicholas had actually fingered him to the boys in blue.

'I promise that I'll pay him a visit soon, Mum.' He meant it, too. It would be a memorable visit with far reaching consequences, albeit not the kind that his dying mother was trying to desperately arrange. Revenge was going to be so sweet that it would make his teeth ache. He just needed time to come up with a suitably vicious plan.

EIGHTEEN

Beth sank gratefully into Matthew's arms as they lay curled up together on the settee.

'You're so funny and entertaining,' he murmured, kissing the top of her head.

Beth loved it when he kissed her there, and said so.

'I love kissing you all over,' he responded, holding her even more tightly than he had before. Earlier in the week she'd had bad period pains and he'd insisted on doing her shopping and constantly refilling the hot water bottle which helped soothe her stomach. She'd never felt so nurtured, Beth thought, so adored. It was almost like dating a woman, albeit one who hadn't yet figured out how to make her come.

'So, how was work today?' she asked.

'A woman locked herself out in Nailsea, a man broke the handle off his door in Worle and a pensioner got her key stuck in the lock at Clevedon.'

As usual, Beth tried to get more detail and perhaps an anecdote. 'Must be disconcerting if you're elderly.'

'No, she stayed with her next-door neighbour whilst I sorted things out. I got the impression that she didn't have much money, so I knocked twenty percent off the total charge.'

Beth kissed his hand, noticing that the veins stood out in a way that hers didn't. Not that she cared about the age difference. Remembering that he'd said that he loved to help her, she decided to mention a recent problem with her house.

'The back door has started to stick at times, though it's probably just swelling in the heat. If it continues, I'll get you to take a look at it.'

'Any time in the next thirty years,' Matthew said.

He really was in it for the long haul, Beth thought, and felt glad that he wasn't leaving her in any doubt about his feelings. It was nice to feel that the uncertainty which followed widowhood was over, that it was no longer a life of me, myself and I. He was a good and caring man and he treasured her. What more could she want? OK, it would have been a bonus if he'd been more of a talker but she got most of her conversational fix from her work and her voluntary counselling. She could surely learn to live with someone who was quiet.

'I love the fact that we're so comfortable together,' Matthew said.

Say something loving to him, Beth chided herself but again her throat closed and the words remained unuttered, as always. When he alluded to love, however indirectly, she couldn't respond so settled for complimenting him on his appearance, but she was running out of things to praise. Last week she'd told him that he had nice eyebrows, surely the first time that that particular body part had been praised.

The following day – long after he'd left for work, having again failed to make her climax – she phoned Adam at his home.

'Hi, it's Beth. I've got some queries about my relationship and I just wondered if you had time for a little informal counselling at lunchtime? Around one if you're free?'

It was common for therapists to share their home and work problems, was regarded as a way of splitting the load.

'No problem. My place or the pub?' Adam asked.

'Oh, the pub!'

She'd spent half of her life in pubs since bereavement as most trips with other widows, and dates, seemed to end up there. It was ironic as she'd been a really light drinker prior to her husband's death.

He named a pub which didn't play music, added, 'See you at one in their beer garden.'

'It's a deal,' Beth said. 'And lunch is on me.'

As lunchtime neared, she changed into one of her more flattering tops and her favourite cut-off jeans. Though she had no intention of ever cheating on Matthew (why would she risk losing someone who was so loyal?), she was aware that Adam was an attractive man and that she wanted to look her best in his presence. It was nice to feel feminine and desired – or, in his case, masculine and desired. Neither of them ever had to act on it.

He was disappointingly late and she had begun to consider calling his mobile when he arrived at 1.20 p.m.

'Sorry – my brother phoned and talked for ages.'

'What does he do?'

Adam looked vague and said, 'Nothing worthwhile!' Then it was as if a light had switched on in his head as he smiled broadly at her and said, 'Tell me about all of the boyfriend's faults.'

'Oh, it's not him – it's me. He's really loving and nurturing but I just can't reciprocate. I mean, I really care for him but I can't verbalize it. It's as if my throat actually closes up.'

'I've had lots of widows tell me that,' Adam murmured, nodding.

Why had none of them said it to her? Did they perhaps feel guilty about dating, fear wrongly that she'd judge them harshly? Or was it difficult to talk about a new relationship to a bereavement counsellor?

Beth felt relieved that she wasn't the only one going through this.

'The bereavement course which I took mentioned that starting over could be hard, but it didn't go into detail. It's weird, because I don't feel guilty about having sex with Matthew and I've even let him put some of his clothes in Brian's wardrobe but I can't say something simple like "I really care for you".'

'Don't force it,' her colleague said. 'When the time is right, the words will come. Don't let him move in either until you're really sure.'

The waiter, who looked about twelve, came over and took their orders.

'I always have the steak when I'm out,' Adam explained, 'as I eat so much pizza in the house. In fact, my lodger has the pizza place on speed dial!'

She had a sudden vision of a bloated, waddling man. 'He must be enormous.'

'No, he's rake thin. He's a personal trainer who can't drive so he walks to some of his clients' houses with this mini-gym strapped to his back. He burns hundreds of calories.'

'That's right – I remember you said that he was always rushing around, dusting your property.'

'Yeah, the folly of youth – he looks for ways to use up energy whereas most of us conserve it whenever we can!'

'Matthew's a bit like that, walks for miles carrying a heavy toolbox. It means that he can eat anything and not gain weight,' Beth said.

'So, d'you reckon he's The One?' Adam teased.

'Well, he makes me feel like The One,' Beth replied and briefly remembered the Stereophonics song, 'Dakota', about that very subject. There, the relationship had ultimately gone wrong . . .

'And is that enough?'

'I think so, I mean, we're good together and he apparently loves me. What's not to like?'

'Do you love him back but can't say so, or aren't you there yet?'

'I'm not there yet,' Beth admitted. 'But it's not crucial for me. If it happens in time, that's an added bonus. I mean, I do have feelings for him and I'd hate to lose him but I don't think that I can label it as love.'

'Can't hurry it, as the great therapist Phil Collins said.'

They both laughed and Beth added, 'So, what would this be costing me if I was your private patient?'

'A damn sight more than a steak!'

'Your clients are mainly rich?' She loved to know how other people lived.

'Or desperate. I'm sure that some of them dip into their savings in order to pay for help when the alternative is an NHS waiting list.'

'And you see quite a few children?'

Adam nodded. 'Lots. Sometimes their parents want to go private so that the kid doesn't have mental health notes in his NHS file. Or they get a partial cure from the doctor in the form of tranquillizers but feel guilty about drugging the child so opt for an additional extra in the form of the talking cure. I've got a sixteen-year-old at the moment who has ADHD and only partially responded to his medication but he's really blossomed since he started coming to me and his parents are well impressed.'

'So you'll soon do yourself out of a job?'

'Doubt it. It's obvious that his mum needs a break from him and I'm a reliable, if pricey, babysitter.'

'That reminds me, there's a widow I met recently who's having problems with her son. I told her to pop into the drop-in session and speak to you.'

'She just wants to talk there? I mean, she doesn't want to become a private patient of mine?'

'Not sure,' Beth said. 'Obviously it's not my place to make a referral.'

'Not even if I put you on commission?'

Beth laughed. 'I can't be bribed!'

'You probably could,' Adam said softly. 'Everyone has their price.' He must have cottoned on to her look of surprise as he added, 'Only joking, my concerned-looking friend.'

'I've never been very motivated by money,' Beth admitted. 'I've always put freedom and relationships first, especially since Brian died.'

'Same here,' Adam murmured. 'I cut back my hours after losing Helen, took note of the old saying that, on your deathbed, you never wish that you'd spent more time at the office.'

'I always forget that you've been widowed too – you seem so together,' Beth said, briefly touching his arm.

'Trust me – I've had my own dark nights of the soul,' Adam

replied. He smiled as the waiter set down his steak and Beth's tuna. 'But it's given me a whole new insight into the human condition that I didn't have before.'

'Oh, same here.' Beth speared a piece of potato salad. 'I have instant friendships now with widows and widowers of all ages.'

'And is Matthew a widower?'

'No, divorced for seven years.'

'Not on the rebound, which is a good sign. There again, why hasn't he recommitted before now?'

Beth shrugged. 'He won't really discuss his past girlfriends. He just says that he wouldn't talk about me if we ever split up so why would he talk about them?'

'Either he's very discreet or he has very little insight,' Adam said thoughtfully.

'Maybe he came on too strong and scared them off?'

'Depends – how many have there been?'

'Four, apparently.'

'And none of them were ready for commitment?'

'I got the impression that a couple of them were shortlived, not a good match.' She cut into her tuna steak. 'He's very full on, would scare someone who wanted something casual – but I personally like the fact that he's so intense.'

'A keeper?' Adam queried.

'Definitely. He's so caring and makes me feel so safe. And he tries so hard to please, has even done my shopping.'

'So, just keep taking it a day at a time. This man is in love with you so he won't do anything to jeopardize the relationship.'

'You don't think that he'll tire of waiting to hear these three little words?'

'Not if the sex is good,' Adam said, grinning.

It was pretty good for her, Beth thought, and presumably excellent for Matthew. He always cried out loudly when he came and had said that just thinking about how she looked when she was naked would get him through a difficult day.

'Eight out of ten,' she said, smiling back.

'And frequent?'

'Every time that I see him.'

'He'll stay hooked, then, as long as you're warm and affectionate.'

'Oh, I am. I've told him that he's cute, that he's got a great body.'

She'd also gone down on him and told him that he tasted nice but there were limits to what she'd admit to her fellow counsellor.

'You've nothing to worry about, Beth. Sounds like you're ticking most of the boxes.'

'Thanks for that.' She felt much better now that she'd confided the situation to someone else. The woman who ended up with Adam, she thought, would be really lucky. He was a skilled counsellor and a caring individual who would give her his full and undivided attention from the start.

NINETEEN

It had been good to flirt with Beth the other day – but what he was doing now gave him even more of a kick, made him virtually euphoric. Everything was going to plan, he thought, as he returned to the car park in Birmingham and hid his latest purchase under the piece of carpet in the back of his boot. The carefully Sellotaped brown paper bag contained the nastiest and most explicit child porn mag that he could find, was devoted to boys age five and under, all touching – or being touched by – naked and literally faceless men.

Perversion didn't come cheap and he'd had to put tenner after tenner onto the counter in the sex shop until the guy took him into the back office and coughed up the goods. It was the male equivalent of those Lolita magazines that some men enjoyed. For his own part, girls only appealed to him when they started to grow breasts and hips – and he'd never be turned on by a young boy of any age. But then the magazine wasn't for him . . .

Adam carefully relocked the boot and made his way to an area where he knew there were several charity shops. The second yielded what he required – a cheap portable typewriter, a well-preserved model from the Seventies. He bought a pad of paper and an envelope at the post office, got the assistant to put on the stamp. He kept his hands in his pockets as much as possible, keen not to draw attention to the fact that he was wearing gloves.

Now he was ready to act. He took his purchases into the nearest gents toilet and typed a short note in the garish blue colour of the typewriter ribbon: *I know this man in a professional capacity and he's been interfering with preschool children. I daren't give my own name for fear of reprisals but am deeply concerned.* He added Nicholas's name and address, deliberately misspelling the surname as 'Neeve'.

If all went well, his baby brother was going to be in a lot of trouble, would lose his impeccable reputation. Still gloved, he sealed up the letter and posted it to Weston police station. They'd get it tomorrow so he was going to be busy tonight.

He drove home, dumping the typewriter in a skip en route, rested until 2 a.m, then drove to Nicholas and Jill's house, bringing their front door key with him. Months before, he'd taken the one that they kept at his mother's and had a copy cut; none of them knew. He'd thought that it would prove useful if he had to pay off a gambling debt at short notice as Nicholas always had ready cash in the house as well as jewellery which could be sold or pawned.

As he'd suspected, the household was in darkness when he arrived. He parked two streets away and padded to their bungalow, let himself in and tiptoed to the nursery. Tim was sleeping peacefully and didn't stir when he slid the kiddie porn under the side of his mattress. He put it within easy distance of the chair which sat beside the child's bed. It would be easy for the police to envisage Nicholas sitting on the seat, reaching for the magazine and touching himself as he looked at the pictures and at his own little son.

His work done for now, he silently left the building, hurried to his car and drove home. At best, his brother would soon be arrested as a potential paedophile, at worst he'd plant a seed of doubt in Jill's mind and their marriage would never be the same again.

*   *   *

'We've had an interesting development.' Detective Superintendent Bill Winston showed the letter to the police psychologist. 'We've always thought that this man was one of the good guys.'

'Has he ever worked with children?'

'Yes, he's a Sunday school teacher. And he has one of his own.'

The psychologist nodded gravely. 'As you know, these guys gravitate to places where children congregate – and they are often religious. You have to treat it seriously rather than as a hoax.'

'I'm sending two officers round this afternoon to talk to him,' Bill murmured, 'though if he's guilty it puts a whole new complexion on the spiel that he gave us about his brother, Adam. So far, the man hasn't put a foot wrong with our undercover cop or with any of his female patients. In fact, as far as we can ascertain, he's a respected landlord, a dedicated volunteer, and a bloody good psychologist.'

'There's no way that this Nicholas could have killed Helen Neave? I mean, we never thought . . .'

Bill Winston pushed back another rush of doubt. 'I think he had an alibi.'

God, wouldn't it be ironic if Nicholas Neave had killed his sister-in-law and blamed his older brother? The husband was usually in the frame so when Nicholas had told them of Adam's childhood cruelty and ongoing controlling nature, they'd simply assumed the worst. Jill Neave had confirmed that Helen had been unhappy and thinking of ending her marriage, but she could just have been parroting what her husband said.

He'd need to liaise with child protection and get an emergency search warrant, but, as soon as the paperwork was in place, he'd get the house searched from attic to cellar. They'd be looking for incriminating diaries, photos, anything. His years in the police force, Detective Superintendent Winston thought, served as a constant reminder that people could lead shadowy second lives, weren't always what they seemed.

TWENTY

Just how often were they going to land him with this little brat? Didn't they know that he had books to read, computer games to play, philosophies to decipher? He wanted to read Descartes, not look after a four-year-old who alternately moped and screamed.

What was the little bastard doing now? Brandon looked up from his Cartesian tome to find that Ethan had stolen his family-sized bar of milk chocolate and eaten most of it, the brown sweetness coating his hands, face and the bedspread on which he sat. He, Brandon, wasn't supposed to eat chocolate (Adam had advocated a low sugar diet) so how the hell was he supposed to explain this to his folks? They'd take away his computer and PlayStation again and he'd go mad with boredom and have to pretend to be neutered in order to get them back. Unless he washed the bedspread, rinsed away the caramel-scented evidence . . .

Brandon took the cotton counterpane from his bed, put it in the washing machine and selected Eco Wash, assuming that it would be the fastest cycle. It would dry quickly on the clothes line as it was so hot outside. His parents were always urging him to go to the garden or the park or sports field, probably hoping that he'd get skin cancer and die.

'Go outside,' he said now, opening the door into the back yard.

'You go too,' Ethan said mutinously.

'No, I have to use the computer.'

He was winning a game of online chess.

Ethan took a step back into the kitchen and Brandon put a hand on his back and began to propel him forwards. To his disgust, the kid threw up all over himself, a strange mix of what looked like chopped carrots and gravy. Now he'd have to wash a T-shirt and jeans as well. God, how did you stop the washing machine? He stripped off the boy's clothes and canvas shoes, switched the machine off at the mains, reset the switch to zero, opened the door and started again.

'Brr,' Ethan said, jumping up and down and rubbing his arms.

'Stop complaining – it's tropical. Anyway, you're about to go into a warm bath.'

The kid took off at speed as he ran the water – he was even skinnier than Brandon himself – but he found him in the lounge, hiding by the side of the settee.

'Come on – it'll just take a minute.'

The four-year-old made a dash for it but Brandon was quicker, grabbed him, carried him to the bath and put him in. The child tried to clamber out and Brandon put his hands on his shoulders, pressed down. And suddenly he realized that he wanted to press harder, that he wanted rid of this encumbrance for good.

Quickly, he stripped off his own clothes and jumped into the bath, holding his little cousin down with his superior body weight. He could feel him wriggling and kicking but they weren't evenly matched. Die, he thought dispassionately. Go away. Get out of my life for good.

Soon the struggling stopped and the house felt newly peaceful. Hearing a 'We're home,' Brandon quickly left the watery grave, towel dried his body and shrugged into his own clothes.

'Hi Mum and Dad. How was your day out?'

Adam had taught him to say that.

'Good,' his mother said, setting down the sleeveless jacket that she'd been carrying. 'The restaurant was doing two courses for the price of one and we walked on to Marine Lake afterwards.'

'It's thirsty work, though, all that walking,' his father added. 'We needed additional tea by mid afternoon.'

I should care? He belatedly remembered the therapist's words, nodded and adopted an interested expression.

'So, where's the little soldier?' his mother asked.

'Having a bath. He was sick over everything so I've had to start a laundry.'

'Well done, Brandon. That was very thoughtful,' his father said.

'That's OK. He's a nice little chap.'

'I'll just go and check on him,' his mother murmured. A few minutes later, he heard her scream.

She ran into the lounge with the dripping child in her arms.

'Graham, can you do mouth-to-mouth whilst I phone an ambulance?'

He watched as his father took the naked boy from his mother, set him on the settee and began to breathe into his mouth. Running Adam's script through his head, he remembered to ask if the child was OK.

'Does he look OK? He must have slipped down in the water,' his mother said as she dialled.

'He was splashing about so happily. I only left to start the washing machine and then I heard you come in . . .'

He listened as his mother gave their details to the operator, looked at his father then said, 'No, he's still not breathing. Yes, we'll continue CPR until the paramedics arrive.'

She walked over to Brandon and embraced him, said, 'It's not your fault, son.' He forced himself to hug her back. She smelt of old perfume and stale perspiration. He watched the back of his father's head as it bobbed up and down, hands moving in a slower rhythm.

Within moments there were stretcher-bearers at the door and, later, police. He repeated his story.

'These things happen,' one of the policemen said, patting his arm. There were more words and forms and mention of a future meeting, but by mid evening he was back playing online chess.

'Are you alright, son?' his mother asked at nine p.m., popping her tightly-permed head around his door.

'I'm trying to come to terms with what happened, Mother.'

He wasn't really. He felt fine about being a killer. It felt right – well, more than right, it felt good. He'd always known that he was set apart from society, was brighter, impressively different. Further proof of that lay in his ability to take a life. He felt powerful, in charge of his own fate, a work in progress. Yet hadn't he read somewhere that many murderers committed suicide, unable to live with their guilt?

'If you need to see Adam sooner than next week . . .'

Hell, no.

'I need some time to myself, Mother.'

'Brandon, I understand.'

Fuck off, then. The silence lengthened and he moved another chess piece on the virtual board.

'How about a nice herbal tea?'

'No thanks.'

'Water?'

'No . . . no, thank you.'

'We'll be having toast at ten.'

Good for you.

'Right.'

'I could make you some – Adam said that it was OK for you to have yours in your room.'

At least the shrink recognized that he was happiest away from the oldsters, though he didn't approve of him having a purely carbohydrate snack.

'I'd like that,' he said, beginning to crave the buttery slices.

If they could send his meals up on a dumb waiter, he'd like that even more.

'And perhaps a little peanut butter for the protein, Adam thought.'

'A little peanut butter would be perfect.'

Christ, he sounded like his grandmother, but would say whatever it took to get his parents off his back.

'Your aunt wants you to know that she doesn't blame you.'

He almost said 'for what?' then realized that she meant for the death of her son.

'I blame myself for going to greet you.'

He cringed inside as she hugged him. She was becoming horribly tactile, despite the fact that she knew he'd always hated being touched.

'It's our fault for telling you to be polite to us. You were only doing what you thought was best.'

'I miss the little chap already,' he said and wondered if he'd been reading too much Evelyn Waugh. He'd been checking out the classics in order to figure out how polite society worked, what made it tick. If he could play the system, as Adam suggested, he could win his ticket to freedom, to a far away university.

'Oh, you're playing chess,' his mother said.

'To take my mind off things, yes. My opponent's in Russia.'

'That far away. Fancy.'

'We're evenly matched.'

'Toast and peanut butter at ten, then?'

That was a mere sixty minutes away and if he had to speak to her again that soon he might well not be responsible for his actions.

'The game will be at a critical stage by then. Perhaps you could leave it outside the door?'

His mother's smile faltered then she seemed to find strength from somewhere and said, 'Consider it done.'

At the appointed hour (they always incinerated the Hovis just before *News at Ten*), he ate, drank and was his own version of merry, with the added bonus that his mother had taken his duvet cover from the washing machine, dried and ironed it, so he had a nice clean quilt with all traces of Ethan rinsed away. It had been a good day, he decided as he finally powered down his PC at three a.m. – goodnight porn sites – and prepared to wank himself to sleep.

TWENTY-ONE

*B**eth seemed to be attracted to him – and the feeling was definitely mutual.* Adam hummed to himself as he finished talking to her on his mobile, having phoned to discuss a mutual client. Matthew sounded slightly dull and not quite bright enough to hold her attention so he, Adam, might get his chance in a few months. He wouldn't have to drug this one, just seduce her. She wanted – or currently thought she wanted – a forever boyfriend so he'd play that particular line.

Letting himself into the bungalow, he scooped up a solitary letter from the porch and opened it to find that one of his premium bonds had won him five hundred pounds. His dad had bought him the bonds for his twenty-first birthday but this was the biggest win that he'd ever had. He wouldn't mention it to the old man as he'd probably want him to spend it on Mum's eventual funeral. Though doped up to the eyes with morphine, she was still hanging on.

The pair of them sometimes complained about the shortfall in their pension funds after all these years of work, but he didn't know why they were so obsessed with money; after all, Nicholas was always taking them out for meals, daytrips and even a couple of foreign holidays. That said, his sibling would have to spend his wages on paying for a solicitor once the police found that kiddie porn. Adam felt a small glow of pleasure, knowing that legal representation was prohibitively expensive and could go on and on. Nicholas wouldn't get in touch for financial or emotional aid, but he figured that his dad might phone him asking for help.

Fortunately, despite his brother's betrayal, the cops had never been able to pin Helen's death on him and now everything was going really well, he thought as he fished out his pay-in book and wrote up the five hundred cheque. Everything was . . .

The doorbell pealed through the house and he walked to the front door and opened it, his face assuming its familiar welcoming smile.

Two policemen stood there. *Christ.* For a moment he simply stared at them, convinced that they'd come to arrest him for Hannah's murder.

'Mr Neave?' the oldest one murmured.

His voice sounded stronger than he expected. 'Yes, that's right.'

'Can we come in?'

He did a quick mental inventory of the house to reassure himself that there were no illicit drugs lying about. He mustn't dwell on the fact that Kylie's body was frozen in the garage. I mean, it wasn't like they were here for a freezer-to-microwave meal or anything.

'Of course.'

He walked to his study and they followed him in. He always took officials there rather than into the lounge or the kitchen/dining area. Surrounded by his certificates and books, he felt grounded, as if he'd gained the upper hand. A genuine professional was calm and intelligent, didn't show fear.

'We understand that you've been treating a teenager called Brandon Petrie. Can you tell us a little about him please?'

He felt his gut relax. *Thank God – it was the kid that they were interested in.*

'He's highly intelligent with a vocabulary way beyond his years, an exceptional child.'

'We know that he has attention defic–' The man stumbled over his notes.

'Attention Deficit Hyperactivity Disorder.' The term rolled off Adam's tongue. 'ADHD.'

'We understand from his mother that it makes it hard for him to concentrate.'

'It does, though he's come on leaps and bounds since he started taking the medication.'

'And you supply this, Dr Neave?'

He wasn't a doctor but their misconception suited him. The working classes – which clearly included both of these DCs – were in awe of medics. Harold Shipman had literally gotten away with murder for years.

'No, his GP supplies his prescription. I've been modifying his behaviour, encouraging him to think about the world in a different way.'

'Has he ever been violent?'

What on earth had the boy done?Murdered his mother?

'No, quite the reverse. He's very gentle. He loves to read books, write computer programmes, play chess.'

'So why were you modifying him, doc?'

'He's so caught up in his own world that he forgets to hold open doors or say please and thank you. People think that he's deliberately rude and antisocial but he's really just lacking in concentration. The dopamine receptors are abnormal in children with ADHD so their thoughts flit around all the time and they have appalling short-term memory.'

'So he forgets what he's doing, maybe moves on to another task?'

'Exactly. I've been showing his mother how to only give one instruction to him at a time and it seems to be working. If he's given too much information, he can't retain it for more than a moment and he becomes upset.'

'Makes sense,' one of the officers said, looking at his partner.

Adam cleared his throat and strove to sound casual. 'Can I ask what this is all about?'

The older man, clearly the senior officer, nodded. 'Brandon

was babysitting for his four-year-old cousin when the child drowned.'

'In the garden pond?' Kids were always jumping or falling into pools of water.

'In the bath. Apparently he'd vomited and Brandon decided to clean him up before his parents got home.'

'He must be devastated – he doted on that little boy,' Adam said, determined that his patient should look good, sound like a model pupil.

'He was very quiet when we spoke to him and didn't show any emotion, but his mother said that he was deeply shocked.'

'He would be. He might not express himself as readily as you and I, officer, but he feels things very deeply. He was just telling me the other day how much he appreciated being given responsibility for the child. He felt that his parents were beginning to respect him and he was determined to make them proud.'

'Makes sense,' the officer repeated. 'He probably thought his parents would be upset if the child was covered in vomit so he tried to do the right thing.'

'It's so easy for a small child to drown,' Adam clarified. 'I once counselled a young mother who had left her toddler in the bath for a moment whilst she answered the door. He was only sitting in a few inches of water but must have tried to follow her, slipped and banged his head. He fell down face first and was dead by the time that she got back.'

He'd made the story up but both men looked suitably sombre.

'There's no malice in young Brandon then?' the youngest one asked.

'None at all. I'd trust him with Tim, my own three-year-old nephew.'

He would, too, didn't care what happened to the wailing little brat.

'We've spoken to his GP, his former paediatrician and his teachers. Is there anyone else . . .?'

Adam shook his head, determined to keep that negative doctor who kept phoning him out of the picture. The last thing he needed was someone questioning his methods, casting blame.

'Just a tragic accident,' the other detective murmured, putting away his notebook and standing up.

'If I can be of any more help, don't hesitate to contact me,' Adam said as he preceded them down the hall to the front door.

'We'll be in touch if we've any further enquiries, sir.'

He got the distinct impression that they were closing the file, that he wouldn't be hearing from them again.

For a few moments after they left, he sat in his study, sipping a Southern Comfort and mulling over the information that they'd given him. Then he phoned Brandon's house.

'Mrs Petrie? It's Adam Neave. The police just told me about the accident. I'm so sorry.'

'It's so kind of you to phone.'

You should have rung and warned me, you stupid bat.

'Is Brandon coping?' He might get some extra hours of work out of this or even a live-in patient. He could move John into the attic, charge the teen's parents residential fees.

'He seems to be. He's been spending even more time in his room than usual but his father says to leave him there, that he has to sort things out on his own.'

'That's just his way,' Adam said reassuringly. 'He's never going to be gregarious or tactile.'

'He let me hug him the night of the accident,' Mrs Petrie said. 'I was amazed.'

'He'll be traumatized in his own way. I know how much he enjoyed caring for his little cousin.'

'You did? He said so? He never gives much away to his father and I . . .'

'Yes, he mentioned the child several times, said that he felt like a big brother figure. He was so proud that you trusted him.'

'That's the ironic thing.' He heard the woman choke back a sob. 'He bathed Ethan to please us and came to the door to greet us because he's being so polite these days. In those few minutes, the poor mite drowned.'

'A tragic accident,' Adam murmured, echoing the police.

'Would you be willing to see him before next Tuesday?'

'I'd be happy to,' he replied, meaning it. He'd just lost several hundred pounds on spread betting so his premium bond win was already spent.

The next day, he greeted the Petries as if they were his best friends, told Brandon to go on through to his office whilst he spoke to his mother in the hall.

'It might be best if he stays here this week – you know, in case he has nightmares.'

'Oh, he never has, Mr Neave. Not even as a child.'

'But he's never been faced with this level of trauma until now.'

'He's still sleeping well – ever since you got the doctor to change his medication.'

Fuck it – he was hoist by his own petard.

'Perhaps he's brooding during the day?'

'Well, he's got all these online friends who seem to keep him busy.'

'It's no substitute for professional help.'

He watched as her frown deepened. 'It's just that he likes his home comforts, his own bed.'

In other words, she didn't want to deal with empty nest syndrome, however briefly. What would she do all day with no one to fret about?

He gave in gracefully. 'I understand.'

'If he becomes distressed, I'll give you a call.'

'You know that you can phone me anytime, that I'm always here for your family.' He waved enthusiastically as she drove away.

'You OK, Brandon?' he asked as he joined the boy in his office. 'I heard about what happened.'

'I only left him for a moment.'

'Don't blame yourself. There are thousands of women world-wide have done the exact same thing.'

'Yeah?' The kid sat up straighter on the couch, put his book aside.

'Yep. We're all used to multitasking and occasionally something goes wrong.'

'I was trying to clean him up to impress the oldsters.'

'I know. They're aware that your intent was good.'

'The police questioned me at length.'

'I think they also recognize that it was an accident. Just learn from it and move on.'

'Fortunately I don't have any other cousins,' the sixteen-year-old said with a wry grin.

'And the neighbours won't be queuing up to have you babysit.'

As he'd hoped, the youth laughed at his black humour. Adam smiled back.

'What now?' Brandon asked.

'Just tell me whatever comes into your head. They call it free association.'

'And it'll help people to like me?'

'I'm sure that they already like you,' Adam replied.

'I get picked on at school . . .'

'We'll find ways for you to stand up for yourself.'

'And Dad would like a son to play cricket with.'

'Then we'll have to make sure that he impregnates your mum!'

Adam laughed at his own joke and, after a moment's contemplation, the teenager joined in. According to his notes, the boy had never been told that he was adopted so presumably the Petries were withholding the information until he turned eighteen.

'Maybe I could create the perfect son for him in the laboratory,' the boy continued, looking thoughtful.

'Could take a while, though I understand that they can now use stem cell research to grow teeth. I guess you could assemble the perfect smile and add the rest of your sibling's body later.' He contemplated the image for a moment, realizing that it was almost cartoon-like, then looked at his notes. 'Anyway, let's get started on the free association and have some fun.'

Free association my arse. Brandon kept a smile on his face but inwardly he felt yet another rush of derision. These sessions were costing his parents a fortune but the therapist didn't have a clue. He seemed to have decided that he, Brandon, was a simpleton who would switch from morose to happy if he could just become polite and easy-going and connect with the moronic aspects of the world. Did Adam really think that he was so uncomplicated? Didn't he know that people hid the darker aspects of themselves?

'Bee,' Adam said.

Fatal sting which would cause you to die in agony. 'Honey.'

Adam looked pleased. 'Love.'

An illusion. 'Mother and father.'

The therapist nodded almost imperceptibly. 'Books.'

An escape from idiots like you. 'Education.'

The man seemed to look around the room for inspiration: 'Medicine.'

Mind control. He'd stopped taking his. 'Aid.'

'Support.'

Bleeding hearts. 'Family.'

By the time they came to the end of what must have been a ridiculously long list, his mother was ringing at the door and Brandon actually felt almost glad to see her. At least he could blame her stupidity on a lack of formal education as she'd married shortly after leaving school, hadn't gone to university or maintained an interest in books. But this fuckwit had a degree plus several postgraduate certificates on his wall, should be able to do more than just parrot words at him.

'I think that we can safely go back to our normal weekly appointment, albeit for two-hour sessions,' Adam said as Mrs Petrie fussed about in the hall.

Brandon stiffened as he felt his mother's arms around him, but he realized that Adam was watching closely and forced himself not to push her away, to consciously relax.

As usual, the woman sounded deferential when she spoke to the therapist, as if he was doing her a favour.

'We'll see you then, Mr Neave – and thank you.'

'My pleasure.'

A pleasure for your bank balance, Brandon thought. He hoped that he'd run into a couple of the younger kids on the way to school tomorrow morning so that he could steal their pocket money and give them a sly kick or two; despite what he'd told Adam, he was always the bully rather than the bullied. He was feeling really irritated with the world and wanted to take it out on someone else.

TWENTY-TWO

She'd forgotten that she owned this – but now she admitted to herself that it would be very useful. Beth sat on her bedroom floor and weighed the personal massager in her right hand. It was a subtle design which looked like a large flat stone and which vibrated at a low level. You could use it to unknot your neck muscles or shoulders – or run it lightly over the pubis and build and build. She'd gone into the seldom-used drawer under the bed in search of her silk pillowcases and found this rarely-used object. Her husband had bought it years ago as a joke present and they'd only tried it once or twice.

Putting it on its charger, she hurried to get ready for her date with Matthew. She'd wanted to change to the silk pillows as someone had said that you were less likely to have bedhead when you woke up as hair slipped off silk whereas it caught and snagged against cotton. Matthew had the kind of wiry hair which always sat well, whereas she could turn into the last of the Mohicans during the night. He'd made some comment about it the other day, presumably joking, but she'd been slightly disconcerted, wanted to look her best.

That night, when they went to bed, she told him to lie back and think of England.

'What have you got in mind?' He looked vaguely alarmed.

'It's my personal massager. I found it when I was looking for linen and thought that I could use it on you.'

She brought the fully-charged appliance over to the bed and began to take off his clothes.

'Bags I use it on you first!' he laughed and started to undress her.

Beth lay back, smiling, happy for him to take charge. When she was naked, he switched the massager on and put it firmly on top of her clitoris.

'Jesus!' When she came down from the ceiling, she took his

hand so that the vibrator rested close to one of her labial lips. 'Not so close – like that,' she murmured encouragingly. Now that the oscillations weren't so direct, she could become aroused.

But, moments later, he moved the massager back towards her clit: his wife, she thought, must have had the genitals of a rhino. Eventually she put her hand over his, holding the machine where she wanted it. Within moments she climaxed, crying out whilst still holding onto his hand.

'Thank God. I thought that you'd never get there,' Matthew said.

It wasn't the most tactful remark in the world, but he was probably tired, Beth thought. After all, he'd done a manual job all day, driven through to Weston to pick her up and danced for a couple of hours at the nightclub. Her suspicions were confirmed when he let out a loud snore. She'd try the vibrator on him another day, she decided, curling into his back and putting her arms around his waist. She'd give him the best orgasm that he'd ever had.

Matthew woke as the morning sun began to filter through the window. He stared at Beth, who was sleeping on her back, her mouth slightly open. What on earth happened to her hair during the night? It somehow seemed to double in volume so it was like waking up with Ken Dodd.

Something clunked against his elbow and he realized it was the massager that she'd insisted on using last night. It took all of the romance out of the equation for him if a machine came between them. He was sure that she'd orgasm from intercourse if she just relaxed a bit more and wasn't so obsessed with her clitoris. His wife had been able to climax as long as he thrust for fifteen minutes or so, as had one of his previous girlfriends. He'd tried fucking Beth and stroking her clit at the same time but she'd said that she couldn't come with anything inside her, which was surely nonsensical.

Beth stirred in her sleep and wrapped her arms around him for what felt like the umpteenth time. Feeling trapped, Matthew unpeeled her fingers – why did she never paint her nails? – from his waist and slid as silently as possible from the somehow claustrophobic bed. He was glad now that he had a Saturday morning call out, glad for an excuse to get away.

Usually, he brought her breakfast in bed but he didn't want to re-enter the room so just cut himself a piece of fruitcake from the one in the bread bin and ate it as he dressed. He'd pick up a takeaway coffee from the nearest McDonalds enroute to his client, kick-start his brain.

Hearing her stir, he hurried from the house and into his van, quickly started the engine. She was going out with a female friend tonight so it would be tomorrow before he next saw her, went to bed with her. Perhaps he'd go home afterwards rather than spending the night. That said, he was glad of their forth-coming date as he hated spending Sundays alone – it was such a couples time. Maybe by then he'd feel close to her again.

TWENTY-THREE

'**N**icholas Neave? We have a warrant to search your house and seize all of your computers.'

Nicholas stared at the two uniformed officers and at the plain clothes woman who accompanied them. Suddenly he felt rooted to the spot, as if he'd never be able to move from his own doorway. With difficulty he found his voice.

'What on earth are you looking for?'

'Indecent images,' one of the men said, looking grim.

Had they got the wrong house? He only had a few holiday photos on his PC, and Jill wore a tankini in most of them as she was self conscious about her post-baby stomach, showed very little flesh.

'And this is Mrs Holden, who will take your child to the medical centre for an examination,' the older of the officers said.

My God, had someone molested Tim? For a second he thought of Adam, the only evil person that he knew, but he realized that even his brother had his limits, wasn't attracted to children. Even as a teenager, his youngest conquest had been thirteen.

'What makes you think . . .?'

'We have our sources,' the officer said.

'Can I phone my wife?'

She was out shopping but might have her mobile switched on.

'You can indeed. She can meet us at the centre if you want.' The man gave him a local address.

He phoned Jill but only got through to her answering service. He hung up, unsure what to say in a message. He put off the DVD that his son was watching and picked the little boy up, but he immediately began to wail. The social worker took him and he quietened in surprise, unused to strangers. Nicholas was belatedly aware that she was staring at him, giving him what appeared to be a knowing look.

'He loves that cartoon,' he said numbly. 'Likes to watch it over and over.'

'We've lots at the centre.'

Shaking slightly, he followed them down the path. A neighbour was standing talking to someone at the door and Nicholas nodded on automatic pilot then saw the man's look of surprise as he got into the waiting police car. Were they still called Panda cars? Had he been arrested? He couldn't remember them reading him his Miranda rights, but vaguely remembered a cop show in which someone said that these had been changed.

They parked outside a building which he didn't recognize and went in, was ushered into an empty room lined with plastic orange-coloured chairs. A woman whom he'd never met before sat down next to him, quietly said hello and began to leaf through a sheaf of papers. He had the distinct impression that she was his guard. He sat silently, but feeling increasingly nauseous, for an interminable period, wondering what they were doing to his son. There were posters on the walls aimed at children and a box of soft toys, with teddies and a feathery ostrich sticking out of the top. He wanted to pick the bird up, to hug it close for comfort, but realized that would look strange to his supervisor or captor or whatever she was.

Eventually his son came into the room with the social worker and both were smiling. Tim hugged his leg.

'Can I take him home?' he asked, glad that he appeared to have passed some vital test.

'I've just got to—' the woman started, then two officers walked in and one said that he was under arrest for the possession of child pornography.

This was making less and less sense.

'You've got the wrong man,' he said, feeling like an actor in a film. This couldn't be happening. He half listened to the stream of verbiage which followed, said that, yes, he understood.

At the police station, they showed him what they'd found, flicking through the obscene pages with their gloved hands, and he felt sick.

'I've never . . .'

'But you like kids.'

'Of course I do, but not in that way.' He'd never thought much about child porn before, had a vague idea that it would involve photos of naked young children, but now they'd made him look at pictures of grown men doing terrible things to little boys.

'Sometimes a man is abused and it plays havoc with his mind. He's a victim in a way of his own childhood.'

But he'd had a great childhood. There again, so had Adam – the first few months excepting – and he'd somehow gone awry.

'Can you check if my brother's fingerprints are on there?' He indicated the mag, tried not to look at it more closely. 'Mine won't be,' he added, starting to feel slightly stronger, on firmer ground.

'Either of you could have worn gloves.' The heavier of the detectives paused. 'Does he have access to your house?'

'He's visited, if that's what you mean, but I didn't like the way that he looked at Jill so I stopped his visits.'

The detectives exchanged looks. What had he said now?

'So there was no love lost between you and your brother?'

'I've already told you that.'

'Maybe he had good reason to dislike you,' one of the men said.

'It's mutual. Can I ask where you found the mag?'

'In your son's bed.'

He felt sick, wondered for a second if Jill could have . . . But no, that was ridiculous. So someone might have been sitting by his son's divan and touching himself or, even worse, touching his child.

'He wasn't . . . I mean, no one has molested Tim?'

'He hasn't had penetrative sex, no.'

What other kind was there? What exactly did a grown man do to a little boy? He glanced at the magazine in front of him and realized that the answers were there and that he didn't want them soiling his previously tranquil mind.

'I want a lawyer.' He'd refused one when he first arrived, aware that he'd done nothing wrong, but now this interview was going on and on and they wouldn't believe him.

'You're entitled to a phone call.'

He called a number from the phone book, feeling almost disembodied, then sat back in his chair and waited for his brief.

TWENTY-FOUR

A *t last he was getting his act together at work and at home. He'd even returned to cooking, something that he hadn't done since his student days.* John smiled as Adam entered the lounge.

'I've made a vegetable chilli if you're hungry.'

'You have?' Adam looked amazed.

'Well, this course that I took taught us to really examine our behaviour patterns and I realized that I eat too much junk, don't take in enough vitamins and fibre. I also spend far too much on processed food.'

'Join the club,' Adam said with what sounded like real feeling.

'From now on it's club sandwiches rather than a burger in a bun!'

'I'm impressed.' Adam left the room and returned with a plate of chilli and a side salad.

'Eat your heart out, Gordon Ramsay,' John replied, and grinned.

'So, what are we watching?' Adam glanced at the screen.

'It's a programme by the Food Doctor – but we can switch to *World's Worst Cop Chases* if you like.'

'No.' Adam seemed to shudder. 'The doc will be fine.'

'Were you out on the pull again last night?'

'No, just out at the casino.'

'Bet you wish that they had one here in Weston,' John said. He'd never been to one, but it was obvious that they were Adam's second home: he was always travelling around to different establishments. He said that it took his mind off his patients, that it gave him a buzz. He, John, didn't need the

stimulus of winning or losing hundreds of pounds, was happy
just to speak to a pretty girl or have a couple of pints in a beer
garden with his fellow gym workers. There again, it was a
novelty for him to get close to women whereas Adam had them
queuing up to join his bed.

Thinking of beds reminded him of an ongoing problem.

'I was wondering,' he asked, as they finished the meal, 'if you
could stretch to a new mattress for my room?'

'Spring for one, you mean,' Adam said and they both laughed.
'Could have to wait a while, mate. I've got a lot of overheads.'

'Maybe I could pay half, then? It's just that one of the springs
is pushing through and it's really uncomfortable.'

'You might be able to pick up a second hand one at a low cost.'

'Right.' John felt slightly disappointed at his landlord's
response. He'd mentioned the bumpy mattress within a fortnight
of moving in and Adam had said that, if his tenure worked out,
he'd replace it. But the older man hadn't raised the subject since.

'So, how's work?' Adam asked.

'Improving. I placed an advert in one of the men's health mags
offering cut-price personal training for the first four sessions
providing people prepay for eight. I've already had three phone
calls so it's looking good.'

'I'd rather work with women!'

'Problem is,' John explained, 'they cancel sessions when
they're premenstrual or on the rag.'

'So target post-menopausal ones.'

'It's harder to get their weight down.'

'Early menopause?'

'Same thing – some of them go up a couple of dress sizes and
it's almost impossible to shift.'

'OK, but a larger woman might pay you in kind . . .'

John smiled, so far, no one had been that grateful. 'No, I'm
going to keep work and my social life separate, be professional. I
need to earn more money so it makes sense to take on clients that
are men.'

'Sounds like you've got yourself sorted,' Adam said, opening
a can of beer.

John looked longingly at the remaining cans in the pack then
determinedly picked up his mug of redbush tea.

'I'm getting there. That reminds me – remember you suggested that I start offering dietary tuition?'

He watched as Adam nodded.

'Well, is it OK if I hold a one-day course here on nutrition and exercise? I'd sign up six people at most and hold it here in the lounge.'

'Go for it – maybe you can buy a new mattress from the fees,' Adam said, grinning widely.

It looked like he was going to have to, John thought, as his landlord had apparently gone broke.

TWENTY-FIVE

'I've missed you, 'Beth said, giving Matthew a hug as they stood in the doorway. He'd called round to take her to the cinema but was fifteen minutes early; if they got there too soon they'd have to sit through the endless trailers and warnings about video piracy and she'd lose the will to live.

'Good,' he replied distractedly, giving her a quick kiss on the cheek.

He hadn't said that he'd missed her too, Beth noted as she preceded him down the hall and didn't seem pleased that she'd at last found the courage to say that she missed him. It felt, in an odd way, like a betrayal of her late husband to admit that she had feelings for someone else.

'Do you want a quick coffee before we go?'

'Might as well.'

Again, he sounded slightly distant.

'I've got chocolate muffins.'

She'd started buying in cakes for him as he seemed to thrive on sugar, like a nectar-starved bumble bee.

'Well done you,' he said as she put their cups and cookies down on the occasional table.

'I made them myself,' she joked, 'including the paper wrappers.'

She lowered herself onto his lap as she often did, facing him, with her knees on either side of his body as they relaxed on the settee.

To her dismay, he pinched at the sides of her waist. 'Should you really be eating cakes?'

'Definitely,' Beth replied. She could hear the hurt in her voice, the confusion. Was he suggesting that she was fat? She was a standard twelve dress size and Brian had always said that she had a lovely body, curvy yet petite. She'd never thought much about her figure, she realized, had been the same weight for most of her adult life. That life had been so simple when she was married to someone who accepted her completely; she'd never worried about bad hair days or water retention or premenstrually patchy skin.

The muffin felt dry and tasteless in her mouth but she forced herself to eat it all as a matter of principle. She simply couldn't let a man dictate her diet. Matthew's wife had gained three stone throughout their marriage so perhaps that had left him paranoid about comfort eating but she had no intention of doing the same thing; she also had no intention of starving herself or forgoing the occasional calorific treat. She'd walked to and from the hospital today, a total journey of over an hour and, as usual, had traipsed the long corridors as she talked to various personnel about their nutritional needs, and her evening meal had just been a mackerel salad. She deserved this carbohydrate snack.

Should she ask him if he thought that she was overweight? No, that made her sound too needy. Had he started to find her less attractive? Her period was due so she wasn't looking or feeling her best. But should a man – especially one of his years – be judging his girlfriend solely on her looks and body? Surely that implied a terrible immaturity?

She was still mulling over his behaviour the following day at the bereavement drop-in session so was particularly pleased when Olivia Marsden walked in. Talking to the young widow would take her mind off her own relationship issues.

'So, how have you been, Olivia?' she asked. She worked hard to always remember her clients' names and their most pertinent details. Admittedly it was easy with Olivia as she'd actually been to her house.

'Up and down. Some days I think that I'm doing really well, others I feel so hopeless that I can't stop crying.'

'Grief is like that. It has its own rhythm,' Beth said sympathetically.

'It's especially hard knowing that Zak will never hear Mia's first words, watch her first steps, take her to school or watch her graduate from college.'

'It must be,' Beth murmured, aware that there were no words which could bring consolation in such difficult circumstances.

They both looked up as the door opened and Adam strolled in.

'Sorry to bother you both,' he murmured.

'Anytime!' Olivia said, smiling brightly up at him.

The younger woman was flirting, and Beth felt a momentary surprise. There again, it must be terrifying being widowed with a baby so maybe she was trying to attract a mate in order to survive.

'Beth – there's a woman at the door who specifically wants to talk to you. Something about a neighbour's cousin.'

'Oh, I know the case. Olivia, are you happy to have another woman join us or . . .?'

Olivia looked up at Adam. 'I'd rather be counselled one-to-one.'

'OK,' Adam said, glancing at Beth, 'well, why don't I speak to Olivia and you can go talk to your friend?'

'I guess . . .' Beth murmured, hoping that the widow wasn't going to make a fool of herself by propositioning her handsome colleague. That said, Adam was far too sensible to get involved with a client, particularly one who had recently given birth to her dead husband's child.

TWENTY-SIX

'Your brother has made certain allegations against you, so we wondered if you could account for your movements on Thursday night,' the policeman asked.

Yes, I was recovering from my trip to Birmingham and waiting until it got dark so that I could go round to his place and slip a porn mag under his son's mattress.

Adam smiled inwardly, picturing the man's face if he told the truth. 'I'll just check my diary. Oh, I was here with John, my lodger.'

'And he can verify that?'

'He's in the kitchen, officer. Please go ahead and speak to him.'

The pair of them had watched a triple bill of *Road Wars* and shared a Chinese fried rice. He'd been careful not to mention going to Birmingham as the letter was date-stamped there. He'd thought about sending it locally but figured it might draw more attention to him; as it stood, the sender could be a professional who travelled for business or pleasure and who perhaps had a child who went to nursery school with Tim. When paedophile cases broke, you invariably found a few parents who had seen something vaguely suspicious in the toilets or changing room but hadn't felt confident enough to act on it. Eventually, someone would send the police an anonymous note.

Ten minutes later, the officer was back.

'Thank you, sir.'

'You're welcome. So, what exactly has my brother accused me of?'

The man looked briefly at his feet. 'We found an indecent magazine in his house and he said that you had planted it.'

Adam frowned slightly, a look that he had perfected in front of the mirror as a younger man. 'When, exactly? I haven't been there for years!'

'We don't know the date, to be honest. But we were tipped off on Friday so if anyone planted it . . .'

'He's forever accusing me of things. If I was a less placid man, I'd probably sue him.'

The detective nodded. 'I gather that there's no love lost between you?'

'Well, no. We both left school at sixteen as our parents wanted us to help run the family florist. But I eventually went on to university and Nicholas didn't. I think he really resented me for that. He delivered bouquets throughout Somerset until my parents retired, then took over the day-to-day organization of the shop. It's living-by-numbers whereas I run a psychology practice and also do voluntary work.'

'But we understand that he also teaches at a Sunday school.'

'He does – he's always been more confident around kids than adults. Even at secondary, he went around with the younger crowd.'

'And how is he with his own son?'

'Oh, excellent – a very good father. '

'And what do you think about Jill's parenting skills?'

'A brilliant mother. Totally dedicated.'

'Yet she didn't want you around.'

Adam grimaced. 'To be honest, I got the impression that they both see sin everywhere, you know, because they are so religious? I'd smile at Jill in a friendly way and she'd blush and Nicholas would look like he wanted to kill me. One day he accused me of making a play for her so I stopped going round.'

The other man looked thoughtful. 'So these were just social visits?'

They might hear the truth from his father, so he'd better level with them. 'No, my parents lent me the money to get through university and I was paying them back whenever I could. Nicholas, for some unfathomable reason, decided to get involved and used to invite me round to discuss my finances. I've paid back most of the loan, now, and they've forgiven the rest.'

'They never lent Nicholas any cash?'

'No, they paid his wages every week from the shop takings and that's all he ever required. I'm the first person in the family to graduate so they're very pleased.'

'I can understand that,' the man said, looking around his therapy room. 'Mr Neave, can I ask if you've ever seen your brother behave inappropriately with a child?'

Adam donned a look of surprise. 'No, never. As I said before, he really likes children.'

'You don't think that he maybe likes them too much?'

He hesitated, blinked several times. 'I never thought . . . Oh no, officer, I can't accuse him of that.'

The silence lengthened, the officer presumably hoping that he would remember some relevant incident. He stared back at him guilelessly.

'If you think of anything else, please get in touch with us.'

Nodding agreeably, he accepted the little card.

After seeing the man out, he hurried to the phone and called his father, but the older man didn't answer. Of course, he'd be with Mum at the hospital. Glad that he didn't have any clients until the afternoon, Adam drove there and hurried to the ward. She was still in a side room, still delirious, still hanging on.

'Dad, I'm sorry to bother you, but have you heard from Nicholas?'

'Your brother? He's in the cafe, having an early lunch. He'll be back in ten minutes.'

Damn, so the police had let him go and he hadn't mentioned any of it to the old man, probably didn't want to worry him at this most challenging time. It was clear that the porn magazine wasn't going to be enough to ruin Nicholas's life completely, that he'd have to commit an even more damning act.

He smiled brightly at his younger sibling when he entered the room. 'Hi bro.'

Nicholas glared, seemed to belatedly notice his father, and smiled weakly.

The three of them – all males from the same family but separated by some unfathomable emotional gulf – sat by the bedside for the next fifteen minutes then Adam looked pointedly at his watch.

'Sorry, but I have to see a client. Must go.'

'Thanks for coming, son,' his dad said gruffly. 'I'll phone you if there's any news.'

News about Nicholas? He realized belatedly that the man meant news about his mother. He nodded, touched his hand then that of his comatose relative, pretended to care. She could hang on for days or even weeks; he often counselled the adult children of dying parents. They lived in limbo, waiting – and sometimes even guiltily praying – for the end. Machines kept patients alive who would previously have expired, kept them in an emotional and mental no man's land. That thought aside, there was going to be news of a death by tomorrow, though not the one that his family was anticipating.

Nicholas had been prepared to send him to prison, on a hunch, for at least sixteen years, ruining his day-to-day life and permanently robbing him of his psychology practice. Now he would rob his brother of the thing that he most loved in all the world.

*   *   *

Again, he waited until the early hours before leaving the bungalow and driving to the district where his brother and sister-in-law lived. Again, he parked a couple of streets away and walked quietly, merging with the shadows made by the overhanging trees. He'd never killed a child before but it must be physically much easier than murdering an adult woman, albeit devoid of fun. No, he doubted if he'd get a sexual charge from this particular murder – but he'd have the ongoing emotional satisfaction of knowing that he was putting Nicholas and the equally smug Jill through hell.

He'd opted to commit this crime after reading about Armenian justice. Their gangsters believed that it made no sense to kill your enemy – after all, you were merely sending him to a permanent peace, to oblivion. But if you killed someone who he loved, you ensured that he mourned and suffered for the rest of his life.

Wearing his by now trademark gloves, he slid his key carefully into the lock – good, they hadn't had time to change it. The lack of lights indicated that they had gone to bed, so he made his way soundlessly to the nursery.

Tim was asleep, his little face relaxed and rosy and, for a second, he hesitated, unsure if he could go through with this. Then he remembered the way that Nicholas had treated him, and felt new rage. Reaching down, he held the toddler's nose and mouth firmly shut with his gloved fingers, pressed his forearms down on the struggling body beneath the duvet. He looked away the entire time, pictured his brother's anguished face. The boy seemed to expire quickly but he kept his fingers in place for untold moments, just to be sure. Finally he let go and pulled the duvet up to the child's – well, the corpse's – neck.

A floorboard creaked and then another. Fuck it. He lay down and rolled under the dusty bed, urged himself not to sneeze and held his breath. Jill walked halfway into the room, he could just see her feet, clad in old-fashioned slippers. She stopped for a moment, presumably peered at her son through the darkness, and tiptoed out again. He must just look as if he was sleeping peacefully.

Adam lay there for ten more minutes before deciding that Jill had probably returned to dreamland. He slid out awkwardly but soundlessly and examined his handiwork. It would help matters if he made it look like the boy had suffocated, so he turned Tim's face into the pillow before pulling the covers up and tucking some of them under his head. Mission accomplished. Tiptoeing very carefully and scarcely breathing, he left the way that he had come and drove home.

TWENTY-SEVEN

'Welcome to my humble abode!' John said. He murmured the same greeting six times in total, as, one by one, his clients arrived at the house for the 'Weight Loss & Well-being' course. He showed each of them into the lounge, furnished today with additional comfy chairs from the kitchen. He'd also strewn bowls of peanuts and fruit around. Lunch was already cling-filmed in the fridge, a brown rice salad, hummus and slices of goat's cheese quiche.

'Nice place,' one of the girls said. John smiled. He wouldn't lie outright but was happy to let the three men and three women think that this was his own house, that he was climbing the property ladder. Adam had said that he wouldn't be back until mid-evening as he was counselling a bipolar man in a neighbouring town. He'd said that he could charge extra if he went to the client's house rather than have them come to him, so was especially glad to take on agoraphobics and anyone who was anxious in crowds.

John cleared his throat and recited his opening sentence, one that he'd learned off by heart. 'If I could start by asking each of you what you hope to gain from today?'

The three females all opted for weight loss.

'I'm the opposite, want to bulk out a bit,' the leanest of the men said.

'I'd like to have fewer colds so that I can give more to my work,' the second man admitted.

'Same here – improved health and fitness,' clarified the third guy.

'In other words, we all need to change what we're doing now in terms of diet and lifestyle,' John said. 'Gently modify our behaviour. I can give you tips for the short term so that you'll see almost immediate improvements but also work out a schedule for the longer term so that you continue towards your goal.'

The heaviest man patted his stomach. 'I sometimes eat all the wrong things, end up with indigestion.'

John nodded. 'You can often clear indigestion almost overnight by trying food combining – that is, you don't mix protein and starches at the same meal. So you could have steak and salad or steak with vegetables but not with potato. Similarly, if you had a baked potato for your meal you couldn't top it with tuna, cheese or another protein but you could have it with sweetcorn or a tomato and onion sauce.'

'And how long would you follow that regime?'

'Probably for a week to give your system a rest,' John said. 'Some people follow it for years but it's very restrictive, particularly when you're eating out.'

'Isn't there also some rule about fruit?' one of the girls asked.

'Yes, food combiners recommend that you eat fruit on an empty stomach as it's easier to digest. So melon is ideal for a starter but not for dessert.'

By lunchtime – an unfortunate mixture of protein and carbs which would probably leave Indigestion Man doubled over later in the day – they were all best friends and the topic had flitted from working out to relationships. One of the women had split up with her boyfriend three months ago and lamented that her job as a buyer for a large retail outlet didn't bring her into contact with many men.

'Then, when I do meet someone, I'm worried that my weight is putting them off,' she said anxiously.

John stared at her in surprise. 'Nonsense – you can only be a fourteen.'

'A fourteen to sixteen.'

'Then you're the same size as over half of the women in this country,' he explained and they smiled at each other for so long that several of the others exchanged knowing looks. He'd love to have her, Louise, as his girlfriend, John admitted to himself.

She had such a sweet face and was very open about her doubts and fears.

The hours passed quickly and, all too soon, it was four p.m. but no one wanted the course to end. They continued talking. Two hours later, Louise admitted that she was hungry and the others said that they were too.

John felt almost giddy at his new-found ability to connect with women. 'Why don't I rustle us up a meal and we can watch a DVD?'

He'd make another batch of the vegetarian chilli that he'd tried out on Adam recently. There were tins of mixed beans in the cupboard, spices on the rack and onions in the bottom of the fridge. It would only take ten minutes. All he needed was enough cooked rice for seven.

A thorough rummage through the kitchen freezer produced nothing of use. In fact, it mainly consisted of frozen vegetables and a couple of microwave fish meals, no good when two of the course members were vegetarian. He'd have to go out to the big freezer in the garage and see what he could find. Fortunately Adam had found the key after next door's Maine Coon had become trapped there, and it was presumably in his study. After a few minutes of rooting around, he found it in the little slide-out compartment of the writing bureau where his landlord kept every-thing from staples to paperclips. Humming to himself, he approached and unlocked the outhouse. The hole in the roof, he noticed, was now patched with what looked like balsa wood: Adam must have repaired it when he was at work. That was unusual as his landlord usually put off DIY and baulked at the cost of calling in a professional, generally let various home maintenance tasks build up.

He opened the large white chest and surveyed the family-sized bags of pasta, roast potatoes and slices of roast beef in gravy, frozen into individual portions. Surely Adam hadn't run out of pre-cooked rice? They sometimes heated a portion to accompany a takeaway curry as it was cheaper and less oily than buying it from the Indian restaurant.

John lifted a few of the bags from the freezer and set them carefully on the floor. He was now looking at a layer of gammon and beef steaks, bought cheaply as they were close to their sell-by date. Third time lucky: he started to pile some of the steaks to one side.

'What the fuck are you doing?'

The sudden, angry voice made him jump and he turned around sharply to see his landlord standing in the doorway.

'Looking for rice.'

'I told you we were low on things in here.'

'But we're not.' He indicated the piles of food. 'I'm sure that there's rice in here somewhere. Remember the last time we were at Tesco and you said—'

'Anyway, it's not safe in here. The roof could fall in,' Adam muttered.

Really? But the hole in the roof was at the other side of the garage.

'I thought that you'd fixed it?'

'Just a patch-up job. Some of these tiles are unstable.' Adam almost leaped into the building and began to toss the groceries back into the freezer, rather than stacking them neatly in place.

John swallowed hard. He'd been having such a nice day yet suddenly he was in the doghouse and he didn't understand why. He and Adam had arranged to do a bulk shop once a month and split the cost, so at least half of the food in here was his. And, until recently, it hadn't been a no-go area: in fact, quite the reverse.

'I've got six guests to feed,' he explained. 'And I'm making them a chilli. I just wanted some of that white-and-wild rice mix that we've used before.'

'Right, you go back to your mates and I'll see what I can do,' his landlord muttered. 'D'you want a few cans of lager as well?'

'Better not – half of them are trying to diet and one of the guys has a dodgy gut so anything which ferments will make it worse. I'll just give them black tea.'

'Redbush for you, I presume?'

'Thanks, Adam.' John nodded and smiled, glad that the therapist was back to his usual, easy-going self.

Fifteen minutes later, he served the meal, complete with the rice which Adam had found in the freezer. His landlord joined them but only had the chilli, explaining that he wasn't hungry enough for both.

'So, is this meal protein or carbs?' Louise asked.

'Both, as beans are made up of the two,' John admitted, pretending to look shamefaced and everyone laughed. 'Hey, I never said that I actually *practised* food combining,' he added good-naturedly, 'just said that it was an option to give your digestive system a break.'

'Apparently chillies are mildly addictive,' Adam cut in, 'which explains why so many of us crave a weekly curry or get hooked on Mexican food.'

'But this is much lower calorie?' Louise asked, looking at John for clarification.

'Definitely – it's very low in fat.'

'You can move into my kitchen and cook for me anytime,' she added, spearing another kidney bean.

In the fullness of time, John thought happily, he might get to do just that.

TWENTY-EIGHT

uck it – last night he'd murdered his nephew and today he'd have to move Kylie's body. Adam continued to smile and chat to John's guests but his mind was racing and forming a plan. He daren't risk John uncovering the girl's corpse the next time that he fancied a bowl of Häagan Dazs. It was unfortunate as, until now, she was still merely being regarded as a missing person, whereas as soon as her body turned up, police would start treating it as a murder case. But, what with marauding cats and unexpected visits from the boys in blue, it was getting too dangerous to keep her on the premises.

He'd have to drug his lodger to make sure that he didn't get up whilst he was removing the frozen corpse from the garage or ferrying it through the garden and out of the side gate to his car. She'd be incredibly difficult to manoeuvre but he couldn't wait around until she thawed out. Earlier in the month, he'd had a heart-stopping moment when a nearby housing area had had a power cut thanks to a lightning strike. That would be all he needed, the smell of Kylie decomposing amidst the thawed legs of lamb. He'd been pleased that he'd literally weathered the storm, had thought that nothing else could happen to thwart him, but today he could have had seven people suddenly staring down at her icy flesh . . .

He had to act normally for the rest of the evening so that John forgot how oddly he'd behaved in the garage. Then, when everyone left, he'd give his lodger some Rohypnol by slipping it into his lager or tea. It would play havoc with his memory, he'd feel groggy when he awoke and would probably spend the next few hours in a hung-over limbo, making the incident with the freezer the last thing on his mind. His memory loss was important as the police pathologist would know that the body had been frozen, might well go public with the news.

The evening passed slowly but, by nine p.m., John's guests started to murmur that they really must go home.

Go, he thought. I've a corpse to dispose of.

'We must do this again next month. A meal and DVD, I mean – and no charge!' John said, looking both flushed and high.

'Or you could all come to me,' the chunky one – Louise or something similar – said.

'It's a date,' John murmured.

Adam cringed inwardly. Hadn't the youth heard about acting cool?

After a dozen goodbyes, two mañanas and promises to become friends on Facebook, the troop departed.

'I'll make you another redbush,' Adam said.

'Thanks, I could use one.' John flopped down on the settee. 'That was a marathon with everyone here for eleven hours.'

'Looks like it was a big success.'

'It was – but I'm knackered now,' John admitted. 'Probably too wired to sleep tonight.'

Trust me, Adam thought, you're heading towards unconsciousness.

He made the tea, added one of the little white pills and stirred it repeatedly. 'There you go.'

John took the mug and drank deeply.

'Pal for life.'

'You put your feet up whilst I load the dishwasher.'

He cleaned up the kitchen for fifteen minutes then tiptoed back to the lounge. As he'd anticipated, his lodger was already in a deeply-drugged sleep.

Within the hour, darkness descended and Adam hurried out to the garage, tossed out the layers of frozen foods and, with great difficulty, levered Kylie's chilled, sheet-wrapped corpse out of the chest and onto the concrete. Putting everything back, he shut the freezer and dragged the cadaver out into the back garden before locking the garage door. Shivering, he half carried and half dragged her down the path, stopping each time that he heard a noise in either of the adjacent gardens. He also froze (and was aware of how ironic the word was) when the McLellan's security light came on, then he reminded himself that it was activated by movement on his path as well as theirs. They invariably went to bed after *News at Ten*, would be in Dreamland by now.

He sidestepped a clearly lonely Tilly – why couldn't they keep the bloody pest indoors at night? – and continued to pull the leaden, sheet-wrapped corpse towards the side gate. It was like manoeuvring a giant ice pole, a frozen juice treat that he'd often enjoyed in childhood. He could use the energy rush now, was having to get by on sheer adrenaline. He'd had to stay up late last night in order to murder Tim, and the lack of sleep was catching up with him. Determined to see the project through, he manhandled her out of the gate and towards his car.

She couldn't go in the boot as she was unfoldable in her current condition, so he laid her on the floor of the back seat, still mummified in the icy cotton. If a traffic cop stopped him and peered into the vehicle, it would be game over but luck had been on his side all his life.

Driving carefully, Adam set off towards a wooded area in Bristol; after all, it was the ice queen's home town. If he dumped the body there, they hopefully wouldn't connect it to Hannah who had been found in Weston-super-Mare.

Almost, almost . . . Finding a quiet, shadowy area in the woods, he manhandled his grisly cargo from the vehicle and tried to remove the sheet but it had stuck to her body. Damn it. With effort, he rolled her down the slope, neatly sheathed in white cotton, and watched her disappear between the trees. She'd probably be found in the morning but by then he'd be in his study, counselling some other confused and desperate bitch.

Keen to get out of Bristol as quickly as possible, he drove home, poured himself a whisky in the kitchen and threw himself down next to John on the settee.

'Alright, mate?' The younger man was still unconscious, his eyes shut, his tongue lolling, his . . . *Oh Jesus.* He took his pulse to make sure, but it only confirmed that he was dead.

How could it have happened a second time? He'd thought that Kylie must have been allergic to the drug but now he realized that it must be a bad batch if it had also killed his lodger. They'd had a spate of deaths in Bristol a couple of years ago when a particularly potent brand of upper had been going the rounds, and a similar number of deaths when a stronger than usual batch of heroin made it to the south west, but why would John take a drug when he was on his own in the house and had showed no previous interest in narcotics? How the hell was he going to explain this to the police?

On second thoughts, he just wouldn't – he couldn't have them prowling around here and asking questions. It had taken him long enough to convince them that he hadn't killed his wife. He'd been badly shaken when they turned up unannounced to ask him about Brandon Petrie, though he'd anticipated a visit after he planted the child porn mag at his brother's house. There was no way that they'd link him to Tim's death, not when Tim's own father was under suspicion. And anyway, young children did occasionally die of suffocation or stopped breathing with no discernible cause.

But when a fit young male like John died suddenly, the authorities started asking questions. No, he'd have to take his lodger's body somewhere and make it look like a suicide. That wouldn't be so hard to believe as, until recently, the youth had been friendless, underemployed and craving love. Detectives would only have to glance at the number of self-help books in his bedroom to ascertain that he was one of the long-term lost. It was Sod's Law that he'd blossomed since doing that course in London but he, Adam, could describe it as being a temporary high.

Suicide, after all, was the leading cause of death amongst

young men who often felt lonely, misunderstood and pressurized
to live up to a macho image, whilst others had doubts about
their sexuality.

He'd better dispose of the body now whilst it was still dark.
Christ, his muscles were going to ache tomorrow. How many
killers had to dispose of two corpses in the one night? He'd go
to a different pub – hell, a different city or even a foreign country
– for future batches of the date rape drug, wouldn't risk a third
untimely death.

Luckily, John was a lightweight. Adam half carried him out to
the car, doubled him into the boot and drove to a wood in nearby
Uphill village; John would have been able to walk here from the
bungalow. He parked, fetched his ladder from the roof rack,
manoeuvred it over the gate and walked into the nearest copse.
Stopping for a moment, he chose a sturdy tree with lots of branches,
one which a man of John's age could easily ascend on foot.

Placing his ladder against the trunk, he climbed to a thick
branch which was at least six-and-a-half feet off the ground, the
perfect hanging scaffold. Working quickly, he took the rope from
his pocket and tied it around the bark. Whilst at home, he'd
already formed the other end into a noose, making use of the
knowledge he'd gained as a boy in the Scouts.

Now, he clambered down and attempted to pull John's body
up the ladder, but the awkwardness of the situation, with the
youth's clothes snagging against the rungs, almost defeated him.
Eventually, urged on by near-panic, not something that he often
experienced, he managed to get the younger man's head parallel
with the branch and looped the noose around his neck. Then,
sweating and shaking with the effort, he descended and looked
for a second at the swaying body before taking the ladder back
to the roof rack of the car.

Home had never felt so welcoming, though it felt strange not
to hear John's familiar cry of, 'Hi mate,' or the strains of Dave
or Sky 3 coming from the television and, when he put on the
kettle, he automatically put out two of their jokey His and His
mugs. What the hell. Tenants were ten a penny – especially in
a seaside town like this where cafes and restaurants were always
taking on cooks and waiters – and he'd get a new one in a couple
of months when the heat had died down.

TWENTY-NINE

'So now our chief suspect's nephew has died,' Bill Winston concluded.

He had to admit that, though harrowing, the weekly briefing of his staff was never dull.

'And is he in the frame?'

The Detective Superintendent shook his head. 'We've no reason to suspect him. There's no sign of forced entry and the mother is a very light sleeper who even got up and checked on her son in the middle of the night.'

The intelligence officer raised an eyebrow. 'Could she or her husband have . . .?'

'Obviously, if the father had been interfering with the boy, he'd have a motive to silence him, but he seems genuinely distraught. So does the mother and grandfather. The grandmother, thankfully, knows nothing of this as she's so ill.'

He broke off as a messenger entered the room, carrying what turned out to be the coroner's report. He scanned it once, then read it more carefully. 'It looks as if Tim Neave suffocated – his face was found turned into the pillow and he'd got the duvet tucked over his face and under his head.'

'Makes sense,' the officer said, doubtless relieved not to have to cope with further complexity. 'I mean, we've never seen any sign that Adam Neave is attracted to kids.'

'No, we thought that he was a woman hater,' Bill Winston murmured then realized that he was speaking in the past tense, that he was having doubts. The man hadn't put a foot wrong in the time that they'd known him, and now the undercover policewoman's reports were equally glowing. It was beginning to look as if they might be focusing on the wrong man.

'Could he have gone to a friend's?' Beth asked. She was pleased that Adam had confided in her that his tenant had apparently gone missing but she thought it was too early to phone the police when he wasn't a juvenile, geriatric or on vital medication. After all, he'd only been gone for thirty-six hours at the most.

'He doesn't really have any friends – except me, of course,' Adam said.

'What about one of those courses that you mentioned he enjoys? Could he have gone off to one of those at short notice?'

'That's just it – he was really disappointed in the latest one. I think he saw it as his last hope, you know, to learn to understand women and get himself a girlfriend, but he somehow couldn't put the advice into practice. Between you and me, I'm fairly sure that he was . . . is a virgin and he's at least twenty-four.'

'One of life's late developers,' Beth said, wondering if she could introduce the youth to any of her young widows. She'd better check him out first, make sure that he didn't have a raging personality disorder: shyness and mild social ineptitude were OK. She realized that Adam was staring at her and wondered if her fringe was sticking up again. Matthew had mentioned it recently.

'I'm just worried that he may have deliberately hurt himself. He gets so down despite the free counselling I've given him. That's why I thought that I should phone the police.'

He was a lovely man, Beth thought, to care so much about his hapless tenant.

'Phone them, then,' she said, 'even if it's just to put your mind at rest.'

She sat down as Adam called the local station and gave John's details. 'No, I'm not at home at the moment – I'm at the hospital with a colleague. I work as a psychologist.' He listened. 'Yes, I can come in now and give you further details. Yes, I'd consider him vulnerable.'

'Let me know if he turns up,' Beth said, meaning it. It would be good to have Adam as a friend rather than merely a colleague as he was so bright and so interested in everyone.

'I'll phone you – promise.'

She watched him walk through the hospital cafeteria and out through the door.

That evening, as she was getting ready for her date with Matthew – they were going to the local comedy club's open mic night – the phone rang and it was Adam.

'Beth? They've found John. He's hanged himself. The police left half an hour ago but I can't stop pacing about.'

Beth knew that there was a syndrome called widow's pacing where the newly (and not so newly) bereaved felt the need to keep moving, caused by their shocked bodies producing added adrenalin. Adam must be experiencing something similar now.

'Can you walk into town? I could meet you at Argos and we'll walk and talk together.'

They arranged a time, and she hung up then dialled Matthew's number. He answered on the first ring.

'Sweetheart? I'm so sorry but I can't make the comedy club – one of my colleagues has just suffered a bereavement. You can come round later and stay over if you like.'

'No, it's OK.' He sounded apathetic. 'I'll just go out with the kids.' His adult children all lived locally and they often socialized as a family, were more like friends.

'It's a crisis,' Beth said, keen to emphasize that she wasn't changing their arrangements without good reason. 'I promise that I'll make it up to you on Saturday night.'

She could use the vibrator to get him aroused and then go down on him, she thought as she ended the phone call. If she licked him to orgasm, he'd surely be indifferent to her unmanageable hair.

Adam was already waiting when she arrived. On impulse, she gave him a hug and he held her closely.

'The police came round shortly after I got home from the station. Apparently he'd walked to Uphill Woods – you know how much he loved walking. Some local children found him when they were picking flowers. The poor little creatures must be totally traumatized.'

'Did he leave a note?'

Adam shook his head. 'I don't think so – the police searched his room and didn't mention anything. I just wish that I'd paid more attention to the clues . . .'

'He hinted at this?' Beth knew that most suicides had talked about killing themselves in the past.

'Not exactly, but he said that he'd never find a girlfriend, that no one at the gym – that's where he worked when he wasn't doing his freelance personal training – understood him, that even his parents had preferred his brother. And he kept bringing home these self-improvement books. Remember I told you about them?'

'Uh huh,' Beth said, though she couldn't quite remember. He'd mentioned John's love of change-your-life courses when she'd said that some doctor's surgeries were now referring the bereaved to positive thinking classes. Other than that, he'd rarely talked about the youth.

'Will we call in someplace for a drink?' she asked hopefully when they'd been walking for over an hour.

Adam stopped. 'You bet! Make mine a double.'

'Mine too,' Beth said, realizing that her spirits needed a lift.

They found a pub and both ordered whisky. When they were seated, she checked her mobile phone but Matthew hadn't been in touch. She realized that he was contacting her less and less often, yet, for the first few months, he'd sent her daily text messages and often phoned to see how she was. He hadn't even asked her about the nature of tonight's emergency, had seemed just as happy to stay in Clevedon with his kids.

'Planning a hot date?' Adam teased.

'No, I just cancelled one with Matthew.'

'Because of me?'

'Because I'll always put bereaved people first. I remember how I felt when my husband died.'

'I hope that Matthew appreciates you,' Adam said, briefly touching her hand.

Beth hoped so too.

Why was she spending so much time with other widows and widowers? It simply wasn't healthy. Matthew put down his mobile feeling put out and confused. She worked all day in a hospital yet still chose to spend her free time counselling on a voluntary basis. It meant that her life was totally unbalanced, dedicated to the sick and the bereaved. He did a semi-manual job so made sure that his social life revolved around the cinema, meals and pubs, places where he could laze about and rest his muscles. It made for a more rounded life.

Going to his landline, he phoned his youngest daughter, the one who could never resist a night out.

'Do you fancy going to the pub?'

As usual, she sounded pleased to hear from him. 'Love to, but aren't you going out with Beth tonight?'

'She cancelled on me at short notice, says she has to help someone who's bereaved.'

'I didn't realize that she had to work nights.'

'She doesn't.' He didn't feel like defending her. Why couldn't she get her priorities right?

'It's a mate, then?'

'Apparently. She's surrounded by widows all the time.'

'Do you think she's seeing someone else, Dad?' His daughter sounded worried for him.

'Not with that hair,' Matthew said, then laughed somewhat bitterly at his own joke.

THIRTY

Once again, life had returned to normal. Beth had become his friend, the police had informed him of John's suicide, his father had told him about Tim's untimely death and his patients were thriving. He'd just taken on a kleptomaniac so was keeping a close eye on the contents of the room. He'd lost heavily on the horses this week, and no longer had John's rent money coming in, so couldn't afford to let his new patient steal anything remotely valuable.

'How do you feel when you *don't* steal?' he asked the man, a sixty-year-old who had accepted a generous redundancy package and subsequently received a substantial inheritance from his parents.

'Depressed. Sort of flat. Ordinary.'

'So shoplifting gives you a temporary high?'

'Just in the moments immediately before . . . I mean, I don't plan it. I'll be browsing in a department store and suddenly this inner voice is urging me to steal.'

It was the same with raping and killing, Adam thought – sometimes the anticipation was better than the actual event.

'And what do you take?' He knew that many kleptomaniacs preferred a specific type of item. One of his former female patients had amassed a huge collection of contraband lipsticks. She'd even had her lips tattooed with semi-permanent colour but it had made no difference to the need to thieve.

'I mainly take pens.'

Adam relaxed: he didn't own a Mont Blanc.

'And you always hang on to them?'

The man looked surprised that he was even asking the question. 'Of course, I keep them in a special room.'

His patient would never sell these pens – he had lots of money. They were merely the outward manifestation of an obsessive compulsive personality.

'So when did this start?' he asked, genuinely curious. He loved to find out what made people tick. It helped him to manipulate them and others cut from the same cloth.

'After I gave up work. I suppose that I was bored and started going out and drinking more. I got mugged one night and stayed home for a week afterwards, feeling really shaky and just ordering home deliveries. One day I made myself go shopping and, for some reason, took a potato peeler from a display stand in the supermarket. For a few minutes, I felt so much better, but afterwards I was shocked at myself and felt really ashamed.'

'A traumatic event can trigger such behaviour,' Adam said calmly.

'I didn't know that. I just thought that I was sliding into madness,' the man replied, looking relieved.

'No, you might be low on serotonin or have some genetic predisposition to this type of behaviour but you are perfectly sane.'

'I'd like to start dating again – I think I said that I was recently divorced? – but I don't want to keep doing this, bring shame on a new partner.'

Adam adopted his most reassuring tone. 'Counselling and, perhaps, medication, will make all the difference.' He hesitated. 'So, what made you seek treatment now?'

'I was caught but paid the store detective and the owner a small fortune not to take it further. If I keep going, I could face a custodial sentence and I couldn't cope with jail.'

Adam shuddered. He, too, hated the thought of prison. What must it be like to get up when the wardens told you to, to eat terrible food and share accommodation with dirty, violent illiterates? What must it be like to lose life's simple pleasures – a single malt, a game of blackjack, a good fuck?

'Don't worry – we'll devise a plan to keep you away from Her Majesty's establishments. You're alert and motivated, you will find it easy to follow a plan.'

A lot of his job was about sounding confident, getting the client to believe in him. Weak people needed an anchor, in the form of a deity, a holistic practitioner, a guru or a shrink. If they thought that he had the answers, was a source of comfort, they would gladly follow his advice.

'Do you get many patients like me?' the man asked.

'A few, though most don't have the courage to self-refer, come to me through the criminal court system.'

'So, at least I'm proactive,' the man said with a wry smile.

'You certainly are.' It was good to have a client who was intelligent and articulate. Sometimes the person facing him was so withdrawn that it was like talking to the wall.

'And am I older than your average client?'

'There's no such thing as average,' Adam explained, meaning it. 'I have seven-year-old patients with enuresis.' He was tempted to add that he had eighty-year-olds with the same problem, but instead settled for: 'And seventy-year-olds with memory impairment.'

'And they are all improving?'

'They are making great strides,' Adam said self-assuredly. He was especially glad that Brandon Petrie had recovered from his little cousin's accidental death, was turning into an exemplary young man.

He hadn't taken his Ritalin for weeks now, and was feeling so much better. The drug made him feel tired and down, sort of hung-over. Now, he was energized and ready to kick ass.

'Brandon – stop kicking your chair.'

He hadn't even realized that he was doing it until Mr Leston loomed in front of him, hands slapping down hard on his desk.

Brandon stared at the English teacher, who eventually looked, and walked, away. He stared at the other teenagers in the class until they, too, returned to their books.

Should he walk out? Why the fuck was he here, learning about the quality of mercy from a long-dead playwright? He was an ideas person, a radical, shouldn't be constrained by the system and by four walls. Entrepreneurs often left school at sixteen and started wheeling and dealing. Bill Gates had the right idea, dropping out of university.

'Brandon, I won't tell you again.'

Good – he'd have peace, then. With difficulty, he stilled his feet.

As the class filed out, Mr Leston called out to him.

'Brandon, can I have a word?'

Which word? Cunt?

He kicked each chair leg as he went past in a contemptuous gesture.

'Is something wrong?' the teacher said.

Something was always wrong in the world – global warming, mass starvation, the small mindedness of most parents. Couldn't the man be more specific? Didn't he mean 'is something wrong with you?'

He shrugged, stared.

'You've been concentrating so well until recently.'

'Maybe I just don't rate Shakespeare.'

'Admittedly he doesn't appeal to everyone, but remember we spoke about how becoming an adult means deferring gratification, doing some boring and repetitive tasks?'

God, he sounded like Adam now, the all-knowing psychologist.

'But not all adults study Shakespeare.'

'No, but chances are that the successful ones will have studied something which didn't appeal to them. For example, you might prefer science subjects but recognize that you also need a pass in English Lit to get into university.'

'Not all successful people go to university.' He shifted from foot to foot, looked at the door and made a slight movement towards it.

'But you said that you *did* want to go to uni, Brandon.'

'Did. Past tense.' Only the dull and unimaginative never changed their minds.

'Whatever you've decided, I can't let you disrupt the class.'

'Bar me, then.'

'We only do that as a last resort. Brandon, you don't belong with the unteachables. You're intelligent and creative. Please don't waste it. You could go really far in life.'

God, he felt such contempt for this man who taught the same plays and poems over and over. They could replace him with a recorded message or a sheaf of notes.

He said nothing, looked out of the window. He could sense the teacher staring at him and he hated that, loathed making eye contact.

'Has anything changed?' the man asked.

Aha, the million dollar question. What he really meant was 'have you stopped taking your medication?' but the notes from his doctor had said that the teacher wasn't allowed to ask. Similarly, they weren't allowed to give him his lunchtime Ritalin as that would mean that the other students would know that he was on tablets. Instead, they trusted him to take it himself.

'What could have changed, Mr Leston?'

'You tell me, Brandon.'

'I can't imagine.'

Stalemate. He walked towards the door.

'If you ever want to talk . . .'

Oh, he loved to talk – but to the scientists and academics that he met online, not to bog standard secondary school teachers. This time, he didn't bother to reply.

His mother was doubtless parked out at the front, so Brandon went out the back way, and walked home in the rain, feeling trapped and alienated and enraged: he hated these patronizing pep talks, had an increasing need for action. Maybe he'd really give them something to talk about by burning down the school.

THIRTY-ONE

'Is John here?'

I hope not. Adam stared at the small, plump girl and realized that she looked vaguely familiar. He wondered where he'd seen her before.

'I'm Louise,' she added. 'I did his health and well-being course here last week.'

Aha, she'd sat happily on his settee eating the rice that had been next to Kylie's corpse in the freezer. She'd been John's potential love interest, would probably have become his first girlfriend and, eventually, his wife.

'I think I left my mobile here and as I was passing . . .' she continued.

He quirked an eyebrow and she had the grace to blush.

'Do you want to come in and look for it?'

She was obviously lonely, so he might screw her sometime that he had a spare night. She'd be suitably grateful. On the other hand, he liked his women to be slimmer, though she had nice big tits.

'That would be great.' She bounced through the front door and into the lounge. 'It might have slipped down the settee.' She made a show of looking for it.

'Wouldn't I have heard it ringing?'

She blushed again. 'Oh no, I was concentrating on John's words, had it switched off.' She hesitated. 'Is he at the gym? I popped my head in the door but didn't see him. He said that he worked odd hours.'

Damn, he was going to have to tell her and she'd cry and he'd have to do ten minutes of arm patting when what he really wanted to do was walk to the hospital and see Beth. He was sure that there was a growing spark between them and he was keen to capitalize on it. Maybe they could be friends with benefits until she wised up and walked away.

'Louise, you'd better sit down. I've something to—'

The bell pealed through the house and he excused himself and went to answer the door.

Shit. He stared at the police. Couldn't they phone up and arrange an appointment like everyone else?

'Mr Neave? If we could come in?'

He wanted to say no but that would look strange. He had to be calm at all times, border on the charming. He wouldn't even ask what it was all about, would presume, until they said otherwise, that they were here to discuss John or tiny Tim. Or could his mother have died and his father have followed suit due to the shock? In some families, sickness caused member after member to collapse like a pack of cards.

'Of course.' He showed them into his study, then said, 'Excuse me a moment.'

Hurrying to the lounge, he smiled at Louise who was sitting, waiting patiently, on the settee, unsurprisingly *sans* mobile.

'My guests have arrived. Can I phone you about John? Leave your number.' He picked up today's copy of the *Guardian* and a pen and handed them to her. He tapped his foot impatiently as she wrote, afraid that the police would come through here and start talking to her. He had to make them think that John had nothing to live for, was without hope.

'He doesn't have to call if he doesn't want to,' she said tremulously.

I doubt if he can dial, sweetheart.

Forcing himself not to give her a shove, he shepherded her outside, shut the outer door and returned to his study to find both detectives studying his bookshelves. Good. Hopefully they'd treat him with respect.

'So, gentlemen, what can I do for you?'

He sat behind his desk and watched them sit awkwardly on the therapist's couch, like a gay couple coming to a Relate session.

'We need to talk to you further about your tenant, John Jameson.'

'A sad case. He was just so lost.'

'The thing is, Mr Neave, we've had the autopsy report back and he didn't commit suicide.'

'He didn't?' Adam heard his own voice go up an octave. 'He wasn't enjoying life so, when you said you'd found him hanging, I naturally assumed . . .'

'No, we're still trying to ascertain how he died, but he was dead hours before he was strung up. We know that from the way that the blood had pooled and the ligature marks. Someone wanted to make it look as if he took his own life.'

'How odd,' Adam said. He'd watched *Columbo* and knew that people often trapped themselves by supplying additional information. He sat back and looked at the two men and they returned his gaze. He let the silence lengthen, was pleased when they cracked first.

'Did he have any enemies?'

'I don't know. He was only my lodger.'

'But he confided in you that he was unhappy, that –' the detective consulted the notes that their colleagues had presumably taken on the previous visit – 'he had never had a girlfriend and feared that no one would ever care for him.'

'Oh yes, he said that and mentioned that he was unhappy at work – he was a personal trainer but a very thin man, could never build up his own muscles, so I think he felt fraudulent and would become depressed. He was always buying these books to improve his mindset but nothing seemed to work.'

'Could he have made a pass at another man?'

'It's possible,' Adam said, understanding their line of questioning. A straight man might lash out at someone who made a pass and kill him by accident then panic and try to make it look like a suicide. 'I mean, he was desperate to be in a relationship and any port in a storm . . .'

'Could he have walked from here to Uphill Woods?'

'Easily, he often walked for miles for work or leisure.'

'And did he know anyone in Uphill?'

'I doubt it. He was completely without friends.'

'Well, it wasn't a friend who killed him, was it?' said the older detective with an edge of sarcasm to his voice.

'I suppose not.'

He wasn't so sure about that. Weren't most people killed by those they loved?

'Have you any idea who might do such a thing?'

'As I said, I was only his landlord.'

'Can I ask how you met him?'

'I took out gym membership and joked to the receptionist that

I needed a personal trainer. John works – I mean worked – part-time for them in that capacity and he overheard, introduced himself. I had a few sessions with him before my client list became too demanding, but by then he'd mentioned that he was looking to rent a room and I'd been toying with the idea of taking a lodger, so he moved in.'

'Did you need the money, doctor? I always thought that psychotherapy was lucrative?'

When had detectives started using such big words? Adam hesitated. 'It's well paid but it's like any freelance work – the number of patients fluctuates whereas weekly rent money is reliable. There was also a security aspect. I take up to four short holidays a year and worried about being burgled. I felt much more secure after John moved in.'

'So his living here worked out well.'

'It worked out brilliantly. In fact, we'd often phone out for a pizza and open a few beers.'

'In other words, he had numerous options to confide in you?'

Damn. He'd suggested earlier that he didn't see much of John.

'No, we usually kicked back, watched comedy or sport. After all, I'd have been talking at work all day and he'd have been exercising hard so we were both tired out and needed to relax.'

'Was he bad-tempered when he was tired?'

'John? No, really easy-going.'

'Did anything rattle him?'

'He was desperately distraught that he'd never had a girlfriend.'

'It wasn't a girl who did this. It took strength to lift such a tall bloke up a tree,' one of the detectives murmured.

'I can't imagine anyone wanting to hurt John. He was an amicable, if confused, young man.'

'Keep thinking about it, doc,' the older detective said, handing over the inevitable business card after getting heavily to his feet.

He would find it hard, Adam thought wearily, to think of anything else.

THIRTY-TWO

'And now the police say that it wasn't suicide,' Beth finished.

She looked at Matthew, assuming that he'd feel as shocked as she was, but his face remained neutral. 'Adam's devastated,' she added, 'to lose a friend and find that it was foul play.'

'People always seem to be getting murdered here. It's a lot safer in Clevedon,' Matthew said, opening his second beer of the evening.

'It's not just here. Apparently they found a woman's body in Bristol the other day.'

'I hate these big cities – people always seem to be getting drunk and attacking each other.'

'But they've got fantastic theatres and restaurants,' Beth said. He looked unconvinced so she decided to change the subject. 'Did I tell you about Adam's little nephew? His mother found him dead in bed.'

'Don't you think that too much of your life revolves around death?'

Beth stared at her lover in surprise. The question had never occurred to her. 'Not at all. I mean, I counsel widows in order that they can carry on living. The hospital and the hospice deals with death – I help people cope with the aftermath. It's life-affirming in a way.'

'It's been three years since your husband died. Isn't it like constantly reopening a wound?'

He'd never said anything like this before. Beth set down her wine glass on the occasional table and gave him her undivided attention.

'Do I seem wounded to you?'

'No.' He didn't sound convinced.

'I know that I cry sometimes when certain songs are played on the radio, but that goes with the territory, Matt. I've friends who have been widowed for five or even ten years and they still weep at times for their beloved and feel really sad. The sense of loss is permanent. It's a recognized condition, the widow's low.'

'OK.'

Did he think that she didn't have feelings for him because she was still in love with her late husband?

'I do care for you. You know that?' she said. She had a vague memory of using the same words to him before when they were in bed, of him hugging her and looking pleased.

'I know,' he said, but he didn't hug her this time, just returned his attention to the television and to his beer.

Should she ask him if he was having second thoughts? Try harder to reassure him? Beth was still wondering what to do when he spoke again.

'There's a big ice show coming to Bristol next year if you fancy it.'

Hadn't he just rejected the city as a den of iniquity? Or was it acceptable for a day trip but not as a place to live?

'Count me in!' she said lightly, glad that he was still thinking ahead, still planning their future leisure activities. Maybe she was overreacting to his mood swings? Beth sat back on the settee and tried to relax.

THIRTY-THREE

D amn, they'd found Kylie's body now: it had featured on the south west news and they'd mentioned that Hannah's killer was also still undiscovered, but there was no suggestion that police were linking the two or that they had any reason to add John's death to the mix.

He'd have to wait a bit longer before he drugged and raped Olivia, though, the way things were going, she'd probably perform cartwheels for him, naked, without the need for Rohypnol. She seemed to have the biggest crush on him imaginable, and always tried to extend their hourly sessions by a few minutes, hovering cutely at the door.

He'd thought that the baby might curtail their sessions, but she always put him before the little brat, whom she'd called Mia. He'd bumped into her one day close to the bereavement centre and she'd had the wailing child in a pram.

'Free to go for a drink? I can drop her at the crèche,' she'd said boldly.

Unfortunately he'd had a client to see or he might well have enjoyed a little afternoon delight.

Without drugs, he reckoned that she'd be happy to have vanilla sex and would maybe go down on him. With drugs, he could go up the chocolate freeway and he wouldn't have the hassle of having to make her come. It took some women ages to have an orgasm, no matter how much they fancied you. He'd read somewhere that it could take twenty-three minutes to get them there with your tongue. He'd much rather be fucking than sucking them during that twenty-three minutes, wanted to be in charge rather than taking the subservient role. He only brought them to climax if he fancied them enough to want to see them again, a comparatively rare event. The rest of the time, he put his own pleasure first.

He'd got a new batch of Rohypnol now, bought in a Portishead bar, but had to make sure that it wasn't an inadvertent murder weapon. To play safe, he intended to try it out on an easy target, someone who was unconnected to himself and therefore completely disposable.

As the shadows lengthened, Adam walked up to Grove Park and strolled to an area often frequented by the homeless, rough sleepers by any other name. He soon found a man who looked sixtyish – probably a forty-year-old who'd had a hard life – propped up against a bench.

'Want a drink, mate?' The tramp eyed him blearily then snatched the adulterated can. Drinking it down in a few gulps, he muttered something unintelligible and went to sleep.

The following morning, Adam returned to the scene of the potential crime. Excellent – the man was awake and importuning various dog walkers for money. This batch, then, would do for Olivia and anyone else who appealed to him.

That night, he listened to the news but this time Kylie's murder wasn't even mentioned in the same bulletin as Hannah's. Good. He'd gotten away with murder yet again.

*   *   *

Now that Kylie's body had been discovered, the Major Incident Room was busier than ever. Detective Superintendent Winston studied the evidence. Both women had been found in the woods – albeit one in Weston and one in Bristol – and had been rolled down steep inclines after presumably being transported to the dump site in a car or van. Hannah had been found naked, but had previously been wrapped in a sheet, probably to keep her concealed in the back seat of a vehicle: minute threads on her body had testified to this. Kylie had also been wrapped in a sheet before being put in a freezer: she'd still been sheathed in it when she was found.

They'd continue to liaise with Bristol police and had warned women in both areas to be especially careful as there was a killer on the loose. As head of the enquiry, he'd spoken to a psychologist in-depth about the murderer, and apparently some men didn't start killing until their forties, although the mid to late thirties was more usual, and even the late teens wasn't unknown. That put an awful lot of Weston men under the microscope, as well as those who visited the town for leisure or work.

He'd had a couple of firm favourites in mind, including Adam Neave, but the man was proving to be a perfect gentleman, hadn't behaved in the least bit inappropriately with Olivia. Their other chief suspect, a lifelong bachelor, was also leading an exemplary life. There were many other strange characters out there, Detective Superintendent Winston admitted wearily to himself, who were much more obviously misogynistic. He'd better not get tunnel vision, should widen his net.

THIRTY-FOUR

They thought that they could control him now that he was taking a tablet after breakfast, one at lunch and a final half-dose after school. They wanted him neutered, zombified. The school feared his ferocious intellect so tried to bring him down to their level; they were producing tomorrow's factory fodder and mindless civil servants whilst his parents needed an obedient, personality-less son. No one liked the real him, the fast-moving, free-thinking embryonic genius. Everyone wanted the real Brandon to die.

His mother kept checking up on him at night and his father had taken away his computer yesterday because he hadn't kept his room tidy. Had Einstein kept his room tidy? Had Bill Gates? His teachers were equally vapid, merely going through the motions until they reached pensionable age.

He'd show them, make them sorry. One day they would tremble as they recognized his latent power. He was in a state of constant tension by the time that he reached the pet shop but forced himself to breathe evenly, slow down. A sign said that they wouldn't sell animals to minors but he'd been in here before and they had been keen to offload various small furry rodents to anyone with ready cash. Everyone had their price, and it was low during a recession. Today, they were grateful to sell him a small white mouse.

Afterwards, when it was dead, he felt almost sorry. He'd enjoyed its squealing, its frantic abortive efforts to escape, the seismic change as the light finally faded from its little pink eyes. Brandon wiped the blood from his knife onto the grass and threw the tiny cadaver under a bush; he'd return nightly on his way home from school and check up on the stages of putrefaction and decomposition of the skeleton, the ever-changing colours and scents of a body as it broke down. It would be his own biology lesson, something far more up close and personal than the bulls' eyes and locusts which they dissected in the lab.

Next week, when he got his monthly allowance, he might treat himself to a large white rat or a degus, though he'd probably have to drug it before getting his blade out. After all, he didn't want to get bitten or scratched.

What on earth was she supposed to do with a single sheet of toilet paper? Olivia stared at the almost-finished roll in exasperation. Why didn't Marc replace the roll from the stock in the hall cupboard? If she hadn't had a couple of paper handkerchiefs in her jeans pocket, she'd have been left in a disgusting state. After washing her hands (he'd left toothpaste smears on the sink, as per usual), she fetched a new roll, stopping enroute to remove a pair of dirty socks which were sticking out of his boots.

Walking into the lounge, she was immediately confronted by empty beer cans, Pringles cartons and the remains of what looked like a Chinese chow mein. He'd had his friends round last night to watch the football and the room stank of alcohol and stale male sweat. His breakfast mug, perched precariously on the arm of the settee, was still warm, proof that he'd been in here today before going to work. Would it have killed him to clear up?

Adam's house, she thought, was very different – neat and clean – and she was glad that she was going there this morning. Oh, she'd only seen his study and the kitchen so far, but she sensed that he was methodical and tidy. He was neat in his appearance too, whereas Marc regularly got mud on his trouser hems and egg yolk on his shirt.

As usual, she thought about the therapist on the train journey to his place. It was hard not to. He'd started off as a work project, someone she'd expected to secretly despise, but she was increasingly thinking of him in much more positive terms. He actively listened to her troubles and seemed to remember them from visit to visit: she'd never once seen him consult his notes. He also remembered their various shared humorous moments and referred to them, helping to further build their rapport. Sometimes they made eye contact for longer than was strictly necessary and she was aware that her heartbeat was speeding up by the time that she looked away. Was she the most compelling and attractive of his patients? Did he think of her as often as she thought of him? And, if she did walk into his thoughts, did he ever have the urge to touch himself and wonder what it would be like to touch her equally intimately?

THIRTY-FIVE

Matthew smiled at his latest customer, a woman of around forty who had locked herself out. She was wearing a close-fitting shift dress, a waist-skimming jacket and black patent heels with a matching clutch bag. Her shoes were polished, whereas Beth's were invariably scuffed and dull. Not that appearance was everything, but it mattered to him and he took care of his footwear and clothes.

Beth wasn't as feminine as he'd originally thought, had spent most of the warm weather in cotton culottes and vest tops. Now that it was December, albeit an incredibly mild one, she'd settled for a uniform-like jumper and jeans. He liked women who wore gypsy skirts and pretty, midriff-skimming tops in summer and cuddly, cashmere jumpers in winter. Although she was much younger than him, she still wasn't girlish enough.

'Almost finished,' he said to his customer as she sat, watching, from the bottom of the stairs. He wouldn't ask her out as he didn't cheat and, anyway, it was unethical to proposition a customer. But if he was single and in a pub and they started chatting, he'd definitely be up for it.

'I've never done this before,' she murmured. 'I mean, I always keep my key in my bag and I never leave home without it. But last night I popped out to post my Christmas cards, so just put the key in my jacket pocket, meaning to transfer it when I got back.'

'At least it's daytime. Last week, I had a phone call from a woman who locked herself out at four a.m.'

'Had she come back from clubbing?'

'No, she'd been in bed for hours when she thought she heard her cat fighting with another in the garden. She went to investigate – and she has a door like yours which locks on closing. She had to wake up a neighbour and call me out.'

'You must hate those late calls.'

He shrugged. 'They pay the mortgage. Anyway, they are few and far between. Most calls are made a day or two in advance for locks which have started to stick, so the home owner is being proactive. I always change my own locks as soon as they start to play up.'

The customer looked at his heavy tool kit. 'Hoisting that around must keep you fit.'

'It does. I never have to go to the gym.'

Even Beth, for all her faults, seemed to appreciate his body. She was always telling him how cute he looked. Perhaps cuter than she?

'So, what do I owe you?' the woman asked as he swept up the pieces of metal filing around the door.

He wrote her out a receipt, not charging for the last fifteen minutes. She had been good for his ego and he appreciated it.

'I'll recommend you to my friends,' she said.

'I should put you on commission!'

'I'd like that,' she murmured, then grinned.

He'd tell Beth about the encounter, Matthew thought, as he walked back to his van. Maybe if she realized how many offers he got in a typical month, she'd try harder. She'd put on a bit more make-up – preferably understated – and buy some sexier shoes.

He'd also like her to spend less time with other widows, to see herself as young, free and single. Why couldn't she just move on, as he had after his divorce? He had no feelings for his ex-wife other than that of derision; it had been a dead marriage long before she ended it. He'd stayed because of some old-fashioned sense of loyalty and because of the children, plus he hated uncertainty so rarely initiated change. He was glad now that he was a bachelor with a future. He enjoyed having a revitalized social life.

But his girlfriend wasn't quite shaping up, so he'd have to make his criticisms more vocal. She had potential, simply had to raise her game. He wanted her to be a partner of whom he could be truly proud, deserved to be the envy of his friends.

Drat – the sun had suddenly disappeared and the temperature was plummeting. They'd had a sunny start to December but now, mid-month, it was really cold. Everyone had been lulled into a false sense of security by the long, hot summer but now winter had arrived and, with it, the usual stomach bugs and colds.

Beth blew her nose for the umpteenth time that morning and put two little packets of tissues and a tube of menthol lozenges in her bag. She replaced the lightweight jacket that she'd planned to wear to Gloucestershire today with a heavier suede garment. They were planning to walk by the water and she couldn't afford to get chilled. She'd gone down with a cold on Monday and missed three days off work. Matthew had brought her comfort foods and collected a parcel from the post office delivery centre for her but he, too, didn't seem to be his usual happy self.

She added a small bottle of energy drink to the growing pharmacy in her bag. She still felt slightly weak and had considered suggesting that they just curl up and watch a DVD together, but he seemed keen to check out the clothing outlets at Gloucester Quays Shopping Centre; they were both atheists who avoided Christmas shopping so presumably he wanted something for himself. She could vaguely remember him mentioning that he wanted another winter coat, liked the fashionable military style.

'Ready when you are,' she said, giving him a hug. She noticed that he didn't hold her as tightly as he used to. Still, when they had made love last night he had called her darling and had swept her hair back lovingly from her face. Maybe he was having one of those mornings when he woke up feeling irritable: he'd mentioned that he sometimes felt that way.

He chatted about his latest customers as he drove towards Gloucestershire and she couldn't help but notice that he stressed how attractive they all were. That was all she needed, Beth thought glumly, when she was feeling bloated and had patchy skin. The area beneath her nostrils was scarlet and no amount of foundation would fully cover it.

Just as she was nodding off to sleep, he said, 'Sorted!' and she opened her eyes to see that they were heading into the shopping centre car park. The place was mobbed and they drove up and up and up until he eventually found a parking space.

'Can we go for a coffee first?' Beth asked. 'I need a fix.'

He nodded, but grimaced when they reached the cafe and he saw the queue of stressed-out couples, most of whom were carrying at least three bags each.

'Can you get me an Americano whilst I'm having a quick look around?'

'Consider it done,' Beth said lightly and smiled but he didn't smile back or wave as he reached the door. He really did seem to be going off her, she thought wearily. Should she say something? She'd never had a boyfriend who'd gone from hot to cold before. She waited patiently in line and was grateful when the male assistant flirted with her: today she felt ugly and tired and somehow unequal to everything. If Matthew would verbalize what was troubling him, she could deal with it – but the only feedback he was giving was in the form of a withdrawal of affection and disapproving looks.

She took the reassuringly large coffees over to a window seat; often she carried the conversation but today she simply didn't have the energy so they'd have to entertain themselves by people watching. Hopefully he'd find the coat that he wanted in a relatively short space of time and they could go home.

He returned empty handed.

'Haven't you seen anything you like?' she asked curiously.

'I don't really need anything. I've got lots of clothes.'

He did, but he was always buying new ones. On the last visit that she'd made to his house, she'd counted thirty dress shirts and so many jackets that he'd had to turn the spare room into a second wardrobe. He was much more interested in fashion than she.

'You always look nice,' she admitted. At first, when she'd complimented him he had looked pleased but now he seemed to be indifferent. Beth turned her attention to her Americano and to the little biscuit that the coffee shop had provided. 'I'll feel better after this,' she clarified, as she saw him looking at his watch.

'There's no rush, but, if we have time I'd like to call into the supermarket on the way back, pick up something for the evening meal.'

He'd already said that he was making dinner for his adult children. He'd cooked for her a couple of times and produced a passable meal.

'I've got lamb chops in the freezer that you can have.'

'Lisa's vegetarian.'

'Damn – I think the nut cutlet drawer is empty,' Beth said, and laughed.

'Oh, I've got jacket potatoes and vegetarian cheese so we won't starve.'

'I'll have something similar myself, something easy,' Beth admitted. She was looking forward to crashing out on the settee alone, having a really lazy night.

'Right, let's get you round the shops,' Matthew said when she was two thirds of the way through her coffee.

'Me? Doubt if I have the energy to buy anything.'

'You should. Gok Wan would have a field day with you.'

OK, now he was being insulting. Beth decided not to let the comment pass.

'No, he wouldn't,' she said, setting down her mug. 'He helps people who are unhappy with their appearance. I've never been a clothes horse, don't particularly care.'

'Don't you want to be admired?'

I am, Beth thought, for my understanding and compassion. But it sounded conceited to say this so she just shrugged. It was horrible being criticized by someone who had previously bolstered her confidence, especially at a time when she was already feeling low.

They trawled round the shops but she genuinely couldn't find the enthusiasm to try anything on. She also felt belligerent about his comments. She'd never been a particularly dressy person yet he'd found her irresistible in the first few months.

He remained quiet during a late lunch and when they walked around the docks, but he seemed to cheer up when he saw a leaflet about a comedian who was coming to the local playhouse in February.

'We should get tickets for that,' he said.

It was six weeks until February 1st so he still saw her as part of his future. Beth felt her spirits lift a little: their relationship was apparently faltering but he'd been distant before and then become more loving, so she hoped that his latest moodiness was just a temporary state. At his best, he was the most adoring partner imaginable and she was reluctant to lose that. She'd so enjoyed being the centre of someone's universe again, something that she'd lost, and deeply missed, when Brian died.

'Why not try that dress on?' Matthew asked as they window-shopped.

Not in this lifetime.

'I'd have to wear tights with it,' Beth explained. 'And I hate them. Trousers are so much more comfortable.'

'Don't you enjoy being ladylike?'

'No – but I'm feminine. There's a difference.'

She'd noticed that, like many men, he wasn't good with nuances of language and now he just looked glum.

'OK, let's head off to the supermarket,' he muttered, 'so that I can do the Jamie Oliver bit.'

He bought the ingredients he needed whilst Beth selected a crusty white baguette, pre-sliced Cheddar and a salad pack: she was going to have a large sandwich for her evening meal followed by a bar of chocolate – and perhaps a medicinal whisky – whilst watching a comedy film on TV.

They drove back, listening to the radio, and he parked outside her house and said that he'd come in to collect his mobile, which he'd left recharging in the kitchen.

'Do you want to stay for a coffee?' Beth asked politely, aware that he'd driven them all the way back from Gloucester and now had another half hour drive to his own house.

'No, the kids are waiting. I'll better go.'

'Well, thanks for a lovely day out,' she said as she walked him to the door. It hadn't been all that brilliant but she was being gracious. She put her arms around his neck and stepped closer so that she could kiss him, but he moved so that his head was over her shoulder and she could feel the tension in his limbs.

'I enjoyed it too,' he said with an odd little laugh. 'It's nice to have a day out with someone you like.'

Someone you like. He'd said that he loved her and now she'd been delegated to mere liking.

'Well, someone you like most of the time,' he added, pushing her away.

My God – he really had gone off her. Beth stepped back, feeling slightly nauseous, and he hurried out of the house and disappeared into his van.

What on earth had she done to warrant such a colossal change? He'd been very critical of her appearance in recent weeks but she was wearing the same type of outfits that she'd worn when she met him. She was also doing the same managerial job at the hospital and the same voluntary counselling work: nothing had changed except his attitude to her.

Could he just have been in an exceptionally bad mood? Would he reflect on his behaviour and get in touch to apologize? They weren't seeing each other till Wednesday night when they planned to go to the cinema but surely he'd want to resolve the situation before then? Beth had been looking forward to her sandwich but now her appetite was vastly reduced and she merely spread butter on a small piece of the baguette and nibbled at it. She felt shocked and somewhat dazed. Somewhat to her surprise, she fell asleep within minutes of going to bed and only woke when her alarm clock rang the following day.

Had Matthew been in touch? She checked her landline and her mobile: nada. She also checked her email but all of her messages were about work, apart from Adam who had sent her a Freudian cartoon with the message: 'thought you'd love this as much as I did.' At least someone appreciated her sense of humour, Beth thought wearily.

Tuesday also passed without a word from her supposed boyfriend and, by the time she woke up on Wednesday, Beth had had enough. He obviously planned to take her to the cinema as if nothing had happened, as if his recent behaviour had been fine. She was worth more than that, Beth concluded, remembering how he'd criticised her weight, her complexion, her clothes and her beloved voluntary work in the past few weeks. He'd clearly lost interest in her but lacked the courage to finish it.

She didn't want to phone him whilst he was driving or with a customer, and it would take forever to send an explanatory text, so she decided to end the relationship by email. He didn't deserve a face to face explanation, given how unpleasant he'd been.

Feeling angry for the first time in years, she composed a terse message:

> It's obvious from what you said when you were leaving on Sunday that you no longer have any feelings for me, and I've no wish to prolong the situation, so let's end it now. Obviously there's no need for you to turn up at any future planned events.

Late that afternoon, she got home from the hospital to find that he'd replied. 'I've no idea what I said, but you've obviously decided that it's over, so that's fine by me.'

So that was it – her first relationship after widowhood wasn't destined to be her last. She was officially single. Beth poured herself a neat whisky and curled up on the settee. The advert break came on the television, promoting a film on DVD that she and Matthew had seen at the cinema eight months earlier. Their romance had been new, then, and full of promise: in fact, he'd only let go of her hand when she wanted to sip her drink.

She needed more drink now. She poured herself a second whisky and, this time, brought the bottle into the lounge. Channel-hopping, she heard a song that he'd mentioned that he liked, something about a couple being able to rule the world if they were together. They were both alone now. Beth flicked onto the next station then slugged down more of the amber spirit, enjoying the sensation as it warmed her throat and stomach, raised her mood.

She wanted to feel pretty, to feel appreciated, to have the hope of a new relationship. Drunkenly, she dialled Adam's home number, was pleased when he picked up the phone.

'Hi, it's Beth. I've just finished with Matthew and could use some company. I wondered if you were free tomorrow night?'

'I knew that you were too good for him. Hang on, I'll just check my diary.' She waited as he rustled through the pages. 'I've got a lot of work on tomorrow, but I'd love to meet up this weekend.'

That suited her fine. 'Saturday night?'

'It's a date.'

She giggled at the innuendo. 'Where shall we meet?'

'Come round to my place for starters,' Adam said, 'and try my new home-made wine.'

'Will do. Oh, hang on – I don't have your address.'

She scribbled away as he gave her the details.

'We can go clubbing after we finish the alcohol. You know, just as mates,' she said.

'We can do whatever we like.'

After ending the phone call, Beth reached for her drink then decided not to finish it. She wanted to look and feel good when she danced with Adam on Saturday night. They wouldn't cross any boundaries, of course – they were both professionals. But it would be nice to flirt a little and feel appreciated again. She was lucky to have made such a bright and handsome new friend, someone she could look up to and learn from. Everything, she told herself firmly, was going to be fine.

THIRTY-SIX

B etter and better – yet another victim had handed herself to him on a plate. He'd look forward to taking Beth up the ass after rendering her comatose. Considering that she was a counsellor, she didn't understand human nature at all.

In fairness to the woman, she had only gone through bereavement training, wasn't fully versed in psychology. That said, he was surprised at how few psychologists recognized that he was a psychopath. He'd realized it years ago whilst perusing the psychiatric literature in order to understand and better manipulate his many girlfriends. He was a classic case: superficially charming and able to zero in on a person's weaknesses but unable to care about anyone except himself. Most psychopaths, of course, weren't killers, so he'd still crossed a line when he murdered his wife.

He was aware that his parents and his brother knew that he wasn't quite right: they'd seen his younger acts of indifference and cruelty before he learned how to mask his true self. Nowadays, he avoided all three as often as possible, lived for the present rather than carry the dead wood of his links with the past. His mother occasionally reached out to him, only to withdraw when he missed a planned get-together or said something hurtful to her. Not that she could reach out to him now, when she kept slipping in and out of consciousness. His Dad left a message on his answerphone every night with an update and he popped round to the hospital every second day for half an hour, just to look as if he cared and so that he had more chance of eventually being left money in his father's will. It was easier to sit by her bedside now that Nicholas and Jill were no longer there, were apparently at home, tranquillized to the hilt and wallowing in grief over their lost boy.

His own life was improving by the minute, especially now that he was going to fuck Beth on Saturday. She'd be feeling vulnerable and confused and he'd be the manly friend who made her feel attractive and charismatic again. They'd listen to some music, maybe dance with their arms around each other or curl up companionably on the settee, start to kiss. He'd add the date rape drug to her drink at some stage after the kissing so that he could go much further than first base.

He wasn't really working on Thursday and Friday night, was actually going to a Bristol casino. He merely wanted to savour the thought of taking her, spend the next two days planning every possible deviant act. He'd keep her drugged for many self-indulgent hours, adding a couple of Valium to the mix if necessary, and would return her to her own apartment in a semi-comatose state. She'd think – and he'd confirm if asked – that she'd spent the evening drowning her sorrows with his home-made wine, that she'd passed out from too much alcohol. It would be good practice for his next victim, the increasingly merry widow Olivia. She'd recovered remarkably quickly from childbirth and, if her flirtatious comments were to be believed, had apparently got her sex drive back. Her eyes said 'take me now, take me hard' and he was increasingly tempted. He'd book her in soon for the last appointment of the day.

The highlight of her week was her visit to Adam, Olivia admitted to herself as she sat in her bedroom, blow-drying her recently highlighted hair. Getting ready to see him was like going on a date with someone that she really fancied and, to her chagrin, she was slightly breathless and her underarms kept getting wet. She felt like a schoolgirl, which was exactly what she'd been when she started dating her first love, Marc. He was at work, of course, had no idea how much effort she put in to her appearance before each undercover assignment. Nowadays, she felt more like a woman and less like a cop.

As usual, she took the train from Dorchester to Weston and, on her arrival, used her special mobile to connect with her colleagues. They verified that they were already doing surveillance from the house across the road. Fortunately they couldn't see or hear her interaction with Adam, though knowing that they watched her arrive and leave made her feel self-conscious, on display. Had they noticed that her tops had become lower, her skirts tighter? Were they commenting on the fact that she'd started to wear fuck-me shoes?

He took longer than usual to answer the door and, for a moment, her mood lowered. Had he gone out? She wanted to complain further about Zak, admitting that her late husband had annoyed her with his various bad habits. In reality, she was often describing Marc.

'Olivia! You're looking well.'

She should do – she'd bought new jeans and a vintage top, smart yet casual. She'd also spent sixty quid on a jasmine-based perfume that she thought was especially sensuous. She wondered briefly if she could claim everything on expenses, almost giggled at the thought.

'I feel well. Mrs Penrose looks after Mia all the time so I'm practically a free agent.'

See me as a young woman rather than a mother.

'Everybody needs good neighbours – or so they tell me! Next door's cat is intent on destroying this place.'

'Oh, I've seen her – she's huge. You wouldn't like your own pet?'

She watched him hesitate. 'I love animals but I sometimes have to travel for my work. It wouldn't be fair.'

'You don't have a friend who could feed it?'

'I had a lodger, but unfortunately he died and most of my friends have moved away to follow their careers. I'm equally short of relatives.'

'A girlfriend?'

'No one will have me,' Adam said and laughed loudly. 'But we're not here to talk about my solitude.'

He indicated the couch and she gratefully stretched out on it, turned on her side to face him. He smiled at her as he took his seat.

'So, how have you been? I mean in emotional terms?'

'Surprisingly OK.' The increasingly live-for-today Olivia that she was creating had very few problems. She was working from home and had a doting older woman to care for her child.

'Sleeping better?'

'Like a rock! Wonder how that particular saying originated?'

Adam smiled and shrugged. 'Probably has its origins in some archaic ritual. You could always Google it.'

'It would make a change from my online widows group.'

'Oh, these things have their place. I mean, you can post at your convenience.'

'But everyone else is so wrapped up in the past. I want to move on!'

'Have relationships, you mean?'

'Uh huh.' She opened her eyes more widely, held his gaze for a flirtatious moment.

'It's a good idea to build your single life first, so that you go into the dating scene from a position of strength. At the moment, you'd just be avoiding pain so the bad feelings would probably return in the long run as depression.'

'I don't think they would.' She took a deep breath, feeling guilty about criticising the non-existent Zak. 'As I've said, my husband and I had our difficulties, so I'm probably more ready than most to move on.'

'Not so,' Adam said. 'We've found that people with difficult marriages take longer to recover after widowhood as there's so much guilt, years of arguments and bad times to remember. In contrast, if you had a good relationship then you know that you made your late partner happy and it's easier to return to an even keel.'

'Oh, I think that I made him happy,' Olivia said in what she hoped was a sexy voice. She shifted her weight on the couch so that her blouse tightened around her breasts, was pleased when she saw that the therapist was looking. It seemed to take an effort for him to look away.

'I'm sure that you did,' he murmured.

Belatedly, Olivia remembered her remit which was to get him to talk about his late wife. 'And did you feel that you made Helen happy?'

'She said that she was, outwith the bouts of depression.' He grimaced. 'But when a spouse commits suicide, it's hard not to feel like you've failed.'

'You feel responsible?'

'Oh, not now that I've had counselling. He made me focus on the fact that Helen had suffered from depression since her teenage years, long before she met me. She was going through hormonal changes, coming to terms with the ageing process and it all got too much.'

'Did she die in the house?'

'No, outside. I'd have hated to come home and find her. It was bad enough as it was when the police arrived at my door.'

'Same with Zak,' Olivia said, remembering her back story. 'I mean, obviously he didn't commit suicide, but he went out and never came back.'

'Do you hate the driver?'

Olivia remembered her brief, which was to sound non-judgemental and alternative. Adam would apparently be attracted to women who thought outside the box.

'No, I remember having a couple of drinks before my first driving lesson, probably explains why there wasn't a second, so there's no point in blaming someone else for getting tanked up!'

'Bad girl,' Adam murmured and Olivia felt herself start to blush.

How bad do you think I can get? she thought and longed, for the umpteenth time, to unbutton his shirt.

'I'd like to start dating,' she said firmly. 'I mean, I'm still young and fit.'

'You've got no argument from me there.'

Again they stared at each other. Olivia felt her pulse quicken and wondered if he felt equally alert to the possibilities. They'd probably be electric together, last for hour after hour.

'So, where do I start?'

'How about an online widows and widowers group, one which offers dating and platonic relationships? You'd be able to find out quite a bit about these men in advance – their language skills, their interests, how long they were married. Remember that you're still vulnerable, that it's vital to protect yourself from further hurt.'

'Have you dated widows since Helen died?'

'No, only divorcees. I suppose that I've been wary of getting into a counselling situation when what I really want is a fun date.'

'But we're not all morose!'

'I know, but I don't want to end up having a busman's holiday.'

Damn, so her imaginary widowhood was actually working against her. Would he have preferred her if he knew her true circumstances, that she was unhappily married? She was doing her best to forget about being a cop.

'I wouldn't mention my situation to a new guy,' Olivia said, striving to sound light hearted. 'I mean, if all I want is a night of dancing and some fooling about . . .'

'Just take it easy, pace yourself, acknowledge what you've been through. Widows often find it harder than they've expected to transfer their affections to a new man.'

'Who said anything about affection? I need to get physically close.'

The police psychologist had told her that she could talk in those terms, just as long as she didn't proposition Adam directly. She was glad that her colleagues in the house across the road couldn't hear her honeyed tone or see her come-and-get-it facial expression and the way that she was thrusting her breasts in his direction. It had been months since Marc had made love to her and now, alone in a small room with an attractive and caring man, her body was crying out for sex.

'Sex with someone new can be equally complicated. After the second or third time, we tend to become emotionally involved.'

'Maybe I should just have a one-night stand?'

'Have you ever had one before?'

'No.' That much was true: the only person that she'd ever been to bed with had been Marc.

'Then now isn't the time to start.'

'Have you? I mean, had one-night stands?'

'We're not here to talk about me,' Adam said, but his voice sounded gentle.

Olivia decided to push the issue. 'I just feel that we're as much friends as widow and counsellor, that I can be frank.'

'OK, yes. Friendship is very important and I don't want to be unduly distant with you. I had a couple of one-night stands as a teenager and one in my early twenties but after that I concentrated on one to one relationships.'

'Because?'

'Because I hurt some of these young women, felt bad in retrospect. They wanted love and I could only feel lust.'

Again she felt her pulse speed up. 'And is lust so bad?'

'No, it's not bad at all, providing you're both singing from the same hymn sheet. But these girls needed romance and a long-term relationship, something that I couldn't provide at such a young age.'

The police psychologist had told her that the teenage Adam had made his same-age girlfriend pregnant and he was doubtless remembering the fallout.

'Committing too young also causes problems. Zak and I made that mistake.'

'Do you feel guilt?'

'No.'

'A sense of regret, then?'

'What's the point?' Olivia answered his question with a question. 'It's not going to change anything.'

'It's just that he didn't have time to give you permission to move on. I counsel a lot of widows and widowers where the spouse died of cancer and they have time for that final talk in which they tell their partner that they'd like them to find someone new to love.'

'Zak would have wanted me to be happy.'

'Of course he would,' Adam said.

They talked about what she wanted out of life now and how she was going to achieve it, then the psychologist looked at his watch and said, 'We're coming to the end of our hour so is there anything else that is troubling you?'

'Apart from the fact that I need a boyfriend?'

'Apart from that!'

'No, I'm doing fine.'

She stood up, stretched and began to walk unsteadily towards the door, knowing that he would follow. He always saw her out.

'Same time next week?' she called out as she sashayed down the hall.

'Perfect,' he said.

She reached the front door, took a deep breath, turned and stood on tiptoe for a moment to kiss him. Her lips brushed his and she felt him return the pressure then she let herself out and hurried down the path. She hadn't stayed beyond her hour, something which would have alarmed her colleagues who were hovering near the window. As far as they were concerned, she was still acting professionally, still doing her job.

But, a few hours from now, she was going to do something

that was just for her, something to make her life wildly exciting. She was going to break all of the rules . . .

Back in Dorchester, she bought a cheap pay-as-you-go mobile and called Adam from it, making the call whilst Marc was still at work.

'Only me,' she said breathlessly. 'I was wondering, can I see you earlier this week as well as at my usual time? It's just that I bumped into a former old boyfriend and he wants us to get together on Saturday night. I remember what you said about not rushing into things but he's gorgeous and I'm really tempted. We used to kiss for hours though we never went too far.' She listened, rejoicing when he said yes, and shakily jotted down the time that he gave her. 'See you then,' she murmured, wondering how much of him that she would get to see.

THIRTY-SEVEN

'It's good to meet you,' Beth murmured as she shook hands with Anya, who'd arrived to be interviewed for the cook's vacancy.

The slightly older woman returned her handshake whilst murmuring, 'I think that we've met before.'

Beth looked at the cook more closely but she didn't seem familiar. 'Have you used the hospital canteen here? Perhaps that's where you've seen me. I help out behind the counter when we're especially busy or short staffed.'

Anya shook her head. 'No, I live in Clevedon so I've never been to the hospital until today.'

At the mention of Clevedon – Matthew's home town – Beth grimaced inwardly. Every time she heard certain songs that they'd listened to together, she felt slightly low and sad.

Telling herself to concentrate, she started the interview. 'So you don't mind the half-hour commute?'

'Actually, my best pal is moving here to take up a nursing job. We're already flatmates and we get on so well that I'm moving with her. That's why I'm looking for work in the Weston area.'

'Brilliant – so you could travel to work together if you get the job,' Beth said.

'Yes, we already car share.'

'And you've found accommodation?'

'We have, so all I need now is work!'

'You have an excellent CV.' Beth studied it for the second time. 'Will you miss the bistro where you're working now? I see that it's a family business.'

'It is. It's run by my father and my sister Maressie, so I can still help out on my days off!'

Matthew had dated a Maressie in Clevedon and it was a comparatively unusual name.

'Did she used to date a Matthew Drysdale?' she asked.

Anya's expression clouded over. 'That's where I've seen you before – you were at a barbeque with him in August.'

Beth nodded. Matthew had spotted Maressie and mentioned that he'd briefly dated her. She'd nodded at him but had looked very uncomfortable, had hurried to the other end of the garden with another female, obviously Anya, and cast sad looks in their direction for the rest of the afternoon. He'd given the impression that they'd only had a handful of dates together and had never been serious, but the woman's body language said otherwise.

'I'm not dating him anymore,' Beth said now.

Anya seemed to hesitate. 'Are you still friends?'

'No, he became so critical of me that the break-up was acrimonious.'

'Same with Maressie,' Anya said, nodding vigorously.

She'd love to hear how he'd conducted his last relationship.

'Did he go from one extreme to the other?' Beth asked curiously.

Anya's nodding intensified. 'He seemed madly in love with her for the first few months then he became really distant and, after that, she couldn't do anything right.'

'He hinted that I was fat,' Beth admitted. She probably shouldn't be talking to a potential employee like this but she'd never stood on ceremony plus it was good to find out about Matthew's past behaviour. Most adults didn't change.

'He did that with Maressie too. In fact, he had a go at her

clothes, her complexion, pretty much everything. She was in love with him and so hurt.'

She, Beth, hadn't fallen in love – though she'd cared for him – and now she realized that she'd had a lucky escape. Only her pride had been hurt and that would revive now that she knew that he'd done this to at least one previous lover. Apparently, unhealthy people became infatuated quickly then backed off when they saw differences between themselves and their new partner, whereas healthy people concentrated on the similarities and accepted the differences with aplomb.

'It was horrible,' Beth said, and shuddered at the memory. 'He made me feel so inadequate, so ugly. Suddenly it was as if I couldn't do anything right.'

'He did that with Maressie's predecessor too, apparently, though we didn't find that out until later. But Clevedon's a small place and people talk.'

'I wondered why all his girlfriends had finished with him,' Beth murmured. 'I was baffled at first as he was so loving. But when he changed, he was so casually cruel.'

'Same with Maressie. We used to sit up at night analysing his comments. In the end, he made one snide remark too many and she ended it.'

'Sounds as if we both had a lucky escape,' Beth said, and realized that she meant it. A lifetime of being criticised and found wanting was no life at all . . .

They returned to the topic in hand – working in the hospital canteen's kitchen – and, by the interview's end, Beth was definitely favouring Anya for the position.

'I just have one more person to see this afternoon,' she said, 'so I'll let you know by tomorrow morning either way.'

Five minutes later, her supervisor, Gill, popped her head around the door.

'Is it going well?'

'It's going brilliantly,' Beth said, realizing that she meant it.

'Excellent. By the way, if you're free this Saturday, my friend's having a girl's night out to celebrate her fiftieth and she says the more the merrier.'

Drat – she was supposed to be going drinking and clubbing with Adam; why did so many good social events clash with each other? Beth thought about it for a moment and realized that Gill's soiree was the more sensible choice. They could talk about the Matthews of this world, their early attempts to woo and their subsequent emotional distance. She needed girl power rather than an evening propping up the bar with a bloke.

'Count me in,' she said and made the necessary changes to her diary.

That night, she phoned Adam's mobile and he answered immediately. From the noise in the background, it sounded as if he was in a pub rather than working. Not that she could blame him for that.

'Sorry, but I'm going to have to take a rain check for Saturday,' she said, trying to sound genuinely regretful.

'You're joking? But I've been brewing the wine!'

'In that case, bring a bottle into work.'

'You'll get us sacked! Have you reconciled with Matthew?'

'No way,' she said with feeling. 'No, I've got an invite to a party. I just forgot.'

'So, come round to my place at the end of the night.'

'Can't – it's in Burnham so I'm crashing out at her place.' She was looking forward to staying with Gill in the seaside resort.

'Sunday, then?'

'I'll be hung-over.'

'We can have the hair of the dog!'

'I'd better not.' She took a deep breath, decided to level with him. 'I was in need of a listening ear the other day, but I've talked it over with a friend and I'm fine now. Adam, we should just keep things professional.'

'You're no fun,' her colleague said, and there was a slight edge to his voice.

'I admit it – I'm a killjoy,' Beth murmured. She waited for his reply but he remained silent and she felt slightly unnerved. 'See you at the next counselling session,' she added warmly and brought the conversation to what she hoped was an amicable end.

THIRTY-EIGHT

Than going to drive to Southampton, a journey of two-and-a-
half hours, and have himself some fun. He'd pick up another
Kylie, a working-class bint with low expectations and no idea
of how to protect herself. He'd screw her senseless either in her
own flat or in the back of his car. That said, his preference was
for her to have her own accommodation: having sex on the back
seat played havoc with his knees and elbows now that he was
no longer in the first flush of youth.

He didn't want to go clubbing until late, would while away
the earlier part of the evening at a Southampton casino. He always
played blackjack, counted cards. He occasionally won hand-
somely, which made the management aware of him, so he moved
around from one venue to another, playing at gambling houses
in Bristol, Bournemouth and various parts of London. Sometimes
he went abroad for a few days and played there.

As usual, he followed the dress code, arrived sober, tried not
to draw attention to himself. He watched the women lose at
roulette and marvelled at how much money they put on the wheel;
it was a game of chance rather than skill so held little interest
for him. He also avoided the card tables with the lonely – and
invariably broke – pensioners who would try to engage him in
conversation: he wanted to blend into the background as much
as possible.

Tonight he was on a losing streak. He cursed inwardly as the
croupier took his chips again and again. First he'd lost Beth and
now he'd lost most of this week's spending money. His eventual
conquest had better be good . . .

At 10.50 p.m., he entered one of the Southampton clubs. The
cost of entry rose at eleven so there was a big queue to get in,
as he'd surmised. He knew just how to play this game. He paid
at the hatch then hurried into the main auditorium with dozens

of others, knowing that the CCTV cameras would hardly be able to make him out amongst the crowds. The footage of these things was remarkably grainy, sometimes looked like an adult version of join-the-dots.

He had a pill in his pocket, anger in his limbs. He was ready for anything. He scanned the room, looking for the weak, the needy, the dispossessed. Society demanded that people be part of a couple, a demand that the conventional took to heart. This was especially true as Christmas neared and all of the traditional songs spoke of love and life partnerships.

It took him an hour, and a couple of false starts, to find her. Small and slender – in other words, easy to overpower. A dyed blonde, so someone desperate for flattery or to fit into some conformist idea of womanhood. No one spent hundreds of pounds and many hours at the hairdressers having their roots retouched unless a certain look was important to them. She was staring at the men in the room, ignoring her mate who was slumped back in her chair and looked close to sleep.

'Too late a night for your pal?' he asked, sitting down.

'Yeah, she's been on the vodka. It always does that to her.'

'Never liked the stuff,' he said, noticing that she was on something darker.

'Nor me, but it's half-price vodka night.'

'So, what are you drinking?'

'Vodka and coke,' she said, looking surprised that he had to ask.

'Fancy another one?'

It would be her last for some time.

'Nah, I'd better get Latoya home.'

Christ, who came up with these girls' names? It sounded like something from the ghetto. His own name had class – Adam, the supposed first man.

'You're not going to drive, are you?' he asked, looking sternly at her half-empty tumbler.

'Well, I couldn't before!' she said, and giggled loudly.

'So how did you get here?'

'Walked.'

'OK, well my car's outside and I've only had half of this.' He indicated his pint. 'I'm happy to give you a lift.'

'To Latoya's?'

No, to Alaska. He fought back the sarcastic remark.

'To her house then to yours. Or we can drop her off and you and I can carry on to another club.'

'It'll cost more now that it's after eleven.'

She hadn't had much to drink if she knew what time it was and remembered the typical club rules, but the Rohypnol would take away her short-term memory. She'd assume that she'd been very drunk.

'Hey, I got a tax rebate so I'm flush.'

'What do you do?'

'Personal trainer.'

'Same here,' she said, looking absurdly pleased.

Fuck – the last thing he wanted was to be questioned at length about his pretend vocation. The best thing to do was to turn the conversation around so that it was all about her.

'I could see that you were fit! Do you do lots of cardio?'

'Lots of everything.'

'Same here. It's all about surprising the body, isn't it?'

Hers was about to get the biggest surprise . . .

'I've just started doing zumba,' she said.

'Is that right?' He had no idea what that was.

'You know, half dance, half aerobics,' she added helpfully.

'A bit too girly for me,' he said with a manly smile.

'I've rugby players come to my aerobics class.'

Probably to letch, he thought sourly. 'I have lots of women in my weightlifting class,' he replied.

'We should attend each other's classes.'

Now, that really would be something.

'For starters, we should get your friend home before she passes out.'

She giggled. 'Will we take an arm each?'

Not in a million years – that way they'd be noticed by security and by other dancers.

'No, let's wake her up properly.'

He shook one of her arms and his intended victim – damn, he'd forgotten to ask her name – shook the other. Latoya opened her eyes and glared at them but got to her feet when they urged her on. She walked unsteadily in front of them, Adam occasionally encouraging her by prodding gently at her back.

They reached the car park without incident and he put both girls in the back seat, got Latoya's address from her and keyed the details into his satnav. Good, she was only a short drive away.

They soon reached her house, a downstairs flat, and he and her friend walked her to the door, helped her find her keys.

'I'll make her a mug of tea, sober her up,' Adam said. An idea was forming. He hadn't enjoyed three-in-a-bed for several years.

He went to the loo whilst the kettle came to the boil, used the time to check out the place. She lived alone, which was ideal for his purposes, and there was no shaving foam or spare toothbrush or any other suggestion that there was a boyfriend in the vicinity who might call round. He made three mugs of black tea, put date rape drugs into two of them and added a little milk to the unadulterated mug. He put all three on a tray, with the milk bottle, and took them into the tiny, airless lounge.

'Pure Stepford husband,' he murmured, 'even if I do say so myself.'

Both girls looked at him blankly: they obviously hadn't seen the film or its various spin-offs. Not that it really mattered – in ten minutes, they'd be so out of it that he wouldn't have to create a rapport.

'Chloe, want to put some whisky in these?' asked Latoya.

Ah, so that was the personal trainer's moniker. Adam smiled conspiratorially at Chloe and she smiled back.

'No, Latoya, we're trying to make you feel better.'

'Looking at him is making me feel much better,' Latoya said.

He looked at Chloe and gave her another smile, one which hopefully reassured her that he wasn't after her mate.

'All that dancing earlier on has made me thirsty,' he murmured and drank deeply of his tea, knowing that it would encourage them to do likewise. Human beings were pack animals and they ate and drank more when they were in company which was why a capitalist society discouraged loners like him. If the need for sex and money hadn't forced him to make connections, he could happily spend day after day in solitude, just driving around the country or reading the latest psychology books and thinking up new mind games to try out on his more vulnerable patients or next girlfriend.

Five minutes later, both girls were close to sleep.

'Let's go into the bedroom,' he murmured. 'Get you comfortable.'

He wanted them to walk there of their own volition, rather than have to be dragged.

Latoya, clearly the more sexed up of the two, got up immediately, giggled, and led the way, her generous hips swaying. Ironically, he much preferred Chloe with her petite frame and longer hair. Both girls stumbled slightly but kept walking until they reached the, unfortunately, single bed.

'Let's all lie down.' He felt as if he was presenting some adult version of a kid's show where everything was outlined in simple sentences. What can we see through the square window? Adam fucking two drugged-up girls . . .

They lay, shoulder to shoulder, for a moment. He watched, listened, they were close to losing consciousness.

'Girls, take off each other's clothes.'

He sat up to watch, impressed at how hard they tried to please him. Whenever they fumbled with a button or a zip, he helped. When they were naked, he rolled them both onto their stomachs and undressed himself. It was party time.

He rolled on a condom and sodomised Chloe first. She moaned but remained immobile. He orgasmed loudly, withdrew and wrapped the sheath in one of the tissues from his jacket pocket. He returned it to his pocket and got a new condom out of the pack. He reached under Latoya and played with her breasts and pussy for a few minutes, felt himself grow hard again. For a forty-year-old, he was wearing well.

Latoya was even easier to bugger and he slid in first time. The drug appeared to have relaxed her completely. He pinched her nipples and she whimpered softly, so, on some level, she could still feel sensation and pain. He took longer to climax this time and she was bleeding slightly by the time that he pulled out of her so he used a few extra tissues to staunch the trickle of telltale red. He wanted everything to appear normal by the morning, for them to believe that they had had consensual sex, or no sex at all.

He dozed in between them for a couple of hours and when he woke up he was hard again. This was the life – no wining or

dining, no pretending to be interested in their hobbies or lengthy
stories about people he'd never even met. He fucked them like
they were hookers but he didn't pay and wasn't limited to a
half-hearted handjob in the car. He used Chloe's mouth this time,
pinching her nose until her lips parted obligingly and he thrust
halfway down her throat.

Afterwards, though he again felt sleepy, he forced himself to
leave. He'd be back in Weston by the time that they woke up,
and they'd realize that they didn't know his name or anything
about him apart from a few details of his car. Most women
didn't even notice the make, only the colour. And it had been
dark in the car park so they might not even have paid attention
to that.

No, he'd gotten away with rape yet again – and it had been
two for the price of one this time. In fact, there hadn't been a
price as he hadn't even bought either girl a drink. He was, Adam
thought, as he drove through the quiet Southampton streets,
invincible. As long as his mind stayed sharp and his manhood
stayed hard, he could go on and on.

THIRTY-NINE

He'd have to take a different approach as his current
strategy wasn't working. They were no nearer to catching
Hannah and Kylie's killer than they'd been at the start.
Olivia had failed to make a breakthrough with Adam Neave,
despite her extensive use of his therapy service. They'd told him
that John had been murdered in the hope that he'd confess, but,
in reality, the post-mortem had been inconclusive and it could
have been suicide. The younger man had apparently had a history
of depression and seemed to have been permanently disappointed
with himself.

Morosely, Bill Winston updated his team about the operation.
The national press returned their attention to the murders whenever it was a slow news week and had been highly critical of his
apparent lack of progress. At the end of last month – December

– they'd produced several features on unsolved murders of the past year. Both of the victims' families were equally anxious to have the murderer – or, more likely, murderers – in the frame. They wanted instant results whereas a murder investigation often took months and even years.

The public thought that he could just arrest the most likely suspects and bully them into a confession, whereas the reality was very different. If he didn't build a watertight case, the Crown Prosecution Service would throw it out. He also had to be careful where his undercover operation was concerned, as the judge would halt the case if he thought that it had been brought courtesy of a honeytrap.

Just to complicate matters, the police were going to have to speak to Adam's colleagues, try to ascertain if he could have framed Nicholas, his more conventional brother. They'd rather have avoided this as it would put him on his guard. They wanted the man to relax and form a bond with the apparently bereaved Olivia, talk to her in detail about his late wife. But everything that Adam had said suggested that Helen had been genuinely low, that he had done everything that he could to help her. He hadn't been critical of his spouse, not even when Olivia heavily criticised Zak. The psychologist had thought that the man would recognize psycho-pathic traits in others, so had encouraged the undercover police-woman to appear increasingly indifferent about her late husband, portray herself as a potential party girl. So far, it had been a waste of time and money as the therapist hadn't taken the bait.

'We'll get him – or them,' he told the sleep-deprived detectives in a desperate bid to boost morale. 'We're making inroads and everything comes to he who waits.'

But how long would they have to wait? And for whom? And, in the meantime, would another young woman have to die?

This was either the bravest thing that she'd ever done – or the most foolhardy. If her superiors found out, she would lose her job but she no longer cared. She was tired of police work, tired of her marriage and thoroughly bored with herself. She'd applied for and accepted this assignment because she craved excitement, and now she was about to find out how exciting life could actu-ally get. None of her colleagues knew that she'd kissed Adam on her last visit – or that she'd made this appointment just for her own gratification, that it was playing no part in her undercover work.

Marc had already left for the office, so she was able to dress with especial care. She put on her new white lace bra and matching panties. Not that she planned to go all the way with the therapist, but the bra pushed her breasts up and made them look especially taut and alluring under her clothes, and the briefs clung to her like the proverbial second skin so left no visible panty line.

For her top half, she selected a tie-dye purple blouse which she left open to her cleavage, and teamed it with purple jeans. She looked trendy yet alternative and youthful without being mutton dressed as lamb. He'd returned her kiss during their last session, but she'd had to leave before her colleagues realized that something untoward was happening. Today she could kiss him at length and run her hands down his back . . .

The train journey seemed to take an age and she had an incredible desire to pace back and forth, but settled for staring out of the window. Was he, too, looking at his watch and wondering how far they would go?

At last she reached the station, hailed a cab, breathed fast and hard as it meandered its way towards Adam's house. He was only the second man that she'd had any form of sexual contact with so their recent kiss probably meant more to her than it did to him. Indeed, he might receive kisses from all of his more attractive female patients. Was she young enough and bright enough to stand out?

'Nice place,' the cabbie said when they arrived.

'It's a friend's house.' She wondered belatedly if the taxi drivers knew the addresses of the local therapists, if they regularly had bunny boilers in the back of their cars. 'Keep the change,' she added, aware that she was giving him an unusually large tip.

'You have a nice day, love,' he said, smiling broadly.

Would she? Olivia wondered as she walked up the path. Or was she about to make a gigantic fool of herself?

He opened the door almost as soon as she rang.

'Saw your taxi arrive.'

'Surprised that you didn't hear him, he was chatting me up so loudly!'

'And were you tempted?'

'No, he's not my type.'

She watched, feeling shaky, as Adam closed the door and turned towards her. 'So, who is your type?'

It was now or never. 'Oh, I have a fetish for therapists.'

She stepped closer and lifted her face towards his.

To her relief and delight, he responded, his mouth coming down on hers, slowly increasing the pressure. Olivia slid her hands around his waist and pulled him closer, just as she had in her dreams. She felt his breathing quicken as she moved her palms down to his buttocks, tracing them through the black cords. Ironically he, too, was wearing a purple shirt, albeit a self-coloured one.

'I could get struck off for this,' he murmured, moving his hands to her hair.

'I won't tell. It'll be our secret.'

'You're a beautiful young woman, Olivia, but I don't want to take advantage . . .'

'You aren't. I want to be more than friends with you.' She pressed her body closer to his, felt his erection pushing into her belly. She whimpered as her body responded, suddenly awash with lust.

He kissed her again, more passionately this time, before she felt his lips moving to her neck, creating new pathways of excitement. He was sensuous and assured yet eager, something that her husband hadn't been for a long time. His mouth traced its way to her cleavage then back up again to her throat whilst inwardly she begged him to touch her breasts.

'I love those,' he said at last, palming her nipples through both layers of thin cotton. Olivia heard herself moan softly. Planning to stroke and kiss his chest, she started to unbutton his shirt.

'We match,' she said huskily.

'Purple, the colour of mystics,' he replied.

'And kings.' She wasn't sure what to talk about but wanted to keep the conversation going, to make a connection.

'Shall we take this to the bedroom?' he continued. 'We'd be a lot more comfortable lying down.'

Olivia hesitated. She'd promised herself that she'd only kiss

and caress him through his clothes, hold out the promise of full
sex for the future. She wanted cosy pub lunches, romantic dinners,
day trips to pretty historic towns. There again, this wasn't a one-
night, or rather one-afternoon, stand as they'd been talking for
many weeks, building up a relationship.

'We won't do anything that you're not comfortable with,' he
added, as if sensing her uncertainty.

'OK. It would be nice to just kiss and cuddle.' She let herself
be led along the corridor, an all-too-willing sacrificial lamb.

'How long will your neighbour babysit?' he asked, sitting
down on the bed and pulling her down next to him.

Olivia felt flustered for a second, forgetting her supposed
motherhood. 'Oh, all day if I let her. Do you have any more
patients arriving this afternoon?'

'No, I sensed that you were conflicted, wanted to give you as
much time as you required.'

If their relationship went anywhere, she'd have to resign from
her job and tell him about her true identity. She'd explain that
she'd given it all up because she believed his version of events,
wanted to be with him more than anything else in the world.
Surely, in the circumstances, he'd forgive her? By then, they'd
have been dating for a few weeks and might even be a little in
love . . .

Her lust intensified as he pushed her down on her back and
rolled on top of her. His weight was exciting but not oppressive,
and he smelt faintly of expensive male perfume or aftershave. He
caressed her again and again through her clothes until a voice in
her head begged him to take them off. Reaching for his shirt, she
finished the unbuttoning, was pleased when he pulled it from his
shoulders and threw it to the floor.

He undid her top and discarded it, was equally adept at unfas-
tening her bra strap. Olivia watched him intently as he tongued
her nipples, loving the dark silkiness of his hair, the nape of his
neck, the look in his eyes as he raised his head and stared at her.
She lifted her hips, indicating that she wanted him to remove her
jeans but he either didn't pick up on her cue or decided to ignore
it, instead continuing to play with her breasts. She stroked his
thick, dark hair, ran her fingers down his back as far as she could
reach, feeling his muscles move beneath her fingers. His arms

were wonderfully hirsute so she stroked them too. She kept pushing her belly against his, wordlessly encouraging him to finish undressing her, was gratified when he at last reached for her zip.

He tugged down her denims, threw them on the floor, reached for her panties. Suddenly self-conscious, Olivia unbuttoned his cords, wanting him to be as naked as she. She winced inwardly as he peeled her briefs away from her pubis and they made a slight squelching sound: she was very, very wet.

She watched as he removed his trousers and boxers to reveal a sizeable erection. He was bigger than Marc and also thicker. She tensed slightly as she felt him probe at her entrance: was this going to hurt? She felt him slide in a little way, cried out at the rush of pleasure. He kept pushing slowly, methodically and she felt herself open up all the way. He stayed still inside her for a moment, as if letting her get used to his girth, then began to thrust.

For a moment, Olivia wasn't sure what to do with her hands. She normally stroked her husband's face as they made love, but it felt like too intimate a gesture to make towards Adam, too maternal. He wanted a modern young lover, presumably someone raunchy, so she grabbed hold of his buttocks and pulled him further in. She also fingered the area at the base of his spine, close to where his crease began, and felt a sense of power when he groaned and increased his thrusts.

She was one of the many women who couldn't come from intercourse, who needed some kind of direct clitoral stimulation, but she loved the feel of a man inside her, the sensation of being filled up, almost of being possessed. The only thing she didn't like was when Marc couldn't come, when he fucked on and on until she dried up and it started to hurt. Would Adam keep going until she felt bruised internally? No sooner had she asked herself the question when he gave a short grunt and flopped more fully on top of her.

Had he come? A moment later, his penis slipped out, accompanied by a deluge of warm liquid. Ugh, she also hated this bit. She realized too late that she should have insisted he wear a condom, but she and Marc hadn't used contraception for years so it hadn't been something she'd thought about in the heat of the moment. Olivia closed her legs and tilted her hips upwards in a bid to stop more of their mingled juices from coating her thighs. She kissed his neck and he rolled onto his back, put his hands behind his head and seemed to fall asleep almost immediately.

Was that it? Wasn't he going to bring her off? Suddenly feeling low – and, if she was honest, slightly used – Olivia closed her eyes and listened to Adam's increasingly deep breathing. For the first time, he reminded her of Marc.

A few minutes later, she stirred as an assured male hand slid down her arm.

'Sorry,' he said. 'You've worn me out.'

'Likewise!'

'Oh, I'm sure that I can revive you.'

She gasped as he reached between her legs and teased her labial lips apart. She could tell that she was still aroused and soaking, that she wouldn't take long to come. She always got there when Marc put his hand over her pubis and gently massaged the entire area, indirectly stimulating her clit.

Ouch! She flinched as Adam put his finger directly on top of the little bud and gave an experimental rub. Feeling awkward, she pushed his hand away, murmured, 'Not so direct, please.'

'Mm?' He returned his fingers to her labia.

'Like this.' She took hold of his wrist and guided his palm to her pubic area, put her hand on top of his and showed him what she liked.

'I love it that you're shaved,' he murmured.

'It's good for oral,' Olivia replied. She felt a frisson – was that word French? – run through her at the thought of Adam's tongue lapping at her most sensitive places. Marc had never been keen on licking her.

But, for now, she had to settle for his hand and he was still manipulating her too firmly. Should she just fake it? It would be a poor start to a new relationship.

'Softer, please,' she whispered, adding, 'I'm too sensitive down there for my own good!'

'Some women like a rougher touch,' Adam said.

Did he like rough sex? In the future, would he hold her down or tie her up? As he began to touch her more lightly, using the circular motion that she loved, she thought the usual shameful thoughts that she used when she masturbated, and soon felt herself getting close to the edge. She had her eyes closed but sensed that he had shifted his weight, then she felt his other hand pinching gently at her nearest nipple. The pleasure went in waves from her breast to her belly and she stiffened as she felt the familiar signal go off in her groin, followed by a few seconds of suspended animation before her climax began. She heard herself emitting the guttural, animalistic groans which always accompanied her orgasm, was vaguely aware of his sigh of satisfaction, presumably at a job well done.

'You needed that,' he said, as she curled into his side.

'It's been months,' Olivia admitted, remembering her role as the frustrated widow. It had, indeed, been ages as Marc was always too tired nowadays.

'Do you often touch yourself?'

'Most nights.' She wanted him to know that she was highly sexed, responsive.

'Same here!' he said, and laughed.

'You must get lots of offers from women.' She wanted to know more about him for personal rather than professional reasons. Whatever she learned now wouldn't be passed on to other cops.

'Some – but I never have sex with my patients.' He gave a short laugh. 'You, of course, are the exception.'

'Why?' She held her breath.

'Because you're not damaged like they are, just recovering from a specific difficult event.'

'But you've counselled other widows like me?'

'Mm, but they tend to be older. You're young and beautiful and lively. What's not to like?'

He hadn't mentioned any of her non-physical attributes, Olivia thought, such as her love of the English language or her irreverent sense of humour. There again, she'd been playing up her sexiness and coolness in the hope of attracting him.

'You've got an amazing body.'

His words broke into her daydream.

'I used to go to the gym a lot.'

'You don't have to. My guess is that you're naturally slim.'

'And you?' She ran her palm down his flat stomach, was gratified to find that he was erect again.

'Oh, I keep fit through copious acts of masturbation,' he said and laughed.

'Want me to . . .?' Olivia asked, wrapping her fingers around his cock and beginning to move them up and down.

'I'd rather,' Adam said breathlessly, 'that you gave him a kiss.'

Drat, she hadn't had any practice at oral sex. She and Marc had hooked up when they were young and entirely inexperienced so had always just aroused each other by kissing and caressing. She'd read up on oral sex in her early twenties, had suggested that they try it, but he'd come up within seconds, spitting hairs, and looking green. Strangely, he had been equally unenthusiastic when she went down on him and, before long, had pushed her head away. In those days he'd wanted sex to be dreamily romantic, another way of getting close to her.

Uncertainly, Olivia kissed her way down the therapist's chest and stomach, paused when she reached his erection. She licked the top in an experimental gesture, felt pleased when he jerked and gasped. She licked it again then felt his hands on her neck, guiding her face further down.

'Suck it like you would a lollipop,' he said.

Had he sensed that she was new to this? Did that make her more or less exciting? Olivia looked at him and was reassured when he smiled back at her. God, he was beautiful. She took the top two or three centimetres of his hardness between her lips and began to move her mouth rhythmically up and down. She was aware of his hand on the top of her head, holding her in place, a gesture she found both faintly troubling and exciting. He was a man who knew what he wanted, unlike Marc.

Up, down, up, down. His fingers were entwined in the hair near her scalp now, tugging slightly. It was strangely arousing and Olivia redoubled her efforts to take him over the edge. She felt a pleasant saltiness coating her tongue, presumably as his pre-ejaculate increased, and was pleased when he began to move his hips up, breathing hard. She felt powerful, sexual, aware of the moment but also of future possibilities. There were so many new things that she wanted to try out in bed with him.

He had to be really close now, as he'd started to make small noises, punctuated by gasps and increased movement. He cried out at the same moment as she felt a thin, warm squirt of liquid on the roof of her mouth. She swallowed, remembering an article she'd read in a magazine which said that men saw it as a sign of acceptance. It was followed by another squirt which she also swallowed down.

'Wow,' Adam said, stretching out.

'You taste lovely,' Olivia said, meaning it. She'd read that some men could take ages to come, even from oral, but Adam had been flatteringly quick. Maybe he'd been fantasizing about her for weeks in the same way that she'd been dreaming about him?

'We aim to please,' Adam replied.

She curled into his side. 'So, what do you do in your spare time?'

She wanted to be able to picture his daily life, his routines.

'I don't have any!'

'You can't work all hours.'

'Not here, no – but, as you know, I also do voluntary work.'

'So, if you were celebrating, where would you go?'

She sensed him hesitate.

'I suppose that I'd choose the casino.'

'You're a roulette player?'

'Blackjack.'

'You must teach me to play sometime.'

She smiled as Adam kissed her on the forehead. 'I'm hardly a maestro.'

'Compared to me you are – I've never played anything more challenging than Snap!'

Again he smiled and, this time, ruffled her hair. 'Ah, the old games are the best.'

'Do you like eating out?' She loved Indian food, was experimental in her choice of dishes.

'Mainly just at the casino as it's handy. Oh, now you have me down as an inveterate gambler!'

'Not at all.' She kissed his upper arm. 'Do you like a curry?'

'Love it!'

She waited for him to ask her out for a meal but instead he

closed his eyes. Olivia cast a quick look at her watch. She'd have to leave now if she was to make it back to Dorchester without arousing Marc's suspicions.

'Got to get home?' Adam's voice broke into her thoughts.

'Sort of. I'll better give my neighbour a break from Mia.'

'Yeah, she'll be needing her mummy.' He looked around the room as he spoke, and she could tell that he wasn't fully concentrating on their talk.

'Oh, she's not clingy. She loves being around new people,' Olivia said. She didn't want him to see her as unavailable or as a brood mare rather than an independent girl. He'd be so pleased when she told him that she didn't have a daughter, that she was free of encumbrances.

'Still, you don't want to take advantage of this older woman.'

'I guess not,' Olivia murmured, feeling dismissed. She reached for her bra and panties and stood up to put them on, straightening quickly after pulling up her knickers, wanting him to see her body looking taut.

'Love the underwear,' Adam said. 'I like the pure look.'

'We aim to please,' she laughed, echoing his earlier remark.

She continued to dress, and watched him putting on his own clothes. Already she wanted him again.

'I'll just nip to the loo and freshen up a bit,' she murmured.

'You know the way.' As she left the bedroom, she heard Adam opening the window. Was he airing the house before his next patient? He'd told her that she was the last client that he was seeing today.

In the bathroom, she used a wet wipe to wash away their mingled juices, used two others to clean under her armpits. She also got out her travel toothbrush and cleaned her teeth before adding new make-up and scent. Now she looked presentable, albeit slightly flushed.

'Alright?' He was already standing by the outer door when she walked down the hallway.

'Sorted.' She smiled at him until she got close enough to give him a kiss. His mouth on hers was receptive but not passionate. Still, the poor man was probably orgasmed out.

'See you soon,' he said and lightly touched her arm.

Was he planning to phone her and arrange the next date? She'd ideally have liked to know now about their next meeting but was supposed to be playing the part of the merry widow, a young woman who didn't fret about anything.

'Absolutely,' she murmured, striving to sound cool. Maybe he wanted a day or two to consider his next move? She'd read that some men needed to create a degree of distance after making love but that they came back stronger if you left them alone. They were going to be fine, Olivia thought as she walked towards the railway station, a dynamic duo. She could still hear the noises of pleasure that he'd made when she sucked him, could feel the sensations left by his hardness between her legs.

FORTY

'You're in a good mood,' Beth said.

'Why shouldn't I be?'

She'd half expected him to be distant with her for cancelling their night of wine-drinking, and possibly song, at short notice.

'No reason – but isn't February supposed to be the cruellest month?'

'That's April. You clearly don't know your T.S. Eliot.'

Beth smiled. 'And you do? Adam, you're such a modern man that I didn't have you down as a poetry lover!'

He smiled back. 'Oh, the mums of my younger clients are impressed if I spout a few lines so I make good use of my *Golden Treasury Of Verse.*'

'That's why I'm just doing voluntary work and you're in private practice! I should bone up on Philip Larkin.'

'You could consider going back to uni, doing a psychology course,' Adam said.

Beth shook her head. 'I did an evening class every winter when Brian was alive, but, after he died, I gave up on further education, just wanted to have fun.'

'And that's where Matthew came into the picture?'

She shook her head again. 'Oh, I started having fun long before dating him! I don't need a man to have a good time. Admittedly, he made me feel looked after for the first time since widowhood but when he changed . . .'

'So you've given up on night classes for good?'

Beth shrugged, not sure if she wanted to talk in absolutes. 'At least for the time being. I don't just talk to widows and widowers here, but do a lot of informal counselling at the hospital so there's not much time left to fit in a weekly class plus additional studying time.'

'I know what you mean – there aren't enough hours in the day!' Adam said and laughed. 'God, my mother used to say that. It's just that you're so good with the bereaved that you really should be doing it full time.'

It was the nicest thing that anyone had said to her for some weeks and Beth felt rather chuffed by the comment.

'Thanks,' she said, touching his arm. They were seated together in the bereavement drop-in centre but snow had been falling all morning so no one had come in. This was her chance, she thought, to get to know Adam better. It would be great to have such an intelligent and sensitive friend.

'So, what made you do a bereavement course?'

'As I think I told you, my wife committed suicide and it was a terrible shock. I wanted to talk to someone professional, but, at the time, there was a big waiting list in this area because of a lack of voluntary counsellors. So I went private in the short term then, when I'd recovered, signed up as a volunteer.'

'As much as you do recover,' Beth said. 'I still have my occasional widow's lows.'

'Same here – well, a widower's low. It goes with the territory.'

'And how do you get through it?'

'Just socialize like a mad thing!'

Beth realized that they were more alike than she'd thought. 'Me too.'

'People who haven't been through it think that you're running away from the grief, but there are enough hours to grieve when you come home from a night out and when you're getting ready for work in the morning. There's no point in wallowing in it further,' Adam said.

She nodded, glad to have someone who understood. 'I feel the same – but it's amazing how many people have opinions on how you should live when they've never been through it. At the six-month stage, I even had my workmates – I used to work in insurance – hint that I was partying too much, that I'd recovered with indecent haste, but socializing was just my way of coping. It's three and a half years now and I still miss him lots.'

'Oh, they all think that they're experts, even when they've never been widowed. You should have heard my parents – they wanted me to turn the house into a shrine for Helen,' Adam replied.

'It must have been a shock for them, though, losing their daughter-in-law so suddenly.'

'Oh, it was. They said that she was like the daughter that they never had. She'd go round and see them all the time when I was working. There were four people in that marriage and I played the lesser part.'

Beth smiled at him sympathetically. He'd obviously been through the same emotional hell as she, was just better at outwardly dealing with it.

'I was especially fortunate – no parents-in-law as my husband's family died young. And my parents emigrated to Canada years ago so we had no interference from either side.'

'But you must have been more isolated when he died?'

'Absolutely – especially when the couple that we'd spent almost every weekend with didn't get back in touch after the funeral.'

'Happens all the time,' Adam said. 'You're seen as predatory now.'

'Yet you aren't?'

'No, we widowers are seen as helpless, get more pity. In fact, my neighbour cooked me a casserole once a week for a year after Helen's death. She must have sacrificed several lambs.'

'All that my neighbours did was cross the road to avoid me,' Beth said heavily. 'I'd never felt so isolated and cast adrift.'

'But you've a good social life now?'

'The best! I go dancing, to the cinema, to see live bands.'

'Maybe some time I could go with you?'

'I'd like that, though we'd better keep things professional,' Beth said, determined to be sensible.

'No problem. I'll keep my hands in my pockets for the entire night!'

'Now, that's just creepy,' she replied and they both laughed.

The door swung open a little and they looked towards it expectantly but it was just the wind.

'Ghosts!' Beth said, and shivered slightly.

'You're not superstitious, are you?'

'No, I'm entirely rational.'

'Same here,' Adam said, looking relieved. 'I hate all that bad poetry which some widows write about their husband becoming an angel.'

'It's even worse when they misspell it and he becomes an angle,' Beth added and they laughed again, albeit somewhat guiltily.

'So, here's to humanism,' Adam murmured, lifting his cup of tea in a mock toast. 'And to our forthcoming platonic night out.'

'To our platonic night out,' Beth echoed, feeling pleased.

Jesus – his balls had hardly had time to fill up again after Olivia when Beth requested a night out with him. If he believed in astrology, he'd have said that these were auspicious days for his particular star sign of Scorpio. As it was, he thought that you made your own luck in this world.

He was surprised at how easy Olivia had been, how available. He hadn't had to buy her a drink, far less a meal. She'd arrived, gift-wrapped in sexy clothes, at his place and started kissing him the second that he ushered her into the hallway. Fifteen minutes later, he'd plunged right in. She'd obliged by giving him oral sex, the only other thing that he wanted from her. She'd handed it to him on the proverbial plate, robbed him of the thrill of the chase. Now that he'd been there and got the T-shirt he'd lost interest, would refer her to another therapist to avoid tears at bedtime and beyond.

The doorbell rang and he walked briskly to the door to greet his newest patient, managed to hide his surprise at her beauty. Maybe there was a god after all.

'You must be Miss Jenkins,' he said, extending his hand as she entered by his side door.

'Susie, please.'

'Susie. As you know, I'm Adam Neave.'

She'd sounded so ordinary on the phone that he'd pictured some mousy little woman. Instead, she had glossy black hair cut in a longish bob, a face to die for and a cafe au lait complexion. If she was suitably submissive, he might well be looking at wife number two.

'Come through to my study, please. I think that I can help you.'

Especially if she wanted her cunt filled.

She followed him through, sat demurely on the couch.

'Tell me more about your problem.'

'Well, as I said on the phone, there were lots of things I couldn't do at school such as tying my school tie and shoelaces or doing up my bag straps. These things have carried over into adulthood. I also can't tell my left from my right.'

'That's surprisingly common,' Adam said smoothly. 'At least five percent of the population has the same problem.'

'Really? Unfortunately I didn't go to school or university with any of them!'

'Can I ask what you studied?' Adam queried, beginning to take notes.

'American Studies. My father already lives in the US so I thought . . .'

'But you're still here.'

A coquettish laugh. 'My boyfriend got me pregnant in my last year, so I married days after graduating and went on to have twins. Moving to California didn't seem practical after that.'

'So, are you still a full time mum or . . .?'

'Oh no. The children have just left home for university and last month I separated from their father. I've taken a job as a dental nurse and receptionist but if I take the drill apart to clean it, I can't put it back together again. The same applies to various pieces of dental and office machinery – I can't even load the stapler. It's my first job and it's very likely that I'm going to get the sack.'

'So, why dental nursing?' Adam asked.

He wanted to understand this woman so that he could appear to be the perfect suitor. She was beautiful and intelligent but had chosen to live a small life so far: she probably had low

self-esteem, could make the perfect spouse. It would be wonderful
to have twenty-four-hour access to that amazing body and he
wouldn't have to get another lodger if he had a second pay cheque
coming in. Moreover, he loved playing mind games, had missed
the daily apologies that he'd managed to wring from Helen, until
she approached the menopause – the one drawback of marrying
an older woman – and became less pliable and a lot more
demanding, more intent on leading her own life.

'Well, I can't drive and I've become totally lost on the few
occasions where I've boarded a bus, so I was looking for local
employment. My dentist lives a ten-minute walk away and I was
telling him that I had to find work and he explained that he was
about to advertise for a nurse.'

'Have you ever taken driving lessons?' Adam asked.

'Dozens! I went through two driving instructors in my late
teens but both said that I'd never learn to drive.'

'I imagine that you found it difficult to stay in your lane,'
Adam said mildly.

Susie nodded. 'I kept veering.'

'And, as you can't tell your left from your right, you hesitated
when asked to make a turn.'

'Uh huh. And I couldn't tell how close I was to other vehicles.
It was a nightmare.'

'In other words, you have motor learning difficulties,' Adam
explained.

'So, is it a recognized condition? My mother always said that
I was a stupid bitch.'

Excellent – she'd been raised without self-belief, the perfect
victim.

'You're probably mildly dyspraxic. In other words, you have a
poor sense of direction, can't read maps and can't fine tune your
movements. I'll bet you couldn't cope with a skipping rope at school.'

'Or catch a ball,' Susie said with a shudder. 'According to the
other kids, I was a spaz.'

'I'll test your IQ now but I'm willing to bet that it's in the
top five percent of the population. You need around 120 to go to
university,' Adam said. 'You're intelligent, merely spatially inept.'

'And would that be caused by a blow to the head? My mother
was always lashing out at me.'

'Could be, or by her abusing drugs or alcohol when you were in the womb. In other cases, that part of the brain doesn't develop at the foetal stage and we don't know why.'

He ran through a series of tests and her prognosis was as he'd anticipated.

'I need time to process your results so can you come back later this week?'

He wanted to see her again as soon as possible, preferably when she had on far fewer clothes.

'That would be brilliant,' Susie said, looking pleased.

He got out his appointments book and gave her the last appointment of the day, the one which not-so-professionals always reserved for the eye candy amongst their patients. It would mean that he wouldn't have to watch the clock, that they could spend more time together. And, in his desire to convince her that he was a nice guy, he'd only charge her for a two-hour session, even if she stayed for three or more. She was a walking wet dream, fantasy fodder. He was so going to enjoy having her in his bed.

FORTY-ONE

I t wasn't every day that she had two policemen arrive at her door. Beth squinted at them through the winter sunshine.

'Can I help you?'

'If we could come in, have a word in private?'

'Of course.' She led them through to the lounge. One of the few good things about widowhood, she reflected wryly, was that you no longer feared the worst when the police showed up. She'd lost the only person that she loved in the world when Brian died, doubted if she could ever bond as closely with anyone again.

'We understand that you work with Adam Neave.'

'That's right.' *Aha, it must be about John's suicide.*

'His brother was arrested recently for having some illegal materials in his household and he blamed Adam for planting the goods.'

'Adam? He's the most public-spirited person that I know.' She saw that they were unconvinced. 'He does voluntary work along-side me and also offers counselling at a reduced rate for people on a lower income. He was devastated recently when John committed suicide.'

'You also heard about his nephew?'

She nodded, remembering the emotion on her colleague's face. 'The little boy who died in his sleep? He told me and was desperately upset about it. It's a difficult time for him, especially when his mother's terminally ill.'

'Don't you find it odd that so many people around him are dying?'

Good grief, did they think that Adam was some sort of serial killer? She sought to reassure them that it was comparatively common to see clusters of related deaths.

'No – we see this in bereavement counselling all the time. A woman's mother dies of cancer and, three months later, her father dies of a broken heart. A sister becomes depressed and commits suicide. Another family member is so distraught that it seriously weakens her immune system and she dies of complications following flu.'

'But Adam's lodger wasn't a family member.'

'True, but he was a lost soul, always searching for something.'

'And his late wife?'

'She was a depressive. I understand that she was a counsellor and there are often unhappy people who go into the therapy field in a bid to heal themselves.'

'So you've seen nothing untoward in Mr Neave's behaviour?'

'Quite the reverse – he's a paragon of virtue.'

'It's a while since I've heard that phrase,' one of the cops said with a wry smile. Then his grin faded. 'We'd appreciate it if you didn't mention our visit to Mr Neave.'

Beth hesitated. 'I won't because he's got enough going on in his life and I don't want to worry him.'

'He's not a serious suspect in this matter but we have to follow up every lead.'

'I got the impression that his brother was highly strung,' Beth said, remembering a couple of her work mate's throwaway comments. 'And maybe a bit jealous of Adam's success.'

One of the men nodded, looking sympathetic. 'As I said, if we get a complaint we have to look into it.'

Beth showed them out then watched as they walked down her path, got into their vehicle and drove away. She knew that the police often arrested the wrong person, but was amazed that they were even considering Adam for any kind of criminal activity. He was an asset to the community and probably the kindest and most charitable man that she knew.

FORTY-TWO

I t had been four days and he still hadn't called. Olivia checked and rechecked the pay-as-you-go mobile that she'd bought specially for their relationship. She was seeing him tomorrow for their usual weekly counselling session but was feeling increasingly nervous about it. Should she act like his patient or his lover? Or a mixture of both? Talk about what had happened between them or be really cool and ignore it? She slept badly, unable to believe that he wasn't interested in her yet all too aware that the lack of contact suggested his indifference.

'You look nice,' Marc said the following morning as she got ready to travel to Weston-super-Mare.

'Well, he's confided in me so little that I have to try harder.'

'It won't be your fault if he doesn't tell you anything. Guys like that often play their cards close to their chest.'

'Guys like what?' She felt irritated at his temerity: he'd never even met Adam.

'Well, psychopaths – or whatever he is.'

'We're all beginning to think that we've got the wrong man,' Olivia said, knowing that this was just her opinion. She hadn't been allowed to discuss the case with her colleagues, just had a weekly meeting with the police psychologist.

'Whatever,' Marc said, and returned his attention to the television. It was his day off, but he clearly didn't intend to do much with it.

By the time that she got off the train in the seaside town,

Olivia was awash with adrenalin. It was only midday but she'd been awake for hours, felt exhilarated yet tired. There were detectives watching from the house across the road so she couldn't stay longer than the allocated hour, but surely they'd talk and kiss in that time, make future plans?

He opened the door and she smiled at him tremulously.

'Hi you,' she said.

'Nice to see you again, Olivia.'

She walked ahead of him as usual to his office, sat down on the therapeutic couch. To her disappointment he didn't join her there, opted to sit behind his desk.

'So, how have you been?' he asked.

Uncertain, confused, almost afraid. 'Busy!'

'Still socializing madly?'

'Of course. You only live once.'

'Don't let a reincarnationist hear you say that!'

'Is that even a word?' Olivia asked, trying to keep her tone as light as his was.

'It is now. The English language is always changing.' There was a longish pause then he added, 'So, is there anything specific that you want to talk about?'

Why haven't you phoned? Am I going to see you again? Don't you still like me?

She shrugged, decided to refer obliquely to their relationship. 'It was nice to become sexually active again.'

Adam cleared his throat. 'About that. I think that it's created an awkwardness between us, that it would be better if you saw another counsellor. I have an excellent one in mind, someone I trained with at university.'

So he didn't want to see her again, not even in a professional capacity. She'd kept telling herself that he was overworked or that he wanted to arrange their next date when he saw her in person – but he didn't want a relationship at all. Olivia felt stunned. She'd spent weeks imagining them talking long into the night and holidaying together, and he'd merely wanted someone new to fuck, and just the once. She'd been a bit on the side, a dalliance, a one-afternoon stand.

She stared at him mutely then realized that his actions would have disastrous implications for her career. If he insisted that she see another therapist, her colleagues at the police station would be instantly suspicious. Maybe Adam would confide in his colleague that they had slept together, and the other man would be questioned by the police and would tell all.

'No, honestly, I'd rather keep seeing you. Platonically, I mean. Last week was just a bit of fun, didn't mean anything. You're a good counsellor and I'd much prefer to keep coming here.'

'You're sure? I mean, you're safe with me – I won't overstep professional boundaries again.'

Damn, Olivia thought, then realized that he'd made the right decision for both of them. She didn't want to merely be a sex object, had longed for a full relationship. How had he managed to look at her with such admiration, with something akin to longing, when all he wanted was a couple of hours in the sack?

'I'm sure,' she said, though inwardly she felt sick and shaky. It was horrible being rejected, especially by someone who was so charismatic, someone who had seemed so right for her. He'd already become the centre of her fantasies and her future plans.

'Excellent! So has what happened brought any other issues to the fore?'

'Not really. It's made me aware that I want to date extensively – but I think that I already told you that? I've registered with one of those dating sites for widows and widowers and already had a couple of emails from guys who are interested. Oh, and there's a singles dance on at a hotel on the seafront this Friday so I'm going there with the young woman who lives across the road.'

'Just don't expect too much of yourself emotionally,' Adam said. 'Most widows struggle when it comes to expressing feelings for their new partner, can be overwhelmed with guilt.'

'I can't imagine feeling guilty, but I'll bear that in mind.'

She didn't yet feel guilty about cheating on her husband, Olivia admitted to herself. She felt almost vindicated because he made so little effort in the bedroom or around the house. She was a lively, intelligent and sexy woman and she needed someone to recognize that.

All that she really had left was her career, she admitted to herself, and she'd almost given it up for a man who felt nothing for her. Now, despite the lowness of her mood and the queasy feeling in her stomach, she had to become a professional again, an undercover cop. But she couldn't ask him about Helen today; after all, people who were dating often talked about their exes, especially when they were both widowed. He had to see her as the perfect patient rather than as a woman scorned.

'I'm thinking about taking a second job,' she said. 'You know, outside the home?'

'Such as?'

Her mind raced but came up blank. She felt shocked, worthless. 'Anything really, so that I get to meet more people and earn a few quid.'

'What did you do before you were married?'

She'd gone into the police force from school, but recounted her sister's resume. Her mouth felt dry.

'Shop work might be a good option in the short term as there are a lot of vacancies and you could work part-time.'

'Uh huh.' She struggled to keep the conversation going. 'Do most widows cope well with going back to work?'

She watched him nod, wished that she didn't fancy him quite as desperately.

'I've known women return to their jobs within a fortnight, particularly if there was no one to cover for them. Others actively choose that option as they don't want to stay home and grieve.'

'Oh, right. So, does it shorten the grieving process?'

'Unfortunately not. The feelings invariably surface. I had one widow who came to me three years after her husband died and she'd only started crying that month. She'd taken on three part-time jobs immediately after his death, filled every waking hour. In the end, she ran out of energy and went into emotional meltdown. It was as if he'd died the previous day.'

'I haven't done that. I mean, I had to spend a lot of time at home during the pregnancy.'

'I know. I don't think that you're looking for short cuts, Olivia. You've simply made a fast recovery because you're a survivor. You're coping brilliantly.'

He saw her as strong, self-assured, whereas she felt as if she was not waving but drowning, that she had no one to cling to, no one who really cared.

'So it's OK to keep trying new things? One of the other clients at the bereavement centre hinted that I was doing too much.'

'You're doing just the right amount. No one else has any right to judge you,' Adam said, then smiled at her encouragingly.

Olivia forced the corners of her mouth upwards, though she remained deflated, her future bleak.

They talked about other ways that she could profitably spend her time and she heard her voice, laughing and joking, coming from somewhere above her head. Every so often she glanced at her watch, willing the hour to be up, for this baptism by fire to be over. She wanted to go home, hide under the duvet and cry like a wounded animal. She longed to be alone.

At last the session ended and he walked her to the door.

'Next week at the same time?' she asked jauntily.

'I'll look forward to it.'

She would dread it, but had no option if she were to keep her job.

Thank goodness that Olivia had gone quietly, acted like a grown up. He was seeing Susie later today: she was his four p.m. appointment, his last of the afternoon. He'd taken care to give her a time when they wouldn't be interrupted – with luck, she'd agree to go out for an early dinner and he could really turn on the charm. No one else had ever understood her dyspraxia so he could be her hero, the only person who truly got her, her soul mate. He'd be the guru, she the willing acolyte.

He polished the furniture with a quality lavender spray, showered and shaved with especial care before her arrival. He also reread everything that he could find about her condition in his textbooks and thought about strategies which might prove helpful, which she could easily implement. Not that he wanted her to become too independent: no, he had to remain the strong one, the one in charge.

She was ten minutes late.

'Sorry, my taxi didn't arrive.'

'Several of my patients have told me that. Apparently there's an influx of new drivers from Bristol who don't know the area.'

'Is that what's going on? I've been let down twice this week.'

'It must be expensive for you, not being able to use buses.'

He knew that she'd struggle to find her way about on public transport, would probably avoid it like the plague.

'It is.' She smiled at him gratefully. 'People don't realize just how poor my sense of direction is. I used to try taking a bus to someplace new but, if I missed my stop, I'd end up completely disorientated. Once I was walking about for four hours in a new district, desperate for the loo!'

'And it compounds the problem that you can't read maps,' Adam said. 'But you shouldn't let it affect your self-esteem as you have a high IQ.'

'No one ever told me that before I saw you.'

'We aim to please,' he said lightly. 'Talking of which, I've sorted out some more tests which will help me ascertain how your brain works. Just tell me what's missing in the following pictures, please.'

As he'd suspected, she answered that nothing was missing, yet there were omissions in every one of the drawings. Unfortunately he wasn't allowed to tell her the right answers as she might be given the test by another professional at a later date.

'So, what can you do for me, doctor?'

The honest reply was 'very little' but he had no intention of letting her escape from him so easily.

'I can help build your confidence in other areas. A short course of cognitive therapy would be ideal.'

'And with regards to my work?'

'I can write to your employer and explain that you are intelligent and motivated but can't put a dental drill back together – or we can look at where your strengths lie and find you a more suitable job.'

'I think the latter,' Susie said thoughtfully. 'I mean, I don't want my boss thinking that I'm substandard.'

'You're hardly that, just wired up a little differently.'

'So what do you think that I *would* be good at?'

Lying on your back and spreading your legs wide and . . . He fought back the thoughts. Instead of answering, he glanced at his watch.

'Gosh, these tests took longer to administer than I thought so we've gone over our appointed time. I missed lunch so I really need to eat, am just popping to a little bistro about ten minutes from here. You'd be welcome to join me. My treat.'

'I'd like that.' She stood up, all long legs and flat stomach and perky little breasts with attitude. God, he was going to enjoy sliding between her thighs.

'I think they do a vegetarian option,' he said as they strolled along the road.

'Oh, I eat meat.'

Better and better. He couldn't wait to have her lips wrapped around his dick.

They ate. They drank. They talked from six until ten that night.

'I'll walk you home – can't have one of my patients getting lost!' he said lightly.

'Do you take all of your patients out to dinner?' she asked as he paid the bill.

'Normally, no. Obviously most of them have mental health issues and are vulnerable, so I'd be breaching my ethical and professional code if I met up with them privately. You're obviously not in that situation, are a very capable professional woman. I've enjoyed our evening and hope that you have too.'

'Oh, I have.'

He took her hand as they walked along the road and she didn't pull away.

'I'd like to see you again,' he said softly.

'No problem.'

'What's your ideal date?'

'Going round a maze,' she said, and they both laughed. 'Seriously? I love nature and the countryside.'

'So maybe we could have lunch on Sunday in a little country pub then go walking?'

'Sounds perfect – you can be my Sherpa.'

She was very receptive to his suggestions – would she put out tonight?

When they reached her front door, he slid his arms around her waist and moved in for the kill. It was, he thought, an unfortunate expression. He wanted this one to live: she might well be a keeper. He wanted to see how far she would go.

He kissed her lightly but when he tried to increase the pressure she pulled away.

'Adam, it's too soon after my separation.'

'Sorry,' he said, holding his hands up in mock surrender. 'I'll be chaste from now on.'

Would he hell – he was so hard that it hurt. He'd drug her at the first opportunity and have his way, otherwise he'd never be able to concentrate on wooing her. He'd fuck her in the pussy rather than the ass so that she wasn't sore when she woke up, would phone her for another date the next day. If she mentioned that her mind was a blank, he'd tell her that she'd been drinking, would carry on the relationship from there. It hopefully wouldn't be long before she forgot about her ex-husband and actually wanted him, Adam, and they could enjoy nightly sex.

'So, a platonic lunch on Friday?' he asked.

She giggled. 'Not platonic, exactly – but no tongues.'

'My tongue and I will be on our best behaviour. Scouts' honour.'

She laughed again. 'You were never in the Scouts.'

Responding to her jokey manner, he shook her hand. 'Thank you for your company, madam.'

'My pleasure, sir.'

It would be his pleasure next time, he thought, as he limped home with his erection digging into his stomach. His libido – and his ego – was going to be very, very pleased.

FORTY-THREE

Something was going to give, Brandon thought. He stared at the two fuckwits who had had the temerity to bring him into the world. How dare they ruin his life with a single comment?

'But I've always planned to go to university.'

It was the only thing that kept him going, his way out, his freedom, his new start.

His father leaned forward in his chair. 'But you haven't been going to school, son.'

Well, he had. He'd been walking in the front door after his mother dropped him off and sneaking out of the back, so technically he'd been there. He always went to the seafront, walked for miles, just dreaming about a more solitary, independent future.

'So? I'm way ahead of the others. I can still pass.'

'They're thinking of excluding you for non-attendance.'

'I can be taught at home, then, or go to a different school.'

'We just don't think that you'll be ready to leave home at eighteen, so, unless you shape up soon, we won't be prepared to pay your fees or living costs.'

It was apparent that the old man had dug his heels in and that his mother, a weak woman at the best of times, wasn't going to contradict him. *Thanks for nothing, Mum.*

He glared, made his voice extra-cold. 'I have the right to my independence – I'll get a flat or a bedsit.'

'Oh, and how will you pay the rent?'

'I'll get a job.'

'Not if you're acting like this, you won't, Brandon.' A lengthy sigh. 'Son, you have to go back on your medication.'

'You can't make me.'

'Of course we can't – you're becoming a young man and we can hardly force-feed you. But remember how much better you could concentrate when you took your pills, how your performance improved in school?'

'No.'

'Well, it did,' his mother said softly. 'We've been talking to Dr Neave on the phone and he agrees.'

'Isn't there doctor-patient confidentiality?'

His father shook his head. 'Not when you're a minor.'

'We're just worried, Brandon,' his mother cut in. 'You can hardly blame us for that.'

Yes, he could. He blamed them for being so fucking dull and unimaginative that he couldn't bear to be in the same room as them and he blamed them for colluding with his shrink. He also blamed them for having the nerve to think that they could tell him what to do.

He fought an almost overwhelming urge to lunge at his mother, grab her by the neck . . . but, if he did, his father would probably knock him to the ground or physically throw him out of the house forever. The man had backhanded him a few times when he was younger and it had really hurt. No, he had to get them in separate rooms before he killed them. They would permanently stand between him and his freedom, so they had to die.

'I'll put the kettle on,' his mother said.

Excellent. He was almost sorted.

'I'll set the tray,' he said and she smiled at him gratefully.

'Thanks, Brandon,' his father said, closing his eyes.

He followed his mother into the kitchen, shut the door. She'd already turned on the tap to let it run for a moment. She always did that – something about getting rid of rust in the pipes. Going into the cutlery drawer, he selected the largest knife, quietly tiptoed behind her and stabbed it through the back of her neck.

He watched as her hand came up, felt the handle, let go. She turned around and stared at him, her mouth frozen in a gape, like a trout at the fish counter. He selected a second knife and prepared to thrust it into her breastbone but she crumpled to the floor and lay there, inert.

Way to go – apart from the shockwave as she hit the ground, she hadn't made a noise. It was almost too easy. His father would be harder, so it would be best to disable him quickly by striking at his head. Fortunately the man kept a heavy wooden club under the marital bed, ready to scare off any intruders. It would make serious inroads into the average – and below average – skull.

Brandon fetched the club and held it behind his back as he re-entered the lounge. He felt almost joyous as he saw – and heard – that his father had fallen asleep. He walked behind him, lined up the wooden block with its target and brought it down with full force. There was an audible crack, after which his victim grunted, jerked spasmodically and began to rise. *No, no, no, no, no!* Heart speeding, Brandon hit him on the back of the head this time, and he pitched forward. Standing over him, he bent down and used the club another three times.

Game over. Walking back into the kitchen, the teenager turned off the tap. He didn't fancy a cup of tea but he could murder a cola. After changing out of his lightly-spattered T-shirt, he took money from his mother's purse and walked jauntily to the nearest shop.

FORTY-FOUR

Tonight's the night, Adam sang to himself. Well, it was this afternoon, to be exact, as he was taking the delectable Susie for a pub lunch. He was driving her out to a country tavern, would slip the Rohypnol into her drink at the end of the meal. He'd get her back to his car before she became drowsy, would drive her to her place and have his oh-so-wicked way.

He wondered if her nipples were pink or chocolate brown, if she had a Brazilian or a forest of pubic hair. It was like unwrapping a mysterious present, discovering new textures, sounds and scents. You slid into some girls like the proverbial knife into butter, whereas others opened up slowly, centimetre by centimetre, as you pushed your cock in.

She was waiting outside her flat when he drew up. That was fine by him – in a couple of hours from now he'd be making himself at home in her currently celibate bedroom. He hoped that she had a double or a king size as some girls got restless on Rohypnol, tended to roll around and moan.

He got out of the car and handed her the flowers that he'd bought, proper ones from the florist rather than the garage shop. First impressions mattered. She hugged him briefly and he breathed in the lovely scent of Tunisian jasmine. He'd find out the name of her favourite perfume at a later date.

'Thanks – they're beautiful. I'll just pop back into the flat and put them in the sink for now.'

'Do you have enough vases?'

'Uh huh – I've got six.'

She'd had other suitors, then, or a very attentive husband, albeit one who had now fled the coop.

He remembered having the same conversation with Helen on their second date, and realizing that she was one of life's unloved when she admitted that she didn't have a vase or urn amongst her possessions. It meant that no one in her recent history had given her flowers, that she'd probably fall heavily for the first

man who did. He'd wanted to woo her quickly and marry in
haste before she saw his true colours, so had sent roses or orchids
every week.

He smiled at Susie when she returned.

'I've booked us a table for midday.'

By mid afternoon, he'd be thrusting for England.

'I love the Somerset countryside, especially after living in
London for so many years.'

He turned the key in the ignition. 'Presumably you couldn't
go on the tube?'

'No, but there were lots of local shops and schools so I was
able to walk everywhere or else Phil took me in the car.'

'You'd probably find trams less daunting as they're slower and
it's easier to see where you're going. Whenever I'm in Manchester
I take one to China Town.'

'Do you go to Manchester a lot?'

'Every two or three months, for a change of scene. I like the
casinos.'

'Oh, Phil used to play but I usually just joined him later for
the meal.'

'Mmm, they've got some good restaurants – silver service.'
He'd take her to a couple of the best London ones and she'd
hopefully be impressed.

He drove, chatted, listened actively and made all of the right
responses. When they reached the pub he nosed carefully into
the car park, determined that nothing would go wrong with the
day.

'They do a good carvery here, including a vegetarian option.'

She'd said that she ate meat but some women were lapsed
vegetarians, appreciated a man who wasn't an all-out carnivore.

'Oh, I love turkey.'

'Same here – as an added bonus, it gives your serotonin a
boost.'

'Do I look unhappy?' she asked, and giggled in what sounded
like a flirtatious way.

He grinned widely back. 'No, but you're atypical – my office
sees more than its fair share of depressives.'

'Including turkeys, if you're encouraging your patients to eat
them,' she said and giggled again.

Was he actually going to need a date rape drug? She might just come through for him without it. There again, why take the chance? He hated being left frustrated, both physically and mentally, loved being fully in charge.

They had the turkey with the traditional roast potatoes and greens, though he took care not to overeat, wanted to have enough energy to fully explore her body. She seemed to have no such brakes, ate enthusiastically.

'Slept in and didn't have time for breakfast,' she explained when she looked up and caught his eye.

'I'm just glad that you aren't one of those women who only eats beansprouts.'

'Have you dated some of them?'

'Only the once, needless to say! I pick up on mental health problems very quickly, steer clear.'

'And I've passed your test?'

'Top of the class.'

'Not even the tiniest hint of neurosis?'

'If you do have any, you're hiding it well.'

But not as well as he was, he thought smugly. He was a master of disguise.

They'd had a pot of tea with the meal but now he suggested a drink in the adjacent lounge.

'Personally, I like to sip a brandy at this point.'

'Whisky for me, please,' she said decisively.

'It makes some of my patients violent.'

'Oh, I'm packing a pistol in case some drunk gets out of hand,' she murmured and they both smiled for what felt like the hundredth time that day.

She was genuinely funny as well as sexy, Adam thought, as he went up to the bar and bought the spirits. He felt almost mean as he put the date rape drug in her glass.

'Here's to life after dyspraxia,' he said, joining her at the cosy table beside the real fire.

'Here's to life, full stop,' Susie replied.

'You seem so confident,' he noted, thinking out loud.

'I am in situations like this. It's just when I have to deal with new streets, machinery, trains, buses – even something as simple as buying a new pair of shoes causes my esteem to plummet as I can't tell which shoe fits which foot, frequently get it wrong.'

'People who haven't experienced it simply don't understand,' he said sympathetically and took a sip of his drink. He was pleased when she sipped hers too.

'Oh, they've got these tins of macadamia nuts,' she exclaimed, looking over at a display behind the bar. 'I haven't seen these for years – nowadays it's invariably bagged ones. I used to buy the tins in Harrods all the time.'

'Allow me.' He bought her a tin and she opened it immediately, shook some into his hand.

An hour from now his hands would be full of her tits and ass. He pushed away the images for fear that he'd get an obvious erection.

'Want any more?' she asked softly.

He did, but he wasn't thinking about the nuts. On the upside, they must have made her thirsty as she made serious inroads into her whisky. He matched her, so that they finished their drinks at the same time.

'I love this song,' he said, as 'It's My Life' started up on the sound system. 'Can you remember who sang it?'

He wanted to see if her memory had started to fade as the Rohypnol took effect.

'Oh, it's that band who specialize in stadium rock. You know, the one with the handsome lead singer.'

Good, that was sufficiently vague.

'Shall we head off through the countryside?' he murmured. 'There are some beautiful views around here.'

'Love to. I used to go walking with my husband on the Mendips.'

He took her arm, but she was still walking steadily. There again, she'd had a heavy meal so it would take longer for her digestive system to process the drug.

'We could call into a cider shop on the way back,' he offered. 'Apparently it tastes best served from glass bottles so avoid these plastic ones which the supermarkets sell.'

'Bon Jovi,' she said.

'Sorry?' He backed the car out of its space.

'The group who sang that song. You couldn't remember.'

'That's who it was,' he said, amazed that her speech wasn't even slightly slurred.

He drove, watching her with peripheral vision and listening carefully for verbal clues. Fuck it, she still wasn't going under. He made a detour to the cider outlet and they tasted a pear cider and a new apple variety that they were trialling.

'Do you want to go walking?' he asked, desperate to prolong the date until she went under.

'Usually I would – but I've had so much to eat that I'm really lethargic.'

'Then let's find a garden centre and have espresso to wake us up.'

'Only if you let me pay this time. I'm not a freeloader.'

'Of course,' he said lightly, 'I'm egalitarian.'

The centre was busy and they queued for ten minutes before being served with the two drinks. He noticed that she gripped the tray tightly and walked slowly. Was the Rohypnol kicking in at last? There again, this was typical behaviour for a dyspraxic as they were clumsy and accident prone.

'So, are you seeing any patients today?' she asked when they found a table.

'No, I'm all yours for as long as you want me.'

'Not for much longer, I'm afraid – my neighbour's coming round at five to tighten something under the sink. It's been dripping.'

'I can do that for you.' The last thing he wanted was some other man muscling in on the act.

She put her hand on his arm. 'Oh, it's OK. She offered first.'

Aha, so it was another woman. He wondered distractedly if she too was druggable.

'Story of my life – surplus to requirements,' he said.

'I'm sure that's not true. I suspect that you do very well with women.'

'Oh, I've had my share of relationships, can't lie about that. But I'm getting a bit too old to play the field.'

'You've never been married?'

'Yes, I have.' He took a visible deep breath. 'My wife was a lovely woman, but prone to depression. She was older than me and the menopause seemed to tip her over the edge. She took her own life by jumping from a multi-storey car park. It was a terrible shock.'

'Was she one of your patients?'

Everyone asked him that.

'God, no. She was a therapist, very well respected in the community. She hid her depression from me until sometime after we were married but apparently it had been there since puberty.'

'I read somewhere that most mental illness is episodic.'

'It is.' To his surprise, he was actually enjoying this date as it gave him a chance to show off his considerable knowledge. 'People cope until they're faced with a specific amount of pressure and then their emotional health breaks down for a while. They regroup and all is well until the next crisis. I've found that a combination of exercise and behavioural modification can really help.'

'Do many of your female patients come on to you?'

'Unfortunately, yes. It goes with the territory. They might be widowed and lonely or they've recently been divorced and want to prove that they are still attractive. Others have come to see me because of sexual dysfunction and, in the process of describing their fantasies, they become aroused.'

'What sort of fantasies?'

He told her a few of the more outlandish ones and she giggled. 'You're making these up!'

'If only. A colleague of mine, Beth, works at the hospital and she gets to hear about the male patients who turn up at X-ray with vacuum cleaner hoses firmly embedded in their rectums. Needless to say, they all claim to have been vacuuming in the nude and to have fallen back on the hose.'

'Did your wife deal with similar cases?'

No, she was too flaky for that. He bit back the words.

'She wasn't really in the psychosexual field – most of her patients were female as her form of therapy was more New Age, more esoteric.'

'You don't seem particularly New Age to me.'

'I'm not.' He only used candles when there was a power cut. 'But it was a case of opposites attract.'

'You didn't win her over to your particular brand of therapy?'

'Nor she to hers. We respected each other's differences. Apart from the periods when she was down, we had an excellent relationship.'

'I've heard that it takes years to recover from bereavement.'

'You move on, but you never fully recover. I still miss her warmth, her sensitivity, her smile.'

'She's a hard act to replace.'

'Very hard.' He touched her arm briefly. 'But I'm determined to give it my best shot and hope that you'll come out with me again.'

'I will.'

'Good,' he said and remained complimentary and upbeat on the journey home.

But he felt frustrated and cheated after he dropped her off, and angry that the drug had turned out to be a placebo. It was getting more and more difficult to buy reliable roofies on the black market – his own recent experience was that they either killed the victim or had no effect. He must research newer and stronger drugs and try them out on another homeless man or someone equally dispensable; with the right sedatives, Susie would be the proverbial putty in his hands the next time that they met.

FORTY-FIVE

They'd started to smell really bad, so he'd buried them in the back garden. Even with the excess energy that he'd had since going off his medication, it had taken hours and hours. Fortunately the neighbours on both sides were on holiday – they always travelled together and it had been a source of contention to his parents that they were never invited – so there was no one to notice as he dug through the night. He'd put them in separate holes as an additional punishment and had planted bushes from the DIY centre on top and also sprinkled grass seed, a variety which apparently grew exceptionally fast. He'd tell people that they'd gone to Spain to start a new life: he knew from the ads that he'd seen on the Internet that oldies did that all the time.

He could go to a local university now that he had no one to flee from. He was a house owner, a grown-up, totally free. All that he had to do was get rid of the paper trail which said that he was difficult and unreliable, or whatever negative words they'd used to define him. For starters, that meant burning down the school. He'd been thinking about it for the last few weeks but Mum and Dad had locked the door so that he couldn't go out in the early hours, whereas now . . .

He went there at three a.m. with his petrol, rags and strategic map. He'd read up on arson attacks on some of the more revolutionary websites. You had to find combustible materials and not leave the premises until they were fully alight.

Now he could spend his life forever in blue jeans. Brandon broke a downstairs window with a half brick. It was easier than he'd thought: he felt fully alive and invincible. He slid his hand in, undid the catch and entered, glad that he was so slim. He knew the building well, made for the sewing room with its bails of fabric and skeins of wool, all advocating an olde worlde life-style. What was the point, when machines could produce clothes so much more quickly and effectively? The materials crackled as they caught alight and he stood, watching, for a while. Gotcha. But there was more to do, so he strode on to the art room with its paper and balsa wood, started another three small fires, exulting as they spread. Later he upped the ante by splashing the assembly room curtains with petrol, put a lit match to the hem and enjoyed seeing them burn.

His next port of call was the secretary's room. How often had he stood outside it, waiting for yet another note to give to his parents? Tonight he was dexterous, managed to pick the lock. He took his file from the metal cabinet and read it with genuine interest, then put it on a fabric-covered chair and set it alight. There might be other report cards in individual teacher's desks or in the staff room, but an inferno would destroy every one of them and it would be Mr Leston's word against his. They might well keep computer files, backed up at a remote location, but he was still convinced that he was doing the right thing. They'd tried to mould him here, to turn him into an obedient, Shakespeare-memorizing machine, devoid of creativity. It was payback time.

When he'd started twenty serious fires (was there any other kind?) throughout the school, he left as quietly as he had arrived and walked swiftly home, fancying that he could smell burning in the air. If only it had included the scent of burning flesh and skin . . .

Later, as he played online chess throughout the night, he realized that he didn't have to go to university at all. He'd only wanted to do so in order to escape the oldies. But now that they were pushing up the daisies – well, the special fast-growing grasses – he could just stay in the house for ever more. He could also . . . For a moment his imagination failed him. But that was alright: he'd come up with another good idea soon. He was intelligent and creative and would no longer have to listen to negative feedback. His folks had been so wrong when they said that he was too impulsive, didn't think things through.

FORTY-SIX

'So they're arresting him within the hour.'

Olivia felt unwell as she took in the enormity of her colleague, Susie's, words. Why had no one told her, until now, that they'd sent a second undercover cop to Adam's? Were they aware that she'd become too close to him? Did they fear that she'd warn him that he was under surveillance at this ambitious woman's hands?

In the two days since she'd last seen him, she had continued to feel second-rate, rejected. Now she felt bloated, having risen for this early morning emergency briefing at five a.m. Unused to getting up at this time, she'd been unable to open her bowels and the cereal that she'd forced down still felt like a brick in the pit of her stomach. She looked around the Major Incident Room at all of the expectant faces and realized that she was the only police officer who was unanimated, low.

She took a deep breath. 'You mean he admitted to killing Helen?'

'No, according to him they had a picture perfect marriage. No, he's being arrested for attempting to drug me.'

'Were you at his office at the time?' When she, Olivia, had lain on his couch, he'd been the perfect gentleman. She'd had to make the first move, and he'd still hesitated, talked about professional boundaries. But she'd continued to flirt until his need for her kicked in.

'I spent time at his office, but on this occasion we were in the pub. Obviously there were several plain clothes officers around for the entire journey. They tailed us in an unmarked car and others posed as diners and bar staff. I kept having to fight the urge to smile and wave.'

I kept fighting the urge to kiss him and then I gave in to it, Olivia thought, and felt a failure and ashamed.

'He drugged your drink?' She wondered briefly if her colleague had set him up, brought along her own sleeping draught. Just how ambitious was she, how determined to get a result?

'He did, but we were proactive and had already arranged for me to swap my whisky for one being held by another officer. All that I had to do was distract him for a second so I sent him up to the bar to buy me nuts.'

'And what had he put in your glass?'

'Rohypnol – the guys took it away for analysis and we got the results back this morning. If I'd ingested it, I'd have been knocked out for several hours whilst he had his wicked way.'

Olivia belatedly became aware that Susie was waiting for a response. 'It'll be enough to shut down his practice,' she said weakly, wondering if she would have to face him in court.

'Exactly, and it'll make it easier for us to lean on him again regarding his wife's death. I mean, this proves that he's immoral. And it puts him more firmly in the frame for Hannah and Kylie's murders. He could have drugged them for sex and they had a bad reaction and died.'

She still didn't like to think of him with other women; he'd made her feel as if they had a bond, a shared love of language and a similar sense of humour. She'd become young and sexy when she was with him, had felt as if all her early potential had been renewed.

'He may have done the same to his lodger,' Susie added. 'You know, if he's bisexual? We'll see what we find in the way of porn and photos when we search his place.'

'He seemed normal to me,' Olivia said, feeling the urge to defend him. 'Very likeable.'

Susie nodded. 'Oh he's charming, like most psychopaths.'

The other woman seemed to be waiting for a reaction. 'So, when exactly are they arresting him?'

Susie rubbed the sleep from her eyes. 'Within the next couple of hours, whilst he's still in bed. They want the element of surprise.'

FORTY-SEVEN

He wished that his mum had stocked the fridge before she died – he was hungry and fast running out of money. He didn't know her or Dad's pin numbers and had spent the money in their wallet, purse and the little bowl in the kitchen where they kept the petty cash. How on earth was he supposed to feed himself or pay the broadband bills? There was no point going to his aunt's house as she spent all her money on cheap vodka and cigarettes. Apparently she'd been even worse since the ostensibly accidental death of her son, Ethan. That surprised him – you'd have thought that she'd be more relaxed without the little brat around.

He'd stayed up all night again playing online games but now it was four a.m. and he had to eat. He belatedly thought of Adam. The man had always offered him wholesome snacks and fresh orange juice when he came straight from school for therapy. Now he could sneak in and take all of the food in the kitchen and go through the man's filing cabinet until he found the information about himself. It probably also made sense to start another fire; if nothing else, it was fun.

It would be comparatively easy to enter the bungalow as the therapist kept the key on a little nail beside the door. Brandon spent a few minutes fashioning a long hook out of two metal coat hangers before leaving the house. He could see that the bushes over his mum and dad were wilting horribly and wondered vaguely if he should replace them with plastic ones. Dad had always brought home plants from the garden centre in his car but he, Brandon, would have to walk all the way there and carry them back and they'd be much heavier and more cumbersome than packets of grass seed. He hated buses, always felt singled out and trapped.

All was quiet when he reached the psychologist's, apart from a large cat which ran up to him, purring. He kicked out but its reflexes were faster than he expected and it sprung sideways, stared at him for a second before running off. In a fair world he would have mastery over the animal kingdom, over all of his inferiors. For now he'd settle for mastering this house.

Angling his hook, he fed it through the letterbox and made several lunges at the key. On his fourth attempt, he knocked it off the nail and it fell to the floor with a tinny sound which echoed for a moment. He froze and listened intently, but no one stirred. It was easy, after that, to drag the key along the lino and towards the door, hook it and pull it carefully through the letterbox. Gotcha. Pleased at his own dexterity, he slid it silently into the lock.

He tiptoed to the kitchen, took four slices of bread out of the bread bin and fetched cheese and a jar of sweet pickle from the fridge. He found a gleaming knife in the cutlery drawer and cut thick slices of Cheddar, making what his gran used to call door-steps, her colloquialism for big sandwiches. He washed them down with a half pint of orange juice, the type that he preferred without fibrous bits in it. His stomach stopped rumbling and he felt even sharper than before.

Now he had to pack lots of food to take home, but he'd forgotten to bring any carrier bags. He began searching through the many drawers and cupboards for some. As he did so, he saw foodstuffs that he liked – tins of baked beans, packets of noodles, cans of pineapple chunks – and began to stockpile them on the table. He also took dairy foods and beer from the fridge.

Hearing a dull thud from upstairs, he grabbed the big knife that he'd used to cut the cheese. He hid behind the open kitchen door, holding the weapon ready in his right hand. His heartbeat quickened as he heard footsteps descending, getting closer all the time. He didn't want to be disturbed, or given a pep talk. He wanted to remain free as the proverbial avian, to do his own thing.

He watched, scarcely breathing now, as his therapist entered the room. The man took a few slow steps towards the table. Brandon slammed the door shut and stood in front of it, clutching the knife.

Adam whirled around.

'Brandon! Christ, you scared me!' He must have belatedly noticed the blade as his eyes widened. 'What can I do for you?' he asked in a gentler voice.

Fuck off, leave me alone. Give me this house. Now, there was a thought – he could move in here rather than transport all of this food to his own place. If he lived at Adam's he wouldn't have to walk past the dying bushes every day, though he should probably go back every so often to water them and . . . well, whatever else his parents had done to keep social services at bay. He had a feeling that he'd have to pay a community charge but that you could do so at the local council office. It would be a steep learning curve but he was up for it.

'Brandon?'

The voice broke into his thoughts.

'What?' he asked, feeling irritable.

'Is there anything that I can do for you?'

'Like what?'

The therapist indicated the tins of food. 'Like cook you a meal.'

'I'm not hungry.'

'Do you want to take these with you?'

'No – I want to eat them here.'

The older man looked confused. 'OK. But not now?'

'Over the next few days . . . you've got loads.'

He watched as the man licked his lips. Was *he* hungry? Had he come down for a sandwich and would he be annoyed that his former patient had eaten so much of the cheese?

'Will I make us a cup of tea?'

'You said that I shouldn't drink caffeine.'

'Juice, then?'

'I've already finished it.'

'That's alright, Brandon. I'll go out now and get more.'

'In your dressing gown?' The therapist must think that he was stupid, must be planning on alerting the authorities. No chance – he wasn't going anywhere.

'Well, at this hour I *could* take the car to the garage shop in my dressing gown – very few people are going to see me!'

Was it early? Nowadays he had no real concept of time.

'Brandon? Shall I go and get you juice?'

'No.'

'Anything else, then?'

'Your PIN number,' he said. He'd forgotten to get his parents numbers before he bludgeoned them to death, wouldn't make that mistake again.

'Why would you want that?' Adam asked in an even softer voice.

Did he have a sore throat? Why was he edging towards the window?

'Sit down or I'll stab you,' he warned.

'OK.' Adam sat down in the nearest wooden chair and turned it slowly until it – and he – was facing him. 'Brandon, remember that I'm your friend.'

'I need money.'

'I've got some in my wallet and petty cash jar.'

'Ongoing money.'

'Have your mum and dad stopped your allowance? I can speak to them.'

'You can't,' Brandon said, glad that, for once, he knew much more than the therapist. 'They're dead.'

He watched Adam Neave pale.

'Recently?' he croaked.

'A few days ago.'

'Are they in the house?'

'Not any more – I buried them in the garden and planted bushes on top.'

He waited for Adam to say well done for showing forward planning, but the man said nothing, just looked quickly around the room.

'I know that they used to upset you,' the therapist said.

'Past tense.'

'Will your other relatives be worried?'

'There's just my auntie and she's been hitting the booze even more since Ethan died.'

He watched with a detached interest as Adam shuddered.

'Should we dig a deeper hole together, Brandon? You know, make sure that you don't get caught.'

'Oh, I won't get caught. Everyone thinks that they've gone abroad to live.'

'But won't your father's employer start to worry?'

'Not if I fake a resignation letter.'

'I could help you write it. We could go out to the post office and get a stamp.'

'Yeah, right.' Brandon pulled one of the other wooden kitchen chairs over to the door and sat on it, holding the long, shiny knife in his lap. It was nice having someone to talk to, he admitted to himself, but, when he tired of the older man's chatter, he'd have to die.

Fuck, fuck, fuck. Who'd have thought that the quiet teenager would turn out to be a total psycho? Worse, a psycho who was now holding him hostage in his own kitchen and brandishing a knife. Adam had used that particular implement to cut large shanks of ham and roast beef, knew how sharp it was. If the kid slashed at his neck or lunged for the heart, he'd be a goner. He had to talk for his life . . .

'Would you like a beer?'

He had a small drinks cabinet in his study and some Rohypnol sellotaped to the cabinet roof. The teen would be comatose in ten minutes flat, and he could disarm him and alert the emergency services.

'No, I'm not old enough.'

'Hey, who's going to know?' Not his parents, at any rate. He belatedly remembered that Brandon's little cousin – Ethan whom he'd referred to moments ago – had died in his presence. He must have killed him, too. But surely he, Adam, could talk his way out of this situation? He'd always prospered in difficult situations before.

He realized that the boy hadn't answered his last question, was staring at him manically. Damn, the kid must have stopped taking his meds. That made him unpredictable, and there was some anecdotal evidence that users sometimes became violent when they suddenly ceased the drugs.

'Brandon, I'm on your side.'

'No, you're on Mum's side. You and she spoke to the doc who put me on the tablets.'

'Because we care about you and thought that they would make you feel better. Remember how well you were doing in school for a while?'

'There's no school, now.'

'Maybe you haven't been getting on with a particular teacher or classmate? Sometimes you can move up a level.'

At this rate, the kid would be going straight to jail.

'No, I mean there's no school. Literally. I burned it down.'

God, the teen really had lost it, big time. He was disappointed that he hadn't recognized a fellow-psycho. The boy had fooled everyone, except that pesky shrink who'd kept phoning for a while.

'Right, well that's one way of ensuring that school's out forever,' he said and attempted a laugh, but it sounded hollow to his ears. He was stuck in this room with a triple murderer and arsonist.

The silence deepened. He wondered if the boy would fall asleep, but, if anything, he looked wired, his eyes constantly searching the room, his movements jerky. He probably felt that he ruled the world at this moment, that no one could stand in his way.

'Mind if I make myself a cup of tea?' he asked casually, aware that he could throw boiling water in the kid's face, tackle him when he put his hands up to shield his burning flesh.

'I mind,' Brandon said.

'You know that we're on the same side?'

'We're not.'

He wasn't going to argue.

'So, what shall we talk about?' he asked softly. He'd always thought that he was cool before but now he sounded like the boy's dad. The kid had woken him from a deep sleep and now he craved coffee, was getting hungry and kept losing his train of thought.

He realized that Brandon, too, had lost his train of thought as the teenager failed to answer him. How much longer would they have to sit here, eyeballing each other? It was lucky that he'd gone to the loo when he'd first got up. The downstairs noise had been sufficiently muffled that he'd half thought it was next door's cat, Tilly, knocking over a plant pot in the garden or the paper boy being especially exuberant. He'd come down here in a half daze, had never expected this . . .

Suddenly, there was an explosion of sound at the front door, the likes of which he'd never heard before. He jumped up instinctively and the boy jumped up too and screamed, 'What have you done?' and lunged at him. Adam felt nothing for a moment and then was struck by wave after wave of dizziness followed immediately by nausea. His legs turned weak and would no longer support his weight so he sank, on his knees, to the floor. It was only then that he saw the handle of the knife sticking out of his chest. Jesus, when had that happened? The blade was all the way in.

His body wanted to fall forward but, with a Herculean effort, he forced himself to slide backwards so that the knife handle wasn't also driven into his flesh. He lay there, completely unable to move, heard male and female voices in the hallway. Then a shocked-sounding voice said, 'Jesus, son, what have you done?' and another said something about fetching an ambulance and then he heard nothing more.

FORTY-EIGHT

'Are you sure that it was him?'

Beth sat in her lounge, facing the detectives. The therapist that she knew simply wasn't capable of murder: he was a kind, community-minded man.

'Well, we know that he put date rape drugs into various women's drinks. We caught him in the act with an undercover policewoman and, after his death, his photo appeared in the newspapers. Since then, various females have come forward to say that they met him in bars and clubs, then everything went blank and when they woke up they were sore all over. They later had flashbacks of being sexually abused.'

'And you think he drugged his wife and she died?'

'No, we believe that he pushed her from a multi-storey car park because she was thinking about leaving him and he had to retain the upper hand. But we strongly suspect that he strangled Hannah Reid.'

Could the man that she'd dined with, worked with, flirted with, really be a sex killer? What would his motivation be when he could attract women in the normal way?

'But why . . .?'

'Our psychologist thinks that killing his wife gave him an incredible buzz, that he wanted to repeat it. We know that Hannah was grieving for the loss of her relatives and probably visited the bereavement centre, got talking to him there. You've said yourself that, when you first saw her photo in the paper, you thought that you'd seen her before, just weren't sure where.'

Beth felt a chill run through her. 'I thought little of it at the time as I meet so many people at the hospital.'

Still, this was just conjecture. They hadn't yet convinced her that he'd murdered Hannah or anyone else.

She sought more information. 'And you also think he killed that Bristol girl?'

'Again, after we went public with his photo, a few clubbers came forward to say that they'd seen a guy matching his description talking to Kylie on the night she disappeared.'

Hadn't she read somewhere that people often wanted to help so put themselves at the centre of an inquiry when they hadn't really been there?

She cleared her throat. 'But don't some people imagine things?'

'Some – but other women have come forward to say that Neave took them home from clubs, drugged and sexually assaulted them. One girl remembered part of his car number plate, whilst another described an unusual mole on his chest, near the nipple. And several of them remember him using the same phrases to them as they meandered in and out of consciousness.'

So it was becoming clear that he had some kind of criminal history – and everyone knew that some people reacted badly to date rape drugs, had a potentially fatal reaction. Had her colleague really cared so little about other lives?

'What about his lodger, John?'

Beth remembered hugging Adam after the younger man had died, trying to console him. Had she really embraced a murderer?

'We'll never know for sure, but maybe John saw something and Adam Neave wanted him out of the way.'

'And his little nephew?'

'He might have killed him to get revenge on his brother, or it might have been one of those occasional inexplicable deaths. In hindsight, it's suspicious, but we'll never know for sure.'

'And Adam's definitely dead?' Beth asked, with a shudder.

Both detectives nodded forcibly and the oldest one said, 'He's dead all right – he was dying by the time we broke in to arrest him and he expired before the ambulance arrived.'

'I trusted him. I feel really stupid now,' she said, thinking out loud. She felt almost contaminated when she remembered how they'd talked and laughed, made eye contact for far longer than was strictly necessary. She'd looked at his lithe body and wondered what it would be like to go to bed with him.

'Don't feel bad. You're not naive – there are thousands of people conned by psychopaths like Neave every year. Even people in the prison and probation services, who should know better, get taken in sometimes We've known of cases where a female prison psychologist married a sociopath serving a life sentence as he convinced her of his innocence.'

'Did Adam have a prison record?'

'No, he was too clever for us, had never been caught.'

'Lots of the widows liked him,' Beth admitted, remembering specifically how Olivia had flirted with the man. 'And apparently he was equally popular with his private patients.'

'That's not so surprising – he told them what they wanted to hear.'

He had indeed. He'd known how to flatter, how to soothe, how to make women feel better. He'd presented himself as a true professional or empathic friend.

'So, what happens now?' Beth asked.

'You're eligible for counselling and help from Victim Support.' One of the men handed her a card.

'I'll think about it,' she said cautiously.

'And if you need time off work, we can explain . . .'

'I don't.'

She wouldn't let Adam turn her into another of his victims, she thought, as she got ready for her hospital job, just as she hadn't let Matthew turn her into some clothes-obsessed bimbo. She was a strong woman, was worth more than that. She would return to her counselling work as a slightly more cautious and wiser individual, would bear in mind that people weren't always what they seemed.

She hadn't really been foolish, Beth told herself. After all, numerous mental health medics, patients and even streetwise clubbers had fallen for Adam's mask of sanity. He had looked and sounded caring and competent and hadn't given any of them a reason to suspect that it was all an act. It had been a shocking period in her life – and in the town's history – but it was, Beth reassured herself, thankfully over. Everything could go back to normal now.

FORTY-NINE

I t had been a difficult few weeks, so she hadn't been surprised to find her appetite reduced, to feel sleepier than usual. But now, for the first time, she felt strangely tremulous and had to sit down. Had the stress of the undercover work and Adam's death caused her blood pressure to shoot up? Or was she more seriously ill?

The sensation passed and Olivia went to the police canteen and bought a banana to keep her going till lunchtime, washing it down with an energy drink and a cup of black coffee. A couple of hours later, as she caught up with her paperwork – she'd returned to her desk job at the station – the odd, disorientated feeling swept over her again.

Later that week, still feeling spaced, she went along to the doctor's surgery. The woman checked her blood pressure, which was slightly on the high side, and also got the nurse to take a phial of her blood so that they could run a series of checks.

'And how are your periods?' she asked.

'As variable as ever!' Olivia admitted.

'Could you be pregnant?'

She was about to say no, that this was impossible, when she felt the first stirrings of doubt. She and Marc hadn't used contraception for years in their quest to have a baby, but they'd both accepted long ago that a pregnancy wasn't going to happen. Their relationship had been so poor that they hadn't had sex for many months. But it was less than three months since she'd been with Adam and she hadn't had a period since.

'It's unlikely,' she said, feeling a new rush of fear and – if she was honest – excitement.

'Well, dizziness can be one of the earlier symptoms so I'll get you to produce a urine sample before you leave. You can phone in for the results.'

For the next forty-eight hours, she monitored her own behaviour, tried to second guess the outcome of the test. Was she urinating more often? Was the weariness she felt due to Marc's boorishness or her boredom at being back in the office? Or was a tiny new life stealing her energy?

By the time that she phoned for the results, she felt almost ill with anticipation. A negative result meant that she retained her old life – the same husband, same house, same job. A sometimes dull life, but a life of certainty. However, if she was pregnant it could signal the end of her marriage and probably the end of her career as she'd want to be a full-time mum until the child went to school.

Her heart beating so fast that it seemed to resound within her head, Olivia listened to the phone ring through to the surgery. When the receptionist answered, she gave her name and waited whilst they presumably brought up her file on the computer screen.

'Yes, it's positive,' the nurse said in a neutral voice.

So, after all those years she was going to have a baby. She'd longed, and even prayed, for this to happen – and now, perhaps, her prayers had been answered, albeit in an unusual way.

'Can you tell me the protocol?' she asked, striving for nonchalance.

'Certainly.' The woman sounded more cheerful now. 'You

come in for a check-up, and we work out your due date and book you a bed in the maternity unit.'

Olivia made an appointment, glad she'd have a chance to talk to someone in the medical profession. She was going to need all the support that she could get.

Determined to be proactive, she bought the local paper and studied the 'accommodation to let' section but was shocked at how expensive a self-contained property was, even an unfurnished one. She didn't want to flat share, not at her age and with a child to raise. And buying was out of the question – Marc paid much more of their mortgage than she did and she simply couldn't afford to go it alone. Would he readily give her back the money that she'd contributed to this house or would she have to take him to court for her share? Now that single parenthood was becoming an increasing reality, she felt frightened and out of her depth.

Would he consider raising the baby as his own? It wasn't such a big stretch, and she'd read of other men who'd forgiven their confused wife a solitary indiscretion. It was the easiest way to maintain the status quo. And look at the upside: he'd have a son to take to football or a daughter to . . . whatever fathers and daughters did together. She was vague on the details as her own dad had always been at work or overtired. Admittedly it wouldn't be Marc's biological offspring but no one in the outside world need ever know.

That would be the ideal, she thought, giving the child the traditional set-up of two parents. It would resurrect her marriage, giving them a fresh focus, a new start. Now that she thought things through, she wondered why they'd both dismissed adoption so readily, been so convinced that they only wanted a baby that was genetically theirs.

Another month passed and she delayed having the talk, put off making any big decisions. What if he rejected her? She'd gone from her parents house to her first marital home, had never lived independently. If only he'd understand . . .

She fell asleep on their bed one evening after work and woke up to find him lying behind her, his hands around her waist. She stirred and murmured, 'Hi, you.'

'Hi sleepyhead.'

She felt his lips on the back of her neck and instinctively tensed, then she felt his palms sliding down her belly and tensed some more.

'Are you premenstrual?' he murmured, sounding concerned. Why hadn't he sounded like that a few months ago? If he'd been solicitous and interested in her life she would never have turned to Adam for solace and sex.

'No.' She took a deep breath. 'In fact, I'm pregnant.'

There was a silence then he said, 'You can't be.'

She forced herself to turn towards him, put her arms around his waist. His face was ashen, his lips trembling.

'I was really stupid, had a one-night stand.'

She felt him stiffen, start to pull away. She held on, feeling desperate.

'You seemed to have lost interest in me and I was so lonely . . .'

'So you decided to fuck another man.'

She'd never heard him sound so hurt, so enraged. She could feel the anger in his limbs as he tore his arms from her waist, moved towards the other side of the bed. For a moment he teetered on the edge, and she fought back a hysterical laugh.

'It was just the one night,' she said again.

'Some bloke at work?' He shifted a couple of inches, propped himself up on one elbow and glared down at her.

She forced herself to meet his gaze, wondered if she looked as distressed as he did. 'No, it was at the end of a girls' night out, just someone I met in a bar.'

'So he could be diseased, AIDS-ridden?'

'He was a professional, wore a suit.' She realized how ridiculous that sounded, added, 'He was quite shy and drunk, probably happily married. I don't think he'd done this before.'

'And where did you . . .?'

She tried to envisage where a drunken couple might go. 'In his car. It was over in minutes and I really regretted it.'

'You thought that I'd never find out.'

It was a statement rather than a question. If she had indeed been barren, they wouldn't be having this conversation now.

She sought desperately to reassure him that it was a one-off. 'I wasn't thinking clearly at the time. It didn't mean anything.'

She watched his lips tighten. 'It means the end of us.'

'It doesn't have to.' She reached for him again but he was rigid with tension. 'We could raise this baby as our own, start again.'

'A stranger's baby.'

'It would be like adopting.'

'No it wouldn't. This would be your child, not mine.'

'This guy even looked like you. No one would know.'

'I'd know.'

'You'll love him or her once they're born, once you hold them.'

'I never want to see this brat. Oh, and I never want to see you again.'

He got off the bed and began to walk around it, heading for the bedroom door.

She jumped up, blocked his way. 'Marc – please. Don't end it like this. Let's talk. Let's go to counselling.'

'There's no point. It's over.' He pushed her away and she watched him leave the room, heard his footsteps pounding the stairs. She sat down again, feeling nauseous, winced as the outer door slammed.

Hours later, as she curled on the settee feeling drained and dehydrated, her mobile rang.

'Marc?'

'No, is he out at this time?'

She recognized her sister's voice immediately, began to cry. 'He's left me.'

'No way.'

She took a deep breath. 'He had good reason.'

'Are you at home? I'm coming over.'

'Thanks, Cathy.' She looked around the room, wondering how much longer she'd be able to call it home.

Cathy took charge when she arrived, making tea and toast, packing the dishwasher, even watering the plants. When the place was shipshape again, she sat down next to her on the settee.

'So, how long has this been on the cards?'

'We just had an argument earlier today.'

'Then it'll blow over. You two have been together forever. He's not going to move out because of a few choice words.'

'It's not . . .' She realized that it was time to tell her sister everything. 'I'm pregnant and he knows it's not his.'

She watched an expression of surprise or shock flit across her sister's face, saw her visible intake of breath.

'A sperm donor?'

If only. She shook her head. 'I had sex with someone else.'

'In order to get pregnant?'

Another head shake. She felt spaced again, somehow dislocated. 'Because I was really attracted to him.'

'No wonder Marc's hurt.'

'I know. But we've not been good together for ages, Cathy. He's either at work or he's too tired to talk. I felt as if I was on the scrap heap. Then I met this beautiful, intelligent guy.'

'And you had an affair?'

'It didn't last long.' She realized that Cathy didn't have to know that she'd been rejected. 'He . . . was killed.'

'Oh my God.' She saw the slow realization in her sister's eyes. 'It wasn't that guy you were doing surveillance on?'

She nodded. 'It went beyond work. We got genuinely close.' She so needed to talk to someone – anyone – about his good qualities, about the special hours they'd shared talking about everyone and everything.

'But he killed two women and drugged others.'

'They *think* he killed them. They'll never know for sure.'

'Well, even if he just drugged . . .'

'I know it's terrible but I think that he really missed his wife, didn't want to get involved again in case he got hurt. They believe that he picked up a few girls in bars – you know, the type that will go with anyone? They didn't put in a complaint at the time, only came forward after the recent publicity so we can't even be sure that they're telling the truth.'

'Olivia, you're not defending him?'

Cathy hadn't seen his human face, his humour and compassion. 'No, of course not. I'm just saying that he wasn't all bad.'

'And do your colleagues know?'

'No, and they're not going to. I'm going to give up work and raise this baby. They'll assume that it's Marc's.'

'When it'll really be a killer's baby.'

Another wave of nausea swept through her, but she forced

herself to look at her sister, keep her voice steady. 'It'll be mine as well.'

She watched Cathy hesitate. 'Olivia, do you remember the Bensons?'

She nodded. They'd been her neighbours for a few years when she was a child.

'Well, after we moved away they adopted a baby girl and gave her everything, but, by the time she was twelve, she was causing chaos. She stole, played truant, started trying to seduce anything in trousers. She must have been thirteen when she got pregnant for the first time and she ended up having babies with four different men.'

'I might have a boy,' she said stubbornly, unwilling to have anyone – not even Cathy – rain on her parade.

'And boys are even harder to raise alone. Listen, love, if we inherit some of our parents' darker characteristics, you could be raising a psychopath.'

'But I'd love him so much that . . .' She could only envisage a smiling, contented baby.

'Didn't that psychologist's parents love him?'

Her sister seemed determined to score points.

'Obviously not enough. I mean, he had a brother who seemed to be pathologically jealous. And Adam himself went through hell when his wife committed suicide. He had a lot to contend with whereas our son will have a better start in life.'

'With a single mother?'

'Mum and Dad will help.' And you, she thought, surely you'll be there for me?

'Will you get police housing?'

She shook her head, feeling sick again. 'I'm going to give up work until he turns five.' All of her instincts were telling her that this would be a boy and that he would look and sound like Adam. He'd have his boyish charm and intellect but not his controlling streak.

'You don't have to do this, Olivia. You've got time to terminate.'

Acid filled her mouth and she only just made it to the kitchen waste-paper basket, knelt by it and heaved copiously. But, apart from the toast which Cathy had made for her, there was nothing to bring up.

'I think you'd better go,' she said, turning around and fetching a kitchen towel to wipe her mouth.

'I don't want to hurt you. You know that? I just don't want you raising a stick with which to beat your own back.'

How could a woman in her thirties use such an archaic term? For a moment, she almost hated her sibling. Then she looked at her white, strained face and could see that she was hurting too.

'I want this baby.'

'You could have another pregnancy. I mean, it looks as if you and Marc weren't compatible but if you went to a sperm bank or started another relationship . . .?'

'I want Adam's child. He was so handsome and bright and funny.'

'You know that I'll support you, but I have to be honest – I think that you're making a big mistake.'

'You won't tell Mum and Dad who the father is? I'll let them think that it's Marc's but that the relationship was already over.'

'I won't tell anyone,' Cathy said with feeling. 'Presumably you could get into trouble at work if people knew?'

'Yes, lots.' Not that she cared anymore. After all, she had what she wanted. Her work now was to have and raise her child.

Months later, days before she was due, Olivia sat in her rented flat and flicked idly through the Sunday supplements. Mum had been very good, bringing her round newspapers and magazines that she'd finished with, and also bringing along home-made quiches, soup and stews. She'd gained just the right amount of weight during the pregnancy, her blood pressure was stable and the midwife was very pleased with her progress. The scan had shown that it was going to be a boy, so her instincts had been right.

Shifting around on the settee until she felt more comfortable, she scanned the features on organic chicken rearing, olive-picking holidays in Spain and the challenges of becoming a vegan. Finally, an article about adoption caught her eye. It was a balanced piece, including interviews with happy adopters and adoptees, but one of the sections was chilling, with a seemingly balanced couple having the same experience that the Bensons had had. The boy that they'd adopted at birth had been a pathological liar by six years, an animal torturer by twelve, an arsonist by sixteen and had finally ended up on a GBH charge in jail.

'We tried everything to put him on the right track but had to give up in the end, wash our hands of him. He was destroying the rest of the family,' the woman – who wished to remain nameless – said. Her statement was followed by that of a geneticist who said that a child could inherit negative traits from their mother or father, though he refused to go so far as to use the term 'bad seed'.

Her son would be good, Olivia told herself. She was too positive and caring a person to raise a killer. She kept repeating upbeat messages to herself as the labour pains began.

FIFTY

It wasn't so bad here now that he'd got to know a couple of the other kids, namely the two brightest teenagers. They agreed on one thing – most of the staff here didn't have a clue, especially the more maternal ones. They were bleeding hearts, convinced that, if their young charges were only loved enough, they would reform and give something back to society. But what could he, with his superior IQ, give to this dumbed-down universe? How could he contribute to a world which was obsessed with talk TV, vapid starlets and anodyne music? He had to stand aside to save his sanity.

Brandon stamped in the direction of a surprisingly large woodlouse which was foolishly hurrying across his plush, warm, dark brown carpet. This room – and the nearby communal rooms – would comprise his home for the next few years. Because of his psychiatric history, he'd been sent to this secure hospital rather than a juvenile detention centre. If he'd gone to the latter, he'd have eventually been transferred to an adult jail. He was probably destined to spend the rest of his life in such a facility unless – or should that be until? – he managed to escape.

The half-squashed woodlouse, now lying on its back, feebly

waved several of its legs in the air. He stamped on it again so that it was unrecognizable. He loved – and longed to recreate – the absolute finality of death. Mum and Dad would never again have the chance to give him one of their extensive pep talks, which invariably involved words like 'responsibility'. Ethan wouldn't have the opportunity to irritate him with his high-pitched squealing and Adam couldn't give him yet another pointless test.

'Alright, Brandon?'

He looked up as one of the nurses popped her head around the door.

'Fine, thanks, Mrs Peters.'

'Dave was wondering if you fancied a game of chess?'

'I'd like that.' He got off of his bed and carefully stepped over the crushed insect: he'd get rid of it later when there weren't any witnesses around. Since arriving here, he'd been presenting himself as a reformed character, someone who had been violent due to external stresses but who was very different in a supportive environment and when taking his medication, something which they made him do religiously. He'd lulled them into a false sense of security now, all friends together, so they'd be unprepared for his imminent blitzkrieg attack.

After much thought – ah, how making plans enlivened his otherwise unexceptional nights – he'd decided to repeat his earlier successes and use a potent mix of arson, stabbing and bludgeoning. This time, of course, he couldn't go from building to building so would carry out all three acts in the one environment. He'd already managed to procure a knife, brought in from the outside for another patient and he was now persuading one of the more vulnerable boys to make him a cosh in woodwork class. He reckoned that he could take out several members of staff providing that he approached them when they were alone in their offices; the others could literally face a baptism of fire.

He'd have fashioned a special key by then, of course, so that he could lock the exits, wait outside in the hospital grounds and listen to the mingled screams. It would be further proof of his pathology, underline the fact that he needed psychiatric care.

Brandon walked jauntily to the games room. He had nothing

to lose by creating a towering inferno and lots of good, multi-coloured memories to gain. He'd also be even more infamous than he was already, would never be forgotten. Smiling, he contemplated the carnage that he could cause for the rest of his life.

Author's Note

Many thanks to the police officer who answered my questions about the setting up of an incident room and the typical protocol in a murder inquiry. The hospital and bereavement centre and all of the characters in this novel are figments of my increasingly warped imagination.